Glory Daze

ALSO BY DANIELLE ARCENEAUX

Glory Be

A GLORY BROUSSARD MYSTERY

DANIELLE ARCENEAUX

PEGASUS CRIME
NEW YORK LONDON

GLORY DAZE

Pegasus Crime is an imprint of
Pegasus Books, Ltd.
148 West 37th Street, 13th Floor
New York, NY 10018

First Pegasus Books cloth edition March 2025

Library of Congress Cataloging-in-Publication Data is available.

ISBN: 978-1-63936-843-3

10 9 8 7 6 5 4 3 2 1

Printed in the United States of America
Distributed by Simon & Schuster
www.pegasusbooks.com

For Kerry Bennett,

Ride or Die

Glory yearned for her old life, before everything had turned itself upside down and sideways. She strode through the heavy doors at CC's Coffee House, the one on Ambassador Caffrey and West Congress, in the same shopping center as Albertsons and a new restaurant called Soulhaus. She had not yet tried this new restaurant, but her daughter Delphine had texted her some videos of a local newscaster consuming piles of food on TikTok. So far Glory had been able to resist because she had received a stern lecture from her doctor about her numbers–and by "numbers" he meant every number that can be measured by modern medicine–but she could sense her resolve weakening.

To help regain a sense of normalcy, she had just returned from church and the monthly meeting of the Red Hat Society of Acadiana, of which she was an outlier on account of her work as a bookie, but also because of a long-ago wave of food poisoning. The membership had insisted the culprit was a cooler of discounted crawfish Glory had purchased from a roadside stand in Abbeville. But honestly, they ought to have thanked her for being resourceful. Crawfish was now twenty dollars a pound on account of global warming. And no one could definitively prove that crawfish was the culprit of the food poisoning, but it had tarred Glory's reputation, nonetheless.

As was tradition, Glory and the members wore red to these meetings. Today she wore wide-legged red pants with a coordinating blazer and a red hat. This particular hat was purchased by her daughter Delphine, who lived in New York City. It featured a wide brim with an exaggerated rosette to one side. Glory squealed when she opened the bundle, packaged in a stunning black-and-white-striped box with the most perfect ribbon you've ever seen. It was the kind of finery that Glory had always loved but only Delphine would spend money on.

By the time she sat down, Noah Singleton, owner of this particular CC's franchise, was walking her way, balancing a tray of small sample cups on a tray. "You have a good Christmas, Miss Glory?"

"Sure did, and you?" Small talk was the glue that held the South together. No matter one's political affiliation or personal beliefs, the connective tissue of Lafayette Parish had somehow remained intact with benign and comforting questions like: *How's your mama doing? You have people over for Mardi Gras? What you fixin' for Easter?* Not that most people minded. It was better than asking questions that might disturb the peace. "You just look mischievous today, Noah Singleton. I can already tell you're up to no good."

He swung a small tray with the sample cups in front of her. "Try this."

She gave him a skeptical look, sipped, and coughed dramatically, as if she had ingested poison. "Noah Singleton, I don't know what you put in that drink, but I suspect I have a case of sudden-onset diabetes. What in the name of the good Lord is this?"

"I'm still working on the right level of sweetness," he said, with a hangdog look that reflected his disappointment. "I'm trying to create a signature drink to go viral on social media. I call it *Praline Perfection*. Chicory coffee, six pumps of praline syrup, whipped cream, and topped with a crumbled praline candy."

Glory had no idea why anyone would ever want to go viral. She had had a brief moment in the spotlight a few months ago and it was more than enough, thank you very much. "Here's an idea," she added. "For an extra $200 you can serve it with a vial of insulin." She thought of Noah like a brother, even if he was always doing too much.

"Did you know that there is no actual pumpkin in a pumpkin spice latte? Not one drop!" And before Glory could respond he added, "And do you know how much money Starbucks has made off that drink? Over a billion dollars! Yes, ma'am, I just need to calibrate my recipe a bit."

Noah gestured for the barista at the counter to bring Glory another cappuccino, on the house, as he often did. Before walking back to the kitchen he pointed at her and said, "I'm going to perfect this recipe. You watch." It was an apology and a declaration. He disappeared behind a pair of swinging doors.

As Glory sipped her cappuccino, her clients streamed in at a steady pace, which was always the case during football playoffs. Glory worked year-round but made a good chunk of her earnings in January and February, when amateur betting and foolishness collided. She had also been busier than usual since everything went down a few months ago. Glory had become somewhat notorious in Lafayette after the murder of Amity Gay, and her role in solving it.

It was attention that she had relished at first, but now it made her itchy with discomfort. Word of mouth had brought a whole new slew of customers. In the world of unsanctioned and illegal betting, publicity is not welcome. But Glory had always had a keen eye when it came to vetting her customers, and those instincts had not faded.

That is why when a lighter-skinned Black woman with caramel highlights and artfully layered hair walked toward Glory, she did a double take. She did not know this woman, or at least, that's what she thought. She knew just about everyone who walked through those doors. But there was something about her that rang familiar, like a relative you haven't seen in many years. She wasn't Glory's age, but wasn't her daughter's age, either. Glory judged her to be somewhere in the middle. This woman could no longer rely on her youth to be naturally firm without effort. And though she had just a few lines that feathered around her eyes and a couple that stretched across her forehead, Glory knew that her still-pretty looks would be deteriorating at a rapid clip from here on out. Glory had been there herself, many years ago.

"Excuse me, are you Glory Broussard?" asked the woman. Glory sized her up further, now that she was up close. She wore a patterned blouse that was too busy for Glory's taste, jeans that clung tightly to her slender frame, and stiletto heels, which Glory noted was not a reasonable choice for a Sunday before noon.

"I'm afraid not, miss. You must have me mistaken for someone else." There was something about the woman that she didn't trust, and having more customers than she knew what to do with at the moment, she was not about to take any risks. Glory peered over her reading glasses and did some calculations to convey that she was not interested in any further conversation. Not even the polite Southern kind.

"Actually, I'm pretty sure you are. I saw your picture in *The Daily Advertiser*," the mysterious woman fired back.

Glory pressed the lead of her pencil harder and scratched away in her notebook, as if the woman did not exist. This was another reason Glory hated all the attention: it had shaken all the crazies loose from the trees. Old men showed up who wanted her to investigate the chattering voices that echoed in their balding heads. Throngs of women pleaded for her to surveil their husbands, who might be stepping out on them. One thing Glory knew from personal experience is that if you think your husband is stepping out, he most definitely is. You don't need to spend hard-earned money to figure that out. And besides, Glory Beverly Broussard was not for hire.

"I'm real sorry to bother you, ma'am," insisted the woman with the pretty-enough face. "But my husband has gone missing, and I thought you'd like to know."

That was it. Glory snapped. "Let me tell you something. I've done had it with you people showing up here with all of this nonsense. What I do know is that I can't help you, and I definitely don't know who your husband is, so please leave me to my business. And support a Black-owned business on your way out. I recommend the Praline Perfection." She shifted her focus back to her ledger. She had never formally studied math beyond basic algebra, but somehow had developed a pretty spot-on way of developing scenarios for a slate of games and estimating her earnings by the end of each weekend. Glory called it her special arithmetic while her daughter called it an algorithm, which must have been one of those ten-cent words she learned working at that law firm.

"My husband is Sterling Broussard."

Glory pressed down so hard on her pencil that the lead shattered. Graphite dust smudged her algorithm. Now it was becoming clearer. The woman was vaguely familiar to Glory because this was the woman, among many women, that Sterling had cheated on her with. Years later, once emotions had been reduced from a rolling boil to a simmer, Glory kicked herself for not seeing it coming. Sterling's purchases of new underwear, the trail of cologne left behind when he was allegedly going bowling. This wasn't a run-of-the-mill infidelity. It was the infidelity that caused him to leave Glory. It was the infidelity that would lead to a new start for Sterling, a new marriage.

The woman took a seat across from Glory. "Look, I know I'm the very last person you ever want to talk with, but I don't know what else to do." Her voice ached with weariness, and there was not enough concealer and tinted face powder to camouflage her exhaustion. "Sterling went out to see some friends two days ago, and I haven't seen or heard from him since. It's so unlike him."

Glory huffed. "Sounds exactly like the Sterling Broussard I know . . ."

"Not the Sterling I know," the woman said, leaning her body halfway over the table. It was a confrontation. *The Battle of Two Wives*. Or, if Glory were framing their relationship correctly, the upstanding, righteous woman who raised him and his daughter, and the hussy who broke a family apart.

Noah's barista delivered Glory's cappuccino at this exact moment, allowing Glory a few moments to regroup. She smiled at the barista, took a sip of her coffee, then delicately placed the small cup on its saucer. "Listen, I done unsubscribed from all that Sterling drama years ago. I'm sorry you've gotten yourself tangled up, but you of all people should have known what you were signing up for." She shoved her notebook into her purse and stood up.

Panic raced across the woman's face. "I thought maybe you'd want to look into it . . . for your daughter's sake."

Glory glared down at her. With fire pulsing through her veins, she snapped. “Keep my daughter’s name out of your mouth.”

♣♦♥♠

The last thing Glory wanted to be doing on a Sunday was driving. It was afternoon now, with a slate of playoff football games about to start. By now, half of Louisiana would have their meat on the grill and two to three beers down their gullets. Some of them would be hitting the road to pick up a missing ingredient for their potato salad or wings, or another case of beer to replace the case that had already been consumed. Glory should have been at home, in her favorite chair, and flipping through channels on the TV.

But because of That Woman, and the disturbance she insisted on dragging through Glory’s door, she was now on I-10, heading west to Jennings, and she would give Sterling a piece of her mind when she got there. Extracting herself from that man had been hard enough. He didn’t deserve to continue to trample on her hard-earned peace with his shenanigans.

And Glory was certain that whatever he was up to, it was definitely shenanigans. She had seen it happen enough during their marriage. He’d have a “gig,” even though he hadn’t managed to make his trombone sound serviceable in years. Then he’d disappear for a few frantic days at a time. Eventually he’d stagger home, enveloped by a cloud of cheap Scotch. Or there would be the times he owed clients money and had “gone fishing” with his buddy Maurice, only to have angry folks pounding on their door, looking for their payday, leaving her to handle it. It was the sloppy way he ran his business that inspired Glory’s no-nonsense professionalism. It had all gotten to be too much. She had gathered him up and dried him out too many times to remember.

Valerie must not have known that he had something of a crash pad in Jennings, which didn't surprise Glory at all, because Sterling was full of secrets. But Glory knew about the place because of their divorce. The house she lived in wasn't in dispute, because it was paid in full and inherited from her mother, in Glory's name only. Not that Sterling would have tried to lay claim. He seemed pretty determined back then to leave the house on Viator Drive as quickly as possible to be with his new love, if that's what you call her. But Glory knew that he had invested a tiny bit of his money in a two-unit duplex in Jennings. He rented out both for a while, until he realized he could just rent one unit and keep the other apartment for himself, his friends, and lord knows what else. Glory was glad to let him have it, uncontested. She had no desire to be a landlord and chase down rent.

On the drive she tried her daughter on the phone for what must have been the tenth time, but no answer. Glory was transported down that nondescript corridor of I-10, with little more than competing Cracker Barrels and Waffle Houses, by pure anger and annoyance. Anger because, against all good sense, she was being dragged into Sterling's funny business again. Annoyance because Valerie LeBlanc had the temerity to show up at her place of employment, and on a Sunday.

Did Glory really care what happened to Sterling? On a personal level, she had stopped pouring feelings into all that long ago. But she did care deeply about her daughter. If only she'd answer that damn phone.

Finally, she arrived in Jennings and pulled up at the curb and parked. The house itself was gray, dull, and lifeless, like any late

January day in Louisiana. The duplex was never fancy, but at least he had kept the grounds tidy. That wasn't the case anymore. Wind whipped a Whataburger bag around a tree, which stopped its graceful tumble on a lawn that was patchy and filled with litter. She made her way through the double carport on the side of the house, in which no cars were parked. The inlay panel of glass on the side door was shattered. Flies buzzed around trash cans that hadn't been emptied for days, judging by their sour smell.

Unsure what to do, she peered through the broken glass. She spotted a retro kitchen table with a Formica tabletop, its edges wrapped in chrome. She recognized it as one of her estate sale finds, one that he complained cluttered the garage. Apparently, he just wanted it all to himself.

For a brief moment, she contemplated calling the police but hesitated. Folks around here don't go calling on the law unless you have no other choice. She preferred to take inventory first.

"Sterling?" She called out, quietly at first, and then louder and clearer. If he was in that house, there was no way he would have slept through her bellowing. From her purse she pulled out a stun gun. Delphine had laughed at her when she bought it at Lafayette Shooters. She explained to Glory that a stun gun only works at close range, and that she couldn't envision her mother in hand-to-hand combat. Glory bought it anyway, not feeling quite ready for a gun, but wanting a little something.

Glory entered the unlocked house, stun gun at the ready. The first thing she noticed upon entering was the odor. She immediately stuck her head out the side door and gagged, her eyes tearing at the stench. She gasped for fresh air and when she gained her composure, covered her nose with a Mardi Gras handkerchief she found in her purse. She told herself she'd do one quick tour of the house and get the hell out of there. But there was no need to tour the house. Sterling was right there, in the kitchen. A black-handled knife pierced his chest. Blood smeared the floor. Maggots mounted his lifeless body.

Glory froze. The only physical reaction she could manage was to clamp her thick hand down on the stun gun. It snapped and threw white sparks from its metallic teeth.

Days later, Glory would revisit what happened after she found the body, because in the moment, all thought and feeling evaporated. She remembered running as fast as she could to her car, which was memorable because she hadn't broken out in a run for at least forty years. The lack of flexibility shortened her strides, and every ligament burned. She dialed 911 and told them to hurry. Then she remembered calling her daughter and somehow managing to break the news. She would never forget the way that Delphine had cried so hard and long that she wrung herself out. Witnessing her daughter in this state, and not being able to ease her suffering, would always be stamped on her soul.

Glory was always envious of the special dispensation her daughter seemed to give Sterling, considering he had abandoned them both. Too many times, Sterling had promised to swing by to take his daughter out for a movie or shopping, only to leave Delphine peering through the curtains hours past the promised time of arrival. Yet she always managed to be happy when she saw him. It's easier to be a father, Glory had fumed. It was a piece of cake to swoop into a clean house, and roughhouse, or go out for ice cream and all the other charming things fathers get to do. The real labor, the kind that keeps a household running, happens behind the scenes. The laundry and coordinating with other mothers for sleepovers and staying up till 2 A.M. because the next day was "wear blue to school day" or some other chore. Glory had done all that and more, but now wasn't the time to keep score.

She could remember, with clarity, the wail of the sirens. It must have snapped them both into the present tense because Glory sensed that Delphine, too, was at least temporarily straightening herself out. "I'm coming down as fast as I can manage. And no matter what, do not talk to the police."

"Delphine," said Glory, treading gently. "I don't see how I can avoid talking to the police." Sirens blared even louder.

"I see your point," said Delphine, sniffling. "Just keep me on the phone."

Glory met the officer at his car, introduced herself, and waited there until the officers toured the house. When they were ready to talk, Glory handed them her phone. Delphine made it clear that her mother had an attorney, and that her client was not to be interviewed unless she was also present, by phone or videoconference. She suggested they find a quiet place for an interview. As a result, Glory unceremoniously found herself in the back seat of a Lafayette Police Department vehicle.

Maybe it was for the best that she was being hauled away in a patrol car. Now that she had broken the news to her daughter and called 911, she noticed that her hands had not stopped trembling. A sticky, sour film coated the inside of her mouth. It was not the first murder Glory had stumbled upon, but she would never grow accustomed to witnessing such godlessness. And as for Sterling, bless his soul, she felt sorry for the man. He may have been an adulterous husband, but he did not deserve to be filleted on a dingy linoleum floor. You can't go around killing everyone who's been unfaithful, even if you can relate to being full of murderous rage toward a man.

At the police station, Glory was led inside an interrogation room. A wreath composed of purple and gold balls was hung so haphazardly from the wall it looked like a strong fan would send it crashing to the ground. A garland of green beads was wrapped around a pole waving a flag with a pelican on a blue background and a ribbon reading "Union/Justice/Confidence" underneath—the Louisiana state flag. No surface was safe from Mardi Gras decor this time of year, even an interrogation room in a police station.

Glory took a seat on a stiff metal chair and took stock of herself. The bottom half of her red suede shoes were now burgundy, exactly at the point where they had sunken into Sterling's waterlogged yard. A layer of mud ringed itself around the perimeter of her soaked shoes. She bent at the waist to wipe it off, which only caused the mud to smear. Then she took a sip of police station coffee to try to erase the sour taste in her mouth, but her stomach began to roil. It wasn't just the bitterness of the precinct's coffee that made her stomach turn, but also finding her ex-husband's body dissected like a frog in a high school biology class.

The police officer behind the table had a sunburned face and wore a hat that looked more park ranger than cop. He struggled with the heavy, department-issue laptop, and after fumbling for several minutes, finally connected with Delphine on the videoconferencing link she had sent for the interrogation. On the other end, Delphine's face was red and puffy with grief. Her head was wrapped in a scarf, which was unusual, but she had only just been notified of her father's murder. She wouldn't have had much time or presence of mind to pull herself together. On the screen, Glory noticed a figure scurry behind her, avoiding the camera. If Delphine had been dating someone since her divorce, Glory had not been informed.

"Confirm your full name," the officer stated.

Glory looked at her daughter on the screen, who nodded. "Glory Beverly Broussard."

"What is your relationship to the deceased?"

"He is my ex-husband."

The police officer tried to hide his surprise, unsuccessfully. "And what prompted you to visit the residence in Jennings this afternoon, in particular?" Glory looked to her daughter to interject, but Delphine sat there, her tearstained face straining through the screen for the same answer. Glory paused and looked around the room. A small video camera was mounted above the Mardi Gras wreath, up high like one of those convenience store video cameras. It gave her pause.

There are moments when it's better to tell the full truth, and moments when it's better to hold back, if only a little. Glory pondered what kind of moment this was. She knew full well that the police were unlikely to investigate this with the full strength of the department. That's just how they do things down here, she thought, and just wait until they knew more about what kind of man Sterling really was. And even if they did pull out all the stops, what did that mean, really? What was the full investigative strength of a local police department in Louisiana, anyway? And then there was the issue of her first-on-the-scene status. You didn't have to be a federal agent to understand that her finding Sterling's body made her suspect, because no good deed ever goes unpunished. And the fact that this was the second murder she had stumbled upon had to look a certain kind of way, especially to a police department inclined to look for easy answers.

"I was just worried about the man. We sometimes checked in with one another, so I just thought I'd pay him a visit. See how he was doing." She was almost convincing. Delphine leaned in closer to her computer with a proactive posture, like she was ready to jump through the screen and end the questioning, if need be.

"Did you keep in touch after the divorce? How often did you two speak?"

"Well," hesitated Glory, struggling to find an answer that satisfied the question without leading to perjury charges down the road. "I guess you could say we had an unconventional relationship. We didn't talk on the regular, but sometimes he would stop by for a chat, or I'd drive by to see how he was doing. Nothing too formal, you know. When you're married for thirty years and have a child, you keep in touch. Just a little."

She went on to describe how she approached the house and what she saw when she opened the door. This didn't require any censure or careful navigation. She wouldn't have known how to lie about it anyway. Impaled in his chest was a knife, with some kind of design carved into the handle.

"Do you know anyone who would want to harm him?"

Glory paused again. If she was telling the truth, yes. There were probably a dozen folks that Sterling had crossed over the years—and those were only the ones she knew about—though she had no way to know if these were active grievances, or lessons learned and chalked up to the game. She suspected Delphine knew this, too, but she didn't want to document years of transgressions in front of her daughter, not when her lip was still quivering.

"Sir, I haven't been married to the man for several years now. I don't know the specifics of his social circle these days, or his comings and goings." And that was the full truth.

He narrowed his eyes on her. If asked to describe the look, she would have said that he was searching for words that were on the tip of his tongue. "Hey," he said, his face lighting up with the satisfaction of sudden recognition. "Aren't you that lady who solved that murder last year?"

Delphine cleared her throat and interrupted, "That's enough questioning for one day. I am making arrangements as we speak to fly down to Lafayette as quickly as possible, and you are free to interview my client again later in the week, when I'll be there in person." To Glory she added, "Do not answer any additional questions, from anyone, until I arrive." Delphine and the police officer exchanged contact information, and the videoconference was disconnected. Glory watched her daughter disappear, yearning to give her just one hug.

"I guess you're free to go, for now," the officer said.

". . . but you drove me here. I'm gonna need a ride back to my car."

The officer exhaled and flapped his lips. Even if she did need a ride, Glory figured she'd be better off with anyone other than this guy and his dramatics. "Is Lieutenant Beau Landry around? Can you check for me?"

His sunburned face looked immediately redder. "I'll find someone to drive you back to your car. You get who you get."

Fluorescent lighting flickered overhead. Maybe the bulbs were flickering, or maybe her borderline blood pressure was getting the best of her. Possibly both? She dug into her purse and found her silver pillbox, dissolving a pink lozenge under her tongue. They were originally prescribed by her doctor for grief after her mother's death, and then refilled after the murder of her best friend Amity Gay. Her doctor had then urged her to get into some kind of therapy, and Glory nodded her head as if she would consider it, knowing already that she was never going to go sobbing to some stranger about her problems. The doctor insisted it would be the last time he filled this prescription unless she also tried a so-called therapeutic approach, so she took them selectively to make them last. This was as good an occasion as any.

Glory busied herself with tearing the rim off a Styrofoam cup. When the door finally opened, Lieutenant Beau Landry walked in. She had never been so relieved to see the boy. She would always see him as a boy, even though he was a grown man with children of his own. But there was once a time when Glory's mama had bathed him, and so he was frozen in time to her.

"My goodness, Miss Glory," he said, dragging a chair her way. "Again?"

"*Again?* I've only known you since you were about three years old. I was hoping you'd lend a little support, not treat me like some kind of common criminal."

"What I meant to say," he hesitated, searching for words, ". . . is that I'm real sorry you stumbled upon that scene, after everything else you've been through lately."

Glory released her shoulders. "There. That is how you console a perfectly innocent person who's been traumatized, repeatedly, through no fault whatsoever of her own."

"Heard you lawyered up. I suppose that means Delphine is on her way?" Of course he would be asking about Delphine at the first available opportunity. Half of Lafayette had seen the moony look on his face whenever she was around, even though he had married into money and really ought to be more discreet if he wanted to keep living that Benoit lifestyle.

"She's booking a ticket now. I suppose she'll be here by tomorrow."

He nodded. Glory registered what she thought was the teensiest bit of a repressed smile cross his face.

"Let me get you home, then."

"You can just drive me back to Jennings. I need to get my car and then I can drive myself home," Glory insisted.

"No, ma'am," he said. "You are in no state to drive. I'll take you home and find a way to get your car back to you." He gave her shoulder a little squeeze before exiting the room.

With the room quiet, and Glory alone, her mind drifted. For a moment she felt compelled to ring up Delhomme Funeral Home to begin making arrangements. It should be mostly solid Catholic hymns—"Amazing Grace," "On Eagles Wings," or "Be Not Afraid." Maybe a little something that felt more like Sterling at the end, like "I'll Take You There" by the Staple Singers. She thought about fetching the navy suit he wore for Delphine's law school graduation but stopped herself. Those were the duties of a wife. It didn't matter that she was married to Sterling for all those years, and he and his new wife were married for a tiny fraction of that. Glory would not have any responsibility for Sterling's final arrangements.

Glory considered notifying Valerie, given that her instincts had turned out to be correct, but there was no need for that, either. The heels that clicked lightly this morning on the coffee house floor were now clomping against the station tile. Valerie walked purposefully down the hallway, briefly snagging eyes with Glory through the metal slats of the interrogation room blinds. The shared glance seemed to shock them both, and Glory looked away.

The only thing that could stop Valerie was the officer with parched skin. She tried to pivot and move past him, as if the truth was just beyond where he stood. He stopped her, bracing his hands against both of her shoulders. Glory couldn't make out what was being said, but he looked like he was stalling, trying to reposition her to a room elsewhere in the station. He couldn't contain her, or her suspicions. It was evident by what he said next, because Valerie's eyes opened wide, and her mouth opened even wider. Her deafening scream was probably heard all the way to Ponchatoula.

3

The next morning, Glory waited curbside at the Lafayette Regional Airport with her motor running. Landry had delivered it some time in the hours after she went to bed and before she woke up. The man was about as solid as they come. According to the internet, her daughter's flight had arrived, and judging by the stream of people shortly thereafter, most of them were making their way through baggage claim and finding their people. Glory looked for her daughter, wondering what was taking her so long. Lafayette Regional Airport had been remodeled, but it was just as big as before, which is to say not much bigger than a mosquito bite.

She scanned for her daughter through the crowds of travelers, then saw a figure in her side mirror, staring at her. Glory slowly pegged the woman as her daughter and unlocked the doors. Delphine lugged a heavy suitcase into the back of the Honda-CRV and slammed the trunk shut.

The reason Glory had hesitated, and didn't immediately recognize her daughter, was her hair. Her soft, shoulder-length curls were gone, and in their place were narrow, tiny braids extending down to the middle of her back.

Delphine slid into the passenger seat and anticipated the topic of conversation. "Mom, I'm exhausted and overwhelmed. I don't need to hear any criticism about my hair. I'm just trying something new. Please don't make it a thing."

Glory clutched her chest. "Delphine, I didn't say a single word."

"I know you better than anyone, and I know you're going to have something to say. Don't worry, you can browbeat me later."

Damned if her daughter didn't know her well. "I . . . I think it looks nice. Just different. Took a second for that recognition to snap in. Don't you fuss at me. Give me a hug." Delphine and Glory embraced, a little longer than usual. For once, Delphine was not the first to turn away.

"Let's go home. I can see you could use some rest." They drove home in wordless silence, like an adult child who visits home a couple times a year does. There was always a warm-up period when they became reacquainted, and now there was a whole murder between them.

Glory pulled up to the home on Viator Drive. The only colors on the dried-out lawn were the Mardi Gras ornaments stuck in the grass on posts—a court jester's hat and two leering masks, in purple and gold. The women shuffled inside. Delphine settled into her childhood bedroom for a nap, and Glory sunk into her recliner for just a few moments, or at least that's what she told herself. One minute she was pondering Delphine's hair, and why she felt the need to add all that fake hair in. Eventually, she woke up, her mouth hanging open and dry on account of her sleeping like that for probably two hours. No wonder she needed a nap, with the way the world was swirling around her.

In the living room stood her Mardi Gras tree, which was not uncommon in Lafayette. This was something of a new tradition, and a great way to procrastinate taking down the artificial Christmas tree. For Glory it was an excuse to buy a bunch of new ornaments at the local shops—peacock feathers, beads, and even more masks than she already had. With the popularity of this decor, a tree could now stand tall in Lafayette living rooms from late November until the end of February.

Glory looked at her watch, then got to work in the kitchen, searching her pantry for the right ingredients. Glory had not spoken with Camille, Sterling's sister, in a couple years, but stopping by with a cake is always the right thing to do in times like these.

She gathered the shredded coconut, evaporated milk, vanilla, sugar, eggs, and butter on the kitchen counter. She opened a tattered Paul Prudhomme cookbook to a page that was transparent in spots from buttered fingers. Not long after, Delphine padded into the room with bare feet, black leggings, and a torn T-shirt.

"Baby, I didn't mean to wake you up, but I wanted to get started on this here cake," said Glory. A cell phone trembled on the countertop, next to a bag of flour. Glory silenced it and put it on the windowsill.

"You didn't wake me." Delphine yawned. "I've been up for a while now."

Glory flicked two sticks of butter from their wrappers and poured a stream of sugar into the bowl of a mixer. She placed a cold brew coffee with almond milk on the table. She had picked it up that morning at CC's specially for her daughter. Delphine sipped; her face filled with gratitude. Suddenly, Delphine gasped. She yanked her knees up to her chest, as if she had seen a mouse. Below her was a black cat with glossy fur and a flickering tail, weaving itself through the legs of her chair. "You got a cat?!"

Glory cracked a couple of eggs into the bowl and gathered the shells into the trash. Under different circumstances, they might have had a good laugh about how that formerly ragged cat—now plump—had come to live an exceedingly comfortable existence on Viator Drive. She would have reminded her daughter of that trailer park psychic they saw who encouraged her to find a symbol of protection to weaken a curse. For various reasons, Glory had come to believe that symbol was this cat. It's not that she really believed in that gobbledygook, but why not help the down-on-its-luck creature? Sometimes people, and animals, just draw bad hands. But she didn't want to launch into the whole story now, given everything her daughter was going through.

"Oh, that's Patti LaBelle. Remember that scraggly cat that had been skulking around my backyard? I decided to take her in." Glory's phone vibrated again.

"Do you need to get that?"

"Damn it, I thought I turned that off." Glory grabbed the phone again and powered it down completely. She didn't recognize the number that had been calling her all day, but had a hunch who it might be. "Nah, just some telemarketers. Do you know someone called the other day asking about a warranty on my boat? I don't even know how to swim."

Delphine returned her feet to the floor and gave the cat a little scratch on one ear. Patti immediately rubbed herself against Delphine's leg. "This is that same cat? Wow, she looks great."

Glory felt a surge of pride in her caregiving skills, especially because this was her first-ever pet. Back when she was growing up, they barely had enough money to make rent, let alone voluntarily sign up for another mouth to feed—especially one with a tail.

"Who are you making a cake for?" asked Delphine.

"Your Aunt Camille. Figured we'd stop by later today. We should pay our respects and bring a little something. Don't forget. She's your *marraine*, and I know she'd love to see you." Delphine agreed.

The whir of the beaters filled the kitchen. "Delphine, I know you're not one to share much about your inner thoughts, but I'd really like to know what you're feeling right now."

Delphine sipped her coffee and, to Glory's surprise, the words started to flow. "I can't believe this is happening, that it's real. I know he was trying to get out of . . ." she paused, searching for the words. "Whatever it was that he was doing these days, but . . ." Her lip trembled. She covered her face with her hands and began to cry. Glory turned off the mixer and gathered her daughter in her arms.

"He didn't deserve to die," Delphine sobbed. "He just didn't deserve to die."

There was no need to ring the doorbell at Camille's house because, judging by the cars, it was a full house. You might as well let yourself in. Glory watched over her daughter, who by now had straightened up her face. The women walked up the stairs to the front door. Glory caught a glimpse of a line of demarcation running along the exterior of the house. The line was a reminder of how high the floods rose during that terrible hurricane years ago, and that Camille lived in an area that was nestled low, even by Lafayette standards. The house had been renovated since, but the line was a permanent marker. Every Louisiana resident is at the grace and favor of the weather and the Lord. You better pray that they both cooperated at the same time. If they didn't, your only recourse was FEMA, which was its own kind of hell.

Delphine opened the door for her mother, who balanced a coconut cake, tented in aluminum foil, on her forearms. Inside was a coterie of people that Glory had seen before, but not in years. Cousins and distant cousins of Sterling's, frail aunts and uncles that had managed to endure, and other miscellaneous relatives connected to you in ways only the family factotum could explain. You might not fully understand it, but you generally accept them as your people.

Glory was relieved that Camille could have a little comfort in her later years in this renovated house. It checked off every interior trend Joanna Gaines had made popular—gray wood flooring, beadboard paneling on the walls, and farmhouse doors that opened to the dining room. Here, trays of homemade food had been delivered. Spread across the table was rice dressing prepared correctly, with ground gizzards, piles of biscuits so high that Glory knew immediately they were prepared with White Lily flour, and desserts. Ambrosia and banana pudding had been prepared in deep bowls, and Glory's coconut cake was the third such specimen of the day.

Glory looked around the room to situate herself while Delphine rearranged platters on the dining table to make room for the cake. She saw a large backside covered in stretch crepe and instantly recognized it as Camille's. She glided across the room to greet Sterling's sister and couldn't help but notice That Woman, Valerie, dabbing her eyes with a tissue.

Glory went half blind with anger. If Glory was a woman prone to acting up, she would have smashed the cake in Valerie's face, the way they do to celebrities that still wear fur. That Woman had not earned the right to mourn alongside Sterling's family, nor did she warrant any sympathy. In Glory's mind she was an agent of chaos, not some helpless, pitiful thing. If anyone was deserving of sympathy in this "rock-paper-scissors" game of grief that Glory was playing in her head, it was her daughter. Yet there Valerie was, in a tight black dress, acting like she was mourning when she was making a right spectacle of herself. Valerie looked up and blew her nose. Just like at the police station, they made eye contact quickly, but Glory broke it off.

"Let's go say hello to your cousin Charity," said Glory, physically steering her daughter away while keeping tabs on Valerie. The problem was that Valerie was also keeping close tabs on Glory, matching her glance for glance.

"Look, your second cousin Earvin is outside, you haven't seen him in a while," Glory said, maneuvering Delphine to the patio. Valerie stood up and tried to head in their direction but was slowed by a steady trickle of well-wishers. These kinds of gatherings are a lot like weddings—everyone wants credit for showing up. They want their attendance noted and appreciated.

After acknowledging everyone in the room, Valerie made her way outside, to the concrete slab of a patio and a grill packed with ribs and turkey wings. She found Delphine through the barbeque smoke and grabbed both hands. "I am so, so sorry for what happened to your father," said Valerie. And then she turned to Glory. "I can imagine this is uncomfortable for you, but I really hope you can put any bad feelings aside and help out."

"Help?" asked Delphine, confused.

Earvin turned the ribs over, but kept looking over his shoulder at the women, trying not to miss a thing. Valerie, bewildered, threw her hands in the air. "I can see that your mother hasn't filled you in on anything. I can't believe it, Glory. I've been leaving you voicemails and texts for the past twenty-four hours, and you haven't even told your daughter?"

Glory stiffened. "What I talk to my daughter about is none of your business."

Delphine interrupted, "What is going on here, Mom?"

Glory rolled her eyes. "Valerie came to the coffee shop to tell me that your father was missing and asked for my help. So, I drove out to Jennings where I expected I might find him, though I didn't think he'd be dead. I did my part."

Valerie jumped in. "In my many, many messages, I asked for her help in solving Sterling's murder, just like she did a few months ago with that nun."

"Well, you'll have to forgive me for not wanting to chitchat with you, of all people," spat Glory.

Valerie groaned. "You might have a hard time believing this, but this is not about *you*, Glory Broussard. You may have known one version of Sterling, but he had *changed*. He was a different man than the person you knew."

"And did you ever wonder how that happened? Did you? I spent the best years of my life raising that man, training him to be an adult and a decent human being. He didn't just come that way. I was raising a child and a grown-ass man at the same time. I guess the one lesson I forgot to teach is *thou shall not cheat*."

In anger, Delphine threw a water glass to the patio floor. It exploded on the concrete, sending shards flying. Glory stood, unable to move or speak from the sheer surprise of it. Valerie winced, clutching her face with both hands as a piece of glass grazed the side of her face.

"Oh my god, Valerie, I'm so sorry," said Delphine. She took the cocktail napkin wrapped around her drink and applied pressure to Valerie's cheek. Glory bristled at how friendly they seemed, and how fast Delphine ran to her aid.

Earvin was slack-jawed at the drama in front of him and made no effort to hide his amazement. "Jesus Christ, Earvin, go inside," said Glory.

"Can't. Who's going to watch my meat?" he asked, oblivious.

"I'll watch your stupid meat. Just take your Black ass inside," yelled Glory.

He smirked and retreated into the house, handing Glory a pair of tongs and pushing through a crowd of spectators that had assembled by the back door.

Delphine lifted the napkin off Valerie's face. A small, puffy gash was still red from blood, and she applied even more pressure. "Mom, why won't you help?"

"I told you I did help. I knew about the duplex he kept and . . ."

Valerie took custody of the napkin from Delphine, freeing her to confront Glory. "Believe me, I'm not wild about asking you for help, and I hate to admit this, but you know Sterling better than anyone. I didn't even know that he owned a house in Jennings. If we are going to solve this case, we're going to need your help."

Glory opened Earvin's grill, coughing at the plumes of smoke rising in her face. As promised, she tended to the ribs, the turkey wings, and the hamburgers in the corner that looked more than done. With a pair of tongs, she removed some of the ribs and put them on a plate. She shook her head in disapproval, yelling in Earvin's direction. "Earvin, you're not supposed to crowd all this meat on the grill. It won't brown properly."

She worked on spacing the meat according to her liking. Looking down at the ribs, she responded to That Woman. "Look, I know folks around here think I'm some kind of detective after everything that happened with Amity, but this is different. Police thought they had it all figured out, but anyone who knew her understood it made no kind of sense. But Sterling? This is a straight-up murder, no question about it. The police are investigating. I'm happy to share anything that might help, but I don't want to be traipsing all over

Lafayette looking for a killer. In case y'all forgot, I nearly got myself killed last time."

Delphine's balled fists were propped on the top of her head, like she was trying to will it all away. She took a deep breath, then faced her mother. "I know you don't want to do this. But if you can't do this for a person you were married to for all those years, then I'm asking you to do it for me. And if you can't do it for me, do it for yourself."

"What do you mean?" Glory continued flipping the meat. Was that *lamb?* She couldn't help but wonder when Black people started grilling lamb.

Delphine continued, "What I mean is that until Dad's murder is solved, it means that they're going to be circling around you, a woman who has found two dead bodies in just a few short months. It might make it hard for you to work . . ."

Glory waved the smoke rising from the grill. Delphine did have a point. She didn't need the police following her around, scaring off her customers. And then there was the issue of her daughter. The amount of residual love Glory had for Sterling was questionable. But for her daughter? Endless.

4

The funeral of Sterling Broussard was the next day. He wore a black suit, and everybody at the service complimented the presentation of the body, especially given the undignified way he met his death. He had been raised in the Catholic tradition like Glory, which was why she was surprised to learn that That Woman and her people were Baptists. There were no Catholic hymns, and Glory had been unprepared for all that hollering and carrying on in a church. It was not the way she would have planned any of it, not that it mattered.

The next evening, Glory and Delphine agreed to meet Valerie at the hair salon where she worked. She would have done anything her daughter had asked of her, especially during this time. But now she was unwillingly in cahoots with the woman who broke up her marriage, driving to her place of employment. After Glory agreed to be a part of this so-called investigation, Delphine had tried to suggest that they meet at CC's, her coffee shop. Glory had to put her foot down. The coffee shop was where she met with clients, but it was also her refuge. Valerie had already violated her sacred space once. She wasn't about to invite her in again. Then Delphine had nearly suggested they meet at Glory's house, but Glory interrupted before could. She was not about to let That Woman violate her home as well as her marriage. Instead, Glory proactively suggested they meet at Valerie's hair salon. It's always easier to leave than to kick someone out.

Glory pulled into the parking lot of the shopping center, which was dotted with small buildings, like those tiny houses Glory had seen on HGTV. These tiny buildings were fine for a little business, but for a home? *Not me*, thought Glory. It's funny that what they used to call a gardening shed they now call a house. One little building was Carrier Jewelers, another was The Pecan Company. And then there was Valerie's salon, The New Woman.

Glory applied some lip gloss in her rearview mirror. "I guess being the *new woman* is not just her approach to married men, but to life."

Delphine sighed. "Are you going to do this all day?"

"Probably."

Since the funeral, Glory had noticed even more changes in her daughter other than the braids. Of greatest concern was a small gold ring implanted in her nose. Of lesser concern were ripped jeans, a bohemian blouse, and a fragrance that might have been patchouli, which smelled like someone's armpit.

"So, you're wearing a nose ring now. That's interesting," said Glory. She just couldn't help herself.

Delphine sighed impatiently. "Not that I owe you an explanation, because I'm an adult woman with full agency, but this is just a clip-in."

"Oh, thank God." Glory felt palpable relief. "Why don't you go ahead and clip that right on out, then."

"No. Are you ready to go inside?"

What had gotten into her daughter? A few short months ago she was prim and proper and dressed to the nines. Now it was like she was embodying a bad impression of Lisa Bonet.

A chime rang when they walked through the salon door. The inside was nothing like the outside. Outside, the structure was quaint, cottage-like. Inside, the vintage look gave way to glossy white tiles and a sleek leather couch in the waiting area. There was even a little corner in the salon decked out with ring lights and a backdrop. Judging by the way a young woman was preening and making a spectacle of herself, it was something of a stage with cameras for what young people called "social media content." It wasn't Glory's kind of place. First and foremost, she was happy with the way Brendan down at Scissor Time cut and colored her hair. He'd been tending to her tresses for nearly as long as she had been married to Sterling. Second, she didn't understand the fascination folks had these days with documenting every picayune detail of their life for the world to see. So, you got a haircut? *Congratulations.*

Delphine and Glory sank into the low-slung black leather couch. A dignified older woman sat under a bonnet hair dryer; her manicured nails busy with a needlepoint project. When Valerie turned the heat off and removed the hood, Glory could see the frail woman was Millie Broward, fellow Red Hat member. Millie Broward was the kind of woman who got a roller set every week and never missed Mass. A fine woman, if you asked Glory.

"Millie, I didn't know you got your hair done here," said Glory.

"Yes, indeed. Miss Valerie keeps me looking young," Millie said, with a wink. There is nothing like a wink from an older Black woman. It feels like an arrow of love exploding in your heart. "Come take a seat and talk to me while I try to look like Marilyn McCoo."

Glory did not want to sit in such close proximity to Valerie, who was unpinning pink rollers from Millie's hair, but it was impossible to turn her down. She was the only Red Hat member who was ever consistently nice to Glory, even before her current, slightly improved standing in the organization.

"So, I hear you're running the big show," she said, referring to the church's Mardi Gras programming. "I hope you placed your king cake order already at Gambino's. Heard they're no longer accepting group orders and it's not even February yet."

Glory did not want to let on that she hadn't even considered this. "Well, I'm thinking that we ought to try somewhere new this year. Maybe Breaux Brothers bakery."

Millie raised an eyebrow while Valerie fluffed and sculpted her client's hair with her hands. "If anyone knows how difficult these women can be, it's you. I recommend you stick with the classics and not reinvent the wheel, or else you might find yourself in a worse position than you were before."

It was true that there was a time when Glory was not in good standing with the Red Hat Society of Acadiana, but that had changed, or so she had thought. But Millie was right, you're never truly in good standing with the members of this fickle group. One day you're in and the next day out, on account of some small transgression, like not poaching the meat for your chicken salad or some other unspoken rule.

"I hear you, but I'm really trying to put my own stamp on it this year," replied Glory.

"Well then, go ahead and put your little stamp on it, but don't say I didn't warn you."

Valerie removed the hairdresser cape from Millie's shoulders with a flourish. "What do you think?" asked Valerie.

As soon as Millie caught a glimpse of herself, her posture straightened. There's a certain inspection a woman does after she gets her hair done. Millie pivoted her hair to the left, then the right. She tucked a tuft of hair behind one ear, then smiled. "Valerie, you got me looking so good I gotta put some lipstick on!"

Valerie laughed while Millie arranged several lipstick options on the counter in front of her. She settled on a bold, bright red.

"Watch out now . . . not the red!" said Valerie in jest. "You know I did good if she pulled out the red lipstick."

Glory noticed the easy way Valerie had with people. Sterling, too, must have been seduced by this breathy laugh that she doled out freely.

"Girl, I can't even believe you're out here doing hair, a day after Sterling's funeral and that god-awful thing that happened to him," said Millie.

"I do not cancel appointments. Ever. Especially not for my regular and most beloved clients." Valerie wiped down her scissors and rolled them up in a leather case. "And besides, it beats staying home and crying. I'd rather try to make myself useful. Keep busy."

Millie stuffed the various tubes of lipstick back in her purse. "The police got any leads?"

Valerie shook her head. "I've been checking in with them every day. They keep telling me that they're working on it, that I've got to be patient, let them do their job."

Glory scoffed. "That's what they say when they ain't got a single bird in hand."

Millie stood up and handed Valerie a fistful of folded-up bills. Valerie stuffed them in her bra like she was a waitress in a biker bar. Millie pointed at Valerie. "It's a good thing you're partnering up with Glory, though I must say I'm surprised you two aren't at each other's throats." Sterling's affair had been a hot topic among the Red Hat Society of Acadiana. Despite her advanced age, Millie had not forgotten a single detail.

"Give it time," said Glory. "Give it time."

Delphine, still seated on the couch, sighed and looked away.

"Thanks again for the hair," said Millie, then gave Glory a final warning. "And I'll tell you one last time. Don't go messing with that king cake!"

Valerie opened the door for Millie, flipped the sign to "closed," then locked it behind her.

"You heard the woman, don't go messing with that king cake," said Delphine in a playful, mocking way. Valerie smiled at this, and it infuriated Glory. Why did it suddenly feel like they were yucking it up in a conspiratorial kind of way? Glory had made it crystal clear that she didn't want to be involved, and instead of being grateful for her participation, they were taunting her. *She* was the one with the unblemished track record of solving murders. They ought to show more respect.

"I love those braids," said Valerie, walking over to Delphine. She inspected them, nodding with approval. "Braider did a good job with this . . . must have taken what, six, seven hours?"

"Nine," Delphine replied.

"You can tell. Real nice job . . . sure would love to offer this here, but we just don't have enough braiders. And the few we have want to charge a fortune. More than the market can bear. Women down here will pay money for their hair, but they ain't paying that much money," said Valerie.

Glory cleared her throat. "You sure your boss is okay with us being here after hours?" asked Glory.

"She sure is," said Valerie. "You're looking at her. I own this salon."

Against her will, Glory's eyes started to blink rapidly, and she sat on the sofa next to her daughter.

"Anyway, I suggest we get down to business," said Glory, holding her purse tightly against her vest like a shield. "I know the police told you to be patient, but that is the very worst thing you could do. The first few days of a murder investigation are crucial."

"Really?" asked Valerie. She pulled a wheeled stool that she used while trimming the ends of clients' hair closer to the sofa and sat down. "How so?"

Glory racked her brain for how to respond. Truth be told, she had seen this on some TV show, but obviously couldn't admit it. "Evidence. People eventually will get rid of evidence, but it takes time. Also, behavior. We need to see who's acting strange or different right now, before they get comfortable again. That means they know something or have something to hide."

Valerie nodded her head like a student.

"Let's start with who attended the funeral. Sometimes folks act slick and show up to the funeral to try to throw everyone off. Let's make a list."

Valerie popped up off her chair and walked over to the reception desk. She returned with a green book that she thrust toward Glory.

"What's this?" asked Glory.

"The funeral guest book. And even if folks didn't sign, I added as many names as I could remember once I got home. I . . . just wanted to remember who showed up for him." Tears flowed down her face. Delphine grabbed some tissues from a nearby hairdresser stand and handed them to Valerie.

"I'm sorry but . . . this is so hard." She wept again, and Delphine clutched her forearm.

As she watched Valerie's theatrics, the veins in Glory's neck popped out like when her mama had a stroke. Delphine's father, an actual blood relation, had died too, and her daughter was consoling *Valerie*, as if she was the only one who was grieving. It must be nice to float around in the world, always putting your own needs first, Glory fumed.

Fed up with Valerie's theatrics, she cleared her throat. "I'll take a look at this tonight. Now, what was Sterling up to these days, and I mean *really* up to."

"He was working at Cypress Downs Casino as a pit manager," said Valerie, still passing tissues over her face to blot the tears.

Glory grew impatient. "Now look, if we are going to get anything done, you're going to have to tell the truth. I know who Sterling is . . . was . . . so you don't have to sugarcoat anything."

Valerie's voice grew more resolute. "I'm telling the truth. He had been working at the Cypress Downs Casino as a pit manager for sports betting. He went down to interview for a dealer position, and by the time it was over he was managing sports betting."

As much as Glory couldn't imagine him working a 9-to-5, something about this rang true. It would be exactly like Sterling to go in for a low-level job and fast-talk his way to management. And no doubt he was a master at sports betting. He had taught Glory the ropes.

"So we go to the casino," declared Delphine.

"We go to the casino," Valerie joined in. This display of solidarity was the last straw for Glory.

"Now listen here, I'm willing to participate because of my daughter, but I'll go about my business alone. I don't need you tagging along like some kind of . . ."

Delphine stood up from the sofa. "Mama, stop!" she yelled. "I know you have your reasons not to like Valerie, but I'm going to need you to put those aside and act like an adult. I've had enough of this sniping and eye rolling."

Glory's hands trembled with rage. It wasn't just that she disliked Valerie, it's more like she despised her with the heat of a thousand summertime Louisiana suns. How else was she supposed to feel about a woman that got tangled up in bedsheets with her husband? Delphine may have been her daughter, but she couldn't erase what Valerie had done, and *when* it happened. It didn't take any of Glory's special arithmetic to know that the timeline of Valerie's relationship with Sterling had not added up.

"May I speak?" asked Valerie.

Glory smirked and pursed her lips, which was about all the permission she could ever grant this woman.

"I know Sterling and I did not behave properly in the past, and I can't make that up to you now," Valerie pleaded. "But if I have to beg to get you involved, then I'm begging. You know that man better than anyone, which doesn't make me feel great as his partner for the last several years, and wife for most of those. But we all know it's true. I don't like it any more than you do, but I do know it's necessary. I'll follow your lead. Please, Glory."

"I'll do my best . . . for my daughter." She tucked the condolence book under her arm, and Valerie unlocked the door to let them out. Delphine waited in the car while Glory walked to The Pecan Company for a bag of sweet and spicy pecans. For later.

5

Glory was fired up by the time she got home. Yes, she was sorry that Sterling ended up this way, but she also believed when all was said and done, they'd find out that he was no angel. The chance of Sterling Broussard being innocent was about the same as a chilly Louisiana day in August.

She changed into her nightgown and tucked herself into bed. Rather, she squeezed herself into the half of the bed that was not sprinkled with belongings like picture frames, paint swatches, and other miscellany. She squirted hand lotion into her palms and wrung them around each other, imaging for a brief moment that it was Valerie's neck.

Delphine's voice traveled from down the hallway, and Glory wondered who she was talking to on the phone at night. Hell, she constantly wondered what Delphine was up to. There were times when she felt close to her daughter, like they were shaped from the same piece of clay. Other times, she felt like an acquaintance. She had little idea how she spent her days, or what her dreams even were. As a child Delphine yearned to get out of Lafayette and go to law school. Now that she had done both, what was next? What did she want from life? Did she want a family, or had the example of Glory and Sterling's marriage scared her off from all that? There was a part of Glory that wished she'd just settle down with a nice guy, but that's what Glory had done. Or at least thought she'd done. And it had caused her nothing but heartache. Sterling was dead and still managing to kick up dust from beyond the grave.

Glory's eyelids grew heavier, but Valerie's green guest book glared at her from her bedside table. She wanted nothing more than to go to sleep, but found herself propping up a pillow and flipping through its pages. Signed in blue ink from a scratchy ballpoint pen were dozens of Broussards, some Fontenots she recognized from Alexandria, and some Blanchards she knew from Baton Rouge. In impeccable penmanship was Delphine's name, with a little hand-drawn heart beside her signature. On the back page were names written in the same script, including *Glory Broussard, born Scott, Louisiana.* It must have been Valerie's handwriting, thought Glory, documenting who showed up with the attention of a genealogist.

There were a few names she didn't recognize. She wasn't much for the internet, but Glory was trying to be more open-minded. She had seen how Delphine could just type in a few words and all kinds of information would flood the screen. One name in particular surprised her. She recorded it in her notebook and made a mental note to follow up in person.

But mostly, she couldn't stop replaying everything that happened in the salon, even commenting on Delphine's hair like they were bosom friends. *Of course*, Valerie would love those braids. Delphine wasn't her daughter, and she didn't have to worry about looking respectable to folks like Glory did, not that she was even trying. Used to be a time when you couldn't even get a job with hair like that. Times might have changed, but the hands of time move slower here in Louisiana than New York City.

Glory was burning anew with anger. The only outlet she could find was talking to the Lord. Some people prayed. Glory talked. She never liked the idea of reaching out to the Lord with her hand out, begging for this and that. She preferred an open and honest line of communication.

Lord, I don't know why you saw it fit to pair me with Sterling Broussard in the first place. The only reason I can think of is my daughter, the only good thing to come out of that union. But now you got me all tangled up with That Woman. Is it the gambling? Is Valerie my punishment because I'm still working as a bookie? I wish I could give that up, but you know I need my work. I'm not willing to go back to working shifts at the grocery store. In fact, I can't, on account of my feet and my joints and everything in my body feeling like it's on fire most of the time, even when I'm lying in bed. The warranty on this body expired a long time ago. So, I'm sorry, but this is what I got to do. There are people that do far worse than me. Go chase after them. I'd appreciate it if you let me live out my final years in peace. Please let this be the last run-in I have with anything pertaining to Sterling or That Woman.

Speaking of which, I'd also appreciate it if you chose another vessel for finding the dead bodies of Lafayette. They say God makes no mistakes, but maybe you could just double-check if I'm truly the intended recipient for all this nonsense. Anyway, if you could let me know, I'd appreciate it.

As she wrapped up her prayers, she remained in a state of consternation for at least another hour. At some point she drifted off for good.

A pounding on her glass storm door is what finally woke her up. The pounding had a frustrated intensity. It was the kind of pounding that probably didn't start out that way, and became louder once previous, more polite attempts went ignored. Glory fumbled for her reading glasses, then her phone, and noticed two things. First was a text from Delphine that said she'd headed out and would be back later in the day. The second was a notification from the doorbell camera Delphine had installed a few months back. She clicked on the notification and did a double take when she realized it was one of her nemeses, Constance Wheeler.

Maybe it wasn't fair to call her a nemesis, because it was Constance who had appointed her as the chair of the Mardi Gras committee. But that was only after years of dismissive behavior that no number of honorifics could erase. Glory's ability to hold a grudge was as deep and long as the Mississippi River.

She swung her feet to the ground. She had no idea why Constance would be showing up at her house at all, especially in the morning on a weekday, but Glory was prepared to give her a piece of her mind and send her packing. She wrapped herself in her bathrobe and struggled down the hallway with a noticeable limp and audible cracking of the knees, the best she could do without time to warm up. She opened the front door, revealing a Constance that was too smug, too proud of herself, and wearing too much perfume.

"Now, I don't know why you've come knocking on my door at this impolite hour," said Glory, winding up. "But whatever Red Hat business you have, you can take it up at the meeting. Y'all just can't be showing up at my front door to holler about king cake or whatever detail you want to review at any old time." She tightened the belt on her robe for extra emphasis and shut the door.

Constance shoved a pink, heeled shoe into the door, catching it before it slammed. She then inserted her entire left shoulder to prop the door open. That's when the perfume walloped Glory. It had top notes of white florals, with base notes of disdain. Everything about Constance felt dated, like she hadn't seen a beauty or fashion trend since 1986. "You really shouldn't treat your court-ordered community advocate in such a shoddy fashion. It could impact my findings. You may think you're above the law, Glory Broussard, but I am here to tell you that you most definitely are not."

Glory rolled her eyes. "You can't intimidate me. All that court order nonsense is done and over with. Now, go ahead and get off my property before I call the exterminator and have you fumigated."

Constance was undeterred, as confident as ever in her meager abilities. "I regret to inform you that your court-ordered supervision is not over, and you must submit to an inspection of your home." The inspections were a result of an unfounded, anonymous call to the city months ago, when her petty sister, who remained angry that their mother bequeathed the house to Glory, reported her house as a hazard to the city.

"I told you, we did that already."

"We did it once. You're required to submit to inspections again at the three-month mark and the six-month mark. This officially marks three months," said Constance, looking as if she had won a debate competition. "But you have nothing to worry about, because I am a professional and maintain the strictest of confidence. I remain righteous in *all* my affairs."

Glory knew that she was taking a swipe at her, and how she made her money. She would have responded with an equal amount of venom if Constance didn't have the ability to make her life more agonizing with an unsatisfactory report.

"The least you could do is be fast so I can go about my day. Unlike you, I make my own money," said Glory.

Constance ran a finger across her mahogany entryway console, inspecting for dust. "I have a job of my own, but yes, I can only imagine how hard it is to be single at your age." She walked into the living room. Glory trailed closely behind.

"I know that's the way you see things, but I wouldn't consider myself single. Not anymore," said Glory. "I am a sole proprietor. I ain't got time to manage any distressed properties. I'm through with fixer-uppers." Both women knew this was a reference to Constance's husband, who might have been a so-called executive with a big office, but also visited Glory's office more Sundays than not.

Constance examined the living room, making notes on her clipboard. "Say whatever you need to make yourself feel better about living in this big old house by yourself."

A black cat jumped in Constance's way and hissed, causing her to startle and clutch her chest. She quickly regained her composure. "I see you've accumulated a beast since my last visit."

"That's Patti LaBelle," confirmed Glory. "She knows who's good people . . . and who's not."

Constance pressed herself against the wall and maneuvered away from the cat. "Please let me do my job in peace, won't you? I cannot conduct my inspection with you talking nonstop and following me around."

Glory backed off and watched from a corner in the living room while Constance inspected every nook and cranny. She opened her curio cabinet, making silent judgments about her brass ducks and glass figurines, and then did the same with the Mardi Gras tree.

Once she had inspected Glory's tree, Constance moved into the formal dining room she never used anymore, which housed her china hutches. Constance moved closer toward her collection, the Waterford Crystal and china of unidentifiable lineage trembling louder at her approach.

"What are you doing with all these dishes?" asked Constance. "You can't possibly be entertaining that often or needing this many service pieces. You need to cull this collection."

There was a time when every piece of her collection had been put to good use. Sterling loved to entertain, and even though Glory would never admit it, he was a fantastic cook—even better than she was. It was common for them to entertain for groups of twenty or more. Sometimes he'd make a big pot of gumbo. Other times, he'd smoke a giant brisket for ten hours while Glory made all the fixings, like macaroni and cheese, red beans and rice with bits of andouille, crispy hush puppies, and smothered potatoes. But since he left, the dishes were little-used. She might as well be collecting postcards at this point—mementos from long-lived memories. Valerie had not just stolen her husband, she had taken the celebrations that once resided in this now-empty room.

Constance dragged a finger across the hutch, catching just a small amount of dust on her fingertip. She walked into the kitchen. "As much as it pains me to say this, it does seem that you've been able to maintain order in this household. I'll be noting this in my report to the judge, though I haven't decided whether or not to include your contemptible attitude." She scratched away on her clipboard.

Glory smirked. "Do you always carry that clipboard around?" Whether in her house or at Red Hat meetings, that clipboard remained glued to Constance's side.

"People don't take you seriously automatically. You have to make them. I find the clipboard reinforces my authority." She wiped her hand against her slacks, as if her inspection of the house had left her sullied. "Anyway, it's eleven in the morning. Is this what you do on the weekdays, just sleep until the afternoon and bark at decent people trying to do their jobs?"

Glory had finally run out of witticisms. "If you want to know the truth, I'm just plain worn out, what with Sterling and all that, and now Delphine's in town, and I got that ex-wife . . . I guess they call her a widow now . . . hounding me to help her find the killer. And I don't want anything to do with any of that kind of business, not no more." She had no idea why she was confiding in this woman like she was a friend instead of a court-appointed busybody, but regardless, she found herself in a confessional mood. She inserted a pod into her coffee machine.

Constance sat down at the kitchen table. "I was sorry to hear about Sterling. I know Clarence was fond of him . . . thought he was a real nice guy. Not going to lie though, I hated when they used to hang out together. He'd always come home a few hundred dollars poorer after doing whatever it was they did together. I—" She stopped abruptly. Her eyes squinted and narrowed in on at least a dozen multicolored Post-it Notes stuck to the refrigerator. She got up from the table and started removing the notes one by one, reading each one out loud. "*Call the bakery? Order linens? Source glassware? Hire the DJ?*" She looked at Glory. "Please tell me that this isn't your Mardi Gras checklist. And please tell me you've completed all these tasks."

Glory opened her eyes wide, searching for the right words, none of which would appease Constance.

"These tasks needed to be done months ago! When I led the committee, I had a spreadsheet with everything that needed to be done, and to keep track of the updates and the confirmation numbers and the vendors. It required the utmost organization."

"You make it sound like I've done nothing at all," said Glory, placing a mug in her coffee maker. "Of course I've started planning. I'm just . . . a little behind."

"Behind with what, exactly?" Constance raised a suspicious eyebrow.

"Everything written on those stickies?" Glory turned around and faced the coffee machine, evading Constance's wrath.

"I knew it! I just knew it," said Constance, clapping her hands like a school mistress in front of unruly children. "We should have appointed a more experienced chair to the Mardi Gras committee and not . . . *you.*"

"I am just as qualified as anyone else to lead Mardi Gras. I just didn't foresee the murder of my ex-husband, the arrival of my distraught daughter, and his former mistress—now grieving widow—all up in my business." The coffee machine gurgled and turned itself off once the coffee was finished. With a sheepish look on her face, Glory added, "Maybe an outstanding member of the Red Hat Society of Acadiana could help out a little?"

"Oh, how the tide has turned!" Constance exhaled a bitter laugh. "If I recall correctly, just a few months ago you were *blackmailing* me. You've spent the last twenty minutes hurling insults in my direction—as a representative of the court, even. I don't see why I should help you at all."

Glory didn't consider it blackmailing in the strictest sense. She had merely wanted access to government databases, which Constance had access to as the regional manager of the DMV. "That wasn't blackmail. I was solving a murder," said Glory. Was a plan of action immoral if it worked? Realizing this tactic was getting her nowhere, she shifted strategies. “Maybe I am not the most experienced person to lead the committee, but how does someone get the required experience unless they have a mentor? How can we, as an organization, build a legacy of success without the proper mentoring and passing down of traditions?” She followed that up with a pleading smile. “On the other hand, you’d get to boss me around and tell me what to do. Isn’t that your love language?”

“If I did this, it would be for St. Agnes and the group, not for you, Glory Broussard. Let the record show.” Another uneasy alliance had formed.

Lieutenant Beau Landry was already seated on the outside porch of the restaurant by the time Delphine arrived. He gave an earnest wave and smile when he saw her, but quickly thought better of it and suppressed his glee. He stood up and gave her a long, heartfelt hug. They had both agreed months ago that what had happened between them at the cabin was done and finished, but that didn’t mean they couldn’t linger in this embrace a bit longer.

“I’ve never been here before,” he said. Spoonbill was an old Conoco gas station downtown that had been converted into an outdoor restaurant. The original red Conoco sign had remained, along with the fluorescent tube lighting that snaked around the awning. Where drivers once tanked up on gas, now stood cheery yellow umbrellas and giant fans cooling customers.

“This is the only place in town where you can get a decent salad. You know how they do salads in Louisiana. Topped with crawfish with cheese poured on top.” She looked across the street toward the courthouse, finding it hard to be present, and even harder to look Landry in the eyes. She hiked her braids up into a ponytail.

He gave her hand a squeeze, and then kept it there, nestled on top of hers. Delphine would have sighed with relief, if that felt appropriate. "I'm real sorry about your daddy. I know the two of you weren't especially close . . ."

"You know, I really wish people would stop making assumptions about my relationship with my father. People around here sure like to talk without having any actual facts." A server interrupted them to share the specials of the evening. Delphine could hardly hear with the blood rushing to her ears.

Landry, which is what Delphine had called him since they were kids, waved the server off and inched his chair closer to hers. He curved his hand between her shoulder blades and leaned into her. "Hey, sorry if I was making assumptions. Why don't you tell me?"

His confident touch soothed her jumpy nerves. She explained to him that, yes, at a certain point she got frustrated with her father's lies and excuses and realized that taking his calls wasn't worth the stress. But then letters started arriving in New York, at first little notes checking in and wishing her a happy birthday or Happy New Year. Then more detailed notes, declaring how much he missed her, and how he wanted to make things right.

"Amends," she said, taking one of those deep breaths that she had learned to do in yoga. One of those breaths that claimed to regulate the nervous system. "And it seemed crazy at the time, after everything he put me and my mom through, but I called him. And I can't explain why, but it felt different this time. Real."

The server showed up with a sandwich for Landry and tomato soup for her, which Landry must have ordered on her behalf, because Delphine had no recollection of looking at a menu.

"And that's when it really started. We talked all the time. And I talked to his wife, Valerie, which at first felt impossible because she was the woman that . . . you know. But it turned out I *liked* her. I even visited them over Christmas, but please don't tell my mom that because she's going to absolutely lose her ever-loving mind. I have enough going on in my life without invoking her hysteria over this."

"Wait, you were here over Christmas . . . and didn't even tell me?"

The truth was that she had wanted to see him, but she couldn't. Not after that night in his hunting cabin, and especially not after everything they revealed to each other, including things that made her heart soar. But he had made it crystal clear that no matter what had transpired between them, and how he felt about her, he would allow nothing to jeopardize his family. Why would she go out of her way to beg for his affection? She may have done foolish things, but she was no fool.

"I knew you'd be busy with your girls and your wife, which is exactly how one should be busy over the holidays," she said, dabbing a spoon into her soup, eating nothing.

Landry stretched, releasing his hand from Delphine's upper back. "The girls are fine. Me and Kerry? Not so great."

"I'm sure you guys will work it out."

"No, we won't. It's over."

Confusion washed over Delphine's face. "What do you mean *over*?"

He took a large gulp of water, steadying himself. "Kerry asked for a divorce. Apparently, she's fallen for some guy her family hired to help run the business, some guy that graduated at the top of his class at Wharton. *A real go-getter*, she told me. If everything goes according to the lawyers I can't afford, I'll get the house and my girls every other weekend."

It was Delphine's turn to offer her condolences. "I'm so sorry. You didn't tell her about . . ."

"No, no," he added. "And she still doesn't know, not that it matters. I guess I was never good enough for the Princess of Lafayette."

"No, she was never good enough for *you*."

A few months ago, she would have been thrilled to hear this marital update from Landry, but now? She was having a hard time reconciling everything that he had told her over lunch. Circumstances had changed, and not just about Landry's marriage or the murder of her father.

The roar of motorcycles interrupted the moment. It was something that seemed to be happening more and more in Lafayette—groups of young men, sometimes women, taking over the streets, popping wheelies, reveling in disobedience.

Landry shook his head. "These guys . . . just making noise and putting themselves and other people in danger. The police department has got to figure this out."

A mention of the Lafayette Police Department was enough to refocus Delphine on her father. "Speaking of police . . . any leads yet, on my father?"

"Regretfully, no." He held her hand again. He seemed to be holding her hand more than was necessary. "This might upset you, but you may want to start wrapping your head around the idea that they may never find out who killed your father."

Anger throbbed in her chest. "*They? They* may never find my father's killer? Or *you*? You're the police, aren't you? Isn't it the literal job of homicide detectives to solve murder cases."

He removed his hand from hers, sensing that the cozy moment was over. "Yes, it is our job to investigate crimes. But we can't solve everything. That's not how policing works. Standard rate for solving a murder is about fifty percent, and even lower than that in Lafayette. We aren't resourced to investigate these kinds of cases over a long period of time."

"*Resourced.* You talk about my father as if he's a project, not a human being with dignity, whose killer deserves to be punished." It was becoming even clearer that she was going to have to take matters into her own hands if she wanted any kind of result, and a plan was already in motion. She kept this to herself.

"Come on, Delphine. We're trying, *I'm* trying. I'm doing everything I can. "

Her head hurt. The thought that her father's death might go unresolved, floating like duckweed in the swamp, enraged her. And yet, there was a seed of grace in her heart that would always reside there for Beau Landry. In this instance, it should have annoyed her, but it didn't. Even during this awful time, their enduring connection was an anchor.

6

The next day, Glory, Delphine, and Valerie had put their differences aside to find Marguerite Dunlop, stable hand and Sterling's tenant. Cypress Downs was both a casino and a racetrack, situated in close proximity to each other. But the horses were kept, groomed, and exercised at the Opelousas Stable, which was about thirty miles north, where the women had driven that morning. They could smell the horses first, then hear them. From the moment she parked her car at Opelousas, Glory despised Sterling even more. She was angry enough at the grief this had caused her daughter and would never get over having to spend time with Valerie. Now, she found herself at a stable with the smell of fresh manure vaporizing her car.

Leaning against a low metal gate was Valerie, dressed once again in exceedingly tight jeans, a low-cut blouse with an inappropriate amount of cleavage, and high-heeled shoes with purple toenails visible from their open-toed front. Glory watched as she talked to a man so small that he had to tilt his head back on his last vertebrae to chat with her. The diminutive man was dressed in tan breeches, knee-high black boots, and dangled a helmet and riding crop from his fingers. Valerie's smile fluttered, in a way that seemed fragile and forced. Despite what seemed like nonstop smiling, the hollowness in her eyes revealed an unspoken sadness. Valerie caught a glimpse of Glory and Delphine in the car and quickly found a way to get rid of the jockey.

"There you two are," Valerie said, looking excitedly behind her. "I was talking to that interesting man, a jockey for Cypress Downs. He seemed to think Marguerite was here today and suggested that we look in the northernmost stalls."

Marguerite Dunlop lived on the top floor of Sterling's duplex. Her signature had been scribbled in the condolence book in pencil, and it took just a few minutes of online searching to figure out who she was and where she worked. Now that she was aware of the presence of the duplex, Valerie was able to contribute a useful bit of snooping and found mail addressed to Marguerite at the residence. Glory had been too shell-shocked when she found Sterling to think about anyone living upstairs, or what they might have seen. But once the shock lifted, Glory knew she needed to talk to the woman who had been his tenant, and possibly more.

"Are you sure you really want to be here?" asked Glory. People always say they want to know the truth, but they never count on the truth stinging. Glory wasn't sure if Valerie had worked out what she herself had suspected, which was that Sterling and Marguerite probably had more than a tenant-landlord relationship. Knowing that man the way Glory did, it was possible—no, likely—that they were having relations of a different kind. "We can try to get to the truth, but that doesn't mean that you're going to like it. The truth doesn't always set people free. Sometimes it keeps you stuck in a place you don't want to be."

"I'm already stuck in a place I don't want to be," said Valerie, fumbling through her purse, finding a pack of cigarettes and lighting one. "Might as well learn the truth while I'm here." She sucked in a dramatic inhale, turned around, and walked to the horse stalls. Delphine followed behind.

Glory reached inside her purse and pulled out a fleur-de-lis handkerchief, the one she ordinarily used to wave at the Mardi Gras floats. She didn't know which was worse, the cigarette smoke or the haze of fresh, pungent manure that enveloped her. As for the stables themselves, they looked more expensive than Glory had expected. The brick flooring was carefully laid in an intricate herringbone pattern. Each stall was made of deep cherrywood on the outside and lined with pine on the interior and the ceilings. A single stall would have been generous enough for two horses but contained only one. The concrete flooring inside each stall was covered with heaps of straw.

Glory walked farther into the stables. A fly buzzed in her direction, which Glory waved off with the handkerchief; that is, until a whiff of manure hit her in the face, and she was forced to choose her evil: the smell or the insect. Ultimately, the smell won, and she covered her face again.

A horse neighed and bucked his head at Glory, almost in jest. She stared at the horse not directly, but gave him the side-eye. Then she lifted her arms in a "V" and said in a booming voice, "Don't you mess with me. A hard head makes a soft behind."

"Mama, what are you doing?" asked Delphine.

"I saw once on TV that is what you're supposed to do when you see a large animal. Make yourself big and loud and don't run, because if you run, then they have no choice but to chase you."

Valerie covered her mouth with the tips of her fingers and let out an exhale of laughter.

Delphine made a look that only daughters exasperated with their mothers can muster. "That's for *bears*, not horses. Do you really think horses in closed stalls are going to break out and violently chase you around the track?"

Glory lowered her arms. "You never know." It was not lost on Glory that Valerie had snickered at her. She was keeping a silent tally of the transgressions Valerie was racking up. How Glory would respond was to be determined, but there would be consequences.

The horse leaned its neck out of its stall, and to add insult to injury, licked Glory's arm. "I swear to God . . ." said Glory, articulated in a way that sounded like a command, an expletive, and a hex, all at once.

They stopped when they encountered a stout woman with a gray buzz cut, a denim boilersuit, and black boots with thick lug soles. She was bent at the waist and lunged forward with a pitchfork, which stabbed into a mess of straw. With each thrust of the pitchfork, the straw rustled and crackled. She plunked briquettes of manure and damp straw into a wheelbarrow, but stopped when she noticed three women gawking at her.

"Jesus Christ, lady, you can't smoke in a stable full of straw," the woman said, pointing a pitchfork in Valerie's direction. Valerie went wide-eyed with surprise at being singled out. "That's a fire hazard *and* bad for the horses. Put that out right now."

Startled, Valerie threw it to the ground immediately. The woman raced toward the lit cigarette and extinguished it with boots sturdy enough to stomp out an entire campfire. She picked up the cigarette butt and threw it in a trash can in the corner of the stable. With her hands on her hips and a look of astonishment deepening in her face, she turned to the women. "Can I help you with anything? Why are you here?"

Glory assumed a leadership position. "My name is Glory Broussard, and I was married to Sterling Broussard."

"No, *I* was married to Sterling Broussard," said Valerie.

"We were both married to Sterling," Glory corrected, annoyed anew that Valerie was here and messing up her flow already. "Though not at the same time. However, there was some inappropriate crossover, which is another story for another day." She snapped her handkerchief at a fly, silencing its flight.

Delphine shot her mother a reproachful look, like she was furious and embarrassed all at the same time.

"You're Marguerite Dunlop, yes? We've come to ask you a few questions about how you came to know Sterling Broussard," asked Valerie, usurping her authority. At first glance, Marguerite was not exactly the type of woman that turned Sterling's head. Her gruff appearance was at odds with Valerie's femme fatale vibe, and she was around the same age as Sterling, a single fact that eliminated her from contention as a potential side piece. On the other hand, a dog with an itch always needs to scratch himself, so Glory wouldn't put it past him.

Marguerite walked to the other end of the stall and grabbed a shovel. "A real pity, the way he went out. It's been the talk of Cypress Downs ever since it happened. I've known Sterling for about twenty years. You see, I've worked in restaurants my whole life, from Santa Fe to St. Pete. I used to tend bar down in the French Quarter at this place called the Peculiar Pelican, and he was always real nice to me when most folks weren't. I was out before that was even a thing, and you know how people are around here, especially back then. But Sterling never treated me no different. In fact, seemed like he always went out of his way to ask how my girlfriend was doing.

"A few years ago, he came down to New Orleans and stopped by the club to say hi, and I was in a bad way. Donna, my partner, was real sick, and we never had any kind of insurance. Spread to her liver and her bones, and when I tell you I felt helpless watching her get chewed up by that disease, I felt *helpless*. When she was gone, I just numbed myself with booze. Sterling found me, got me some help, and helped me get back on my feet. Got me this job and let me stay at that duplex. Eventually, I paid him rent. I knew he could get more than $800 a month for that apartment, but that was the Sterling I knew. Always willing to help someone out, especially someone down on their luck."

This sounded like it might be true, thought Glory. He always did have a soft spot for hard cases. More than once, he had helped out one of his no-good pals in some way Glory disapproved of. Once, he had allowed his friend to drive his Chevy F-10 into their backyard because the guy was behind on his car note, and a repo man was on the prowl. Another time, he tailed a friend who had pawned his Gretsch drum kit for $200 to make rent. Sterling bought it back at the absurd markup of $900, which the drummer never paid back. Glory told him to worry about his own family instead of these fools that weren't even blood relations, but he ignored her.

Valerie stepped forward, edging Glory to the side. Glory crossed her arms in disgust. "Did you hear or see anything the day that Sterling was killed?" asked Valerie.

Marguerite shook her head and swept up the aisle in front of her. "I'll tell you what I told those other guys. I was here until 3 A.M. Two of the horses came down with a case of equine flu, so they had to be isolated and moved to another facility. We had to sanitize this whole place from top to bottom. You can't have a virus like that taking hold in a stable with more than fifty horses. Took all night."

"Other guys? What other guys?" asked Delphine.

Marguerite stopped sweeping and looked at them. "I'm not really sure if I should talk about that. I think I've said enough."

Delphine walked straight into the stall and touched the woman's shoulder. "Sounds like my dad helped you out during a tough spell. I'm his daughter, and I would like to find his killer. I'd sure like whatever help you can provide."

Marguerite paused, then propped her broom against the stall. "The Louisiana Gaming Control Board."

"They came to the duplex to interview you? Why?"

"Look, I don't know why. I guess because he worked in a casino," Margarite said, wiping a piece of straw off her face. "If we're all being honest with each other, I think we all know that formal employment wasn't exactly Sterling's thing. Here's what I do know: Sterling was real excited about his job at the casino, to start. I'd see him coming home from the casino and he'd tell me all kinds of stories about managing the crew, the games folks was betting on, his take on upcoming Bowl games, all that. And toward the end, I don't know, he just didn't seem like the same man. He wasn't half as animated, and he was spending a lot of time downstairs, all by himself. To be honest I'm surprised to hear he left someone behind, because I thought he was divorced. He never talked about having another wife. Anyway, if I were you, I'd look into whatever might have been happening at the casino. That seemed to be the source of his unhappiness."

Valerie's stomach collapsed in on itself, like she had been punched in the gut.

Delphine reached into her back pocket and pulled out a card. "Please give me a call if you hear or remember anything you think might be helpful."

♣♦♥♠

Glory, Delphine, and Valerie had relocated to the bleachers near the practice track. Pocket-sized men in breeches bobbed up and down on silky horses, their tails swaying in the breeze. The horses seemed thrilled to stretch their legs and make the most of the cooler Louisiana weather. The jockeys occasionally leaned down and patted the horses' shoulders—pleased with the workout. Even Glory had to admire how handsome these animals were—from afar.

Glory could tell from the tortured look that had sunk onto Valerie's face that she wasn't focused on the animals. Valerie must have assumed that she'd be immune from Sterling's extracurricular activities, but Glory knew better. If it wasn't Marguerite, it was surely someone else. And you know what they say, a marriage that starts in adultery ends the same way. What a fool That Woman was, to think she could neuter a tomcat.

"So Sterling was on the radar of the Louisiana Gaming Control Board? Good Lord, what did he get himself tangled up in?" she asked.

"No idea," said Delphine. "But I can have my office see if there are any warrants that have been issued that might tell us something. Or maybe I can see if Landry knows something, but you know what a Boy Scout he is. Unlikely to get him to talk."

Glory bit her tongue. She remembered a few months ago when her daughter stayed the night in his hunting cabin due to that big storm, and half of Lafayette had seen the way he was always looking at her. If there was anyone that could get Lieutenant Beau Landry talking, it was Delphine. It's not a secret if it's written all over your face, thought Glory, but she wasn't going to meddle here.

"Ain't no harm in asking," was all Glory could muster. She turned to Valerie, whose bony shoulders were visibly hunched in her halter top. "Did he say anything at all that would lead you to believe that he was under investigation at Cypress Downs?"

Valerie, now free to smoke, puffed on a cigarette and exhaled. "He loved his job at the casino. He was proud of the way he walked in there for one job and walked out with another, that he was able to use his past for good for a change. It made him feel like it was all worthwhile."

Delphine tapped away on her phone, then said, "The law firm has sources in state attorney general offices all over the country. I'm putting in a line to see what leads I might be able to draw in."

"I've got to get back to the salon," said Valerie, standing up from the bleachers. "I say next up is the casino."

"Absolutely. The casino," Delphine agreed, in solidarity.

Glory gave her eyebrows a tired shrug.

7

After the stable episode, Glory decided that she'd go to the casino under two conditions: alone, and on a weekday. She would not tolerate being undermined by That Woman again. Anyway, today was Sunday, which meant that Glory had office hours at CC's Coffee House, and she was not about to surrender her earnings to Valerie.

Gus and Noah were huddled in conspiracy behind the counter. The men whispered, seeming to encourage each other and hyping the other up. Glory noticed a bunch of small cups, quarts of various kinds of milk, assorted squeeze bottles, and syrups in a rainbow of colors.

"What are you two doing back here?" Glory said, causing the men to startle. "This shop is damn near full, and you two are giggling like schoolgirls." She was surprised to see Gus back behind the counter. He had worked there as a barista last year, without distinction. The Discalced Carmelite nuns gave him a beehive to manage, and Glory knew that he was trying to get a honey business off the ground, but maybe that wasn't going so well. Which was a pity, thought Glory, because working with those bees was about all he was good for.

"Woman, mind your own business," said Noah, in a tone only he could get away with. "This is for grown men, you hear me?"

"Gus, don't be like this brute. Tell me what y'all are up to," Glory insisted. "I thought your honey business was going well?"

"It is, Miss Glory, just helping Noah out with his recipe," said Gus, wiping his hands on a formerly white towel, now stained brown with caffeinated substances. "Try this."

"No, thank you," she said. "Last time I tried one of these experimental drinks I felt my blood pressure rise in real time. I had the shakes for the rest of the night."

Gus wiped down a sticky squeeze bottle and countered. "That was an *old* recipe. It was too sweet because Noah was using cane syrup. I told him honey would be better because it has more complexity to it, and a floral note to counteract the sweetness. Try it."

". . . *a floral note to counteract the sweetness*," said Glory, poking fun at his seriousness. "Got you sounding like some kind of Food Network personality. I don't know . . . coffee and honey? Doesn't sound too appealing if you ask me."

Gus tilted the coffeepot until the cup was about two-thirds full. From a large glass measure he spooned a pale blonde cream on top. To finish it off, he sprinkled what looked like sugared nuts. Excitement and anticipation stretched across both of their faces.

Glory smirked and took the cup, reluctantly. She sipped delicately at first, then contemplated what she had just tasted, smacking her lips together for good measure. She then took another, less tentative sip and said, "You know, this is not half bad. It's actually pretty good. What's in here?"

"It has a base of—" Gus started, before he was interrupted.

"It's proprietary," said Noah.

"How's it supposed to be proprietary when you got all the ingredients out for the whole world to see?" said Glory, waving at the crowded countertop. "I can see you got some chicory coffee, some nonfat milk, some sugar-dusted pecans . . ."

Noah scrambled to block everything with his body. "All you need to know is that it's coffee with a honey whipped cream topping, with toasted pecans," he said. Then, with a grin he asked, "But you liked it though, right? Would you order it on your own?"

Glory sipped the rest of her small sample and placed the empty paper cup on the counter. "Yes, I think I might."

Noah and Gus erupted into a small, contained dance. "A cappuccino on the house for Miss Glory," said Noah, a reward for her fine taste and appreciation of their drink.

"I think I'll have that *proprietary* drink instead," she said. Noah and Gus high-fived each other in glee. "I meant to ask you . . . what's the last you heard from Grady Williams?"

"Grady?" Noah's head tilted to the side in thought. "I haven't seen him in ages. Last time I saw him he was limping around, could barely move. Wait a minute . . . he worked with you at that grocery store, right? I think he works at the casino now. Saw him behind the security desk on Thanksgiving. They do a mean spread for the holidays."

Glory felt a tiny bit of shame at that. Noah had seen more grief than a man his age should, outliving his wife and his daughter, the latter of whom got caught up with substances. She'd have to invite him over for Thanksgiving, rather than him eating a turkey dried out from fluorescent warming lights. They may have sparred with each other, but he was a kindred spirit.

"Thank you," she said.

"Why you asking? What are you up to?"

"Up to? Now, why do I gotta be up to something to inquire about someone's whereabouts?"

"Because I know you," he said. "You better not be investigating Sterling's death by yourself. Remember, you nearly got yourself killed last time. You better tell the cops what you know."

"Noah, I am a grown woman of a very advanced age. Make my coffee, please, I need a little caffeine in the bloodstream." Glory assumed her regular spot at the table and tended to her regular customers who placed bets on a range of games, mostly on the SEC and Big Ten conference.

Working as a bookie was a complex thing. On the one hand, she felt a little sorry for her customers, most of whom had little common sense and even less disposable income. She sometimes sent the most desperate cases packing, but a fool always finds a way to be parted from their money. Why shouldn't it be to her advantage? What she liked most about her line of work was figuring out the lines and percentages, which she did on her own. Sterling had his own methods, which Glory came to realize were not methodologically sound. With the help of some online videos from some gambling hotshots in Las Vegas, plus her own inscrutable instincts that helped her refine her so-called algorithm even further, she had come to a system whereby her lines were often more accurate than the biggest casinos.

There was one factor the gambling experts never accounted for—the wind. In Glory's experience, it was usually the biggest factor in which a team won or lost. Was the arena indoors or outdoors? Would there be a wind that was unusual for the geography? Because if there was, it meant an upset would be more likely. Statistically, quarterbacks that know how to throw in the wind will always have the advantage, even with a weaker defensive line. To the contrary, a strong quarterback who's accustomed to an indoor arena will have a bad night with a slight outdoor breeze. Everyone thought Glory must watch ESPN all day, and she never did. Just a bunch of blowhards whose opinions change one day to the next. But The Weather Channel? That was a different story.

Glory was busy with her regulars, who lingered around the coffee shop. They ordered their drinks and muffins and waited inconspicuously to the side until Glory summoned them with a nod of her head. She occasionally handed over a crisp white envelope with money owed based on last week's games, but she took in far more money than she doled out. This system of envelopes in/envelopes out continued until the crowd dwindled down and Lieutenant Beau Landry walked in. He was wearing civilian clothes, but it didn't matter. You could tell he was a cop by the stiffness of his spine and the squareness of his jaw.

None of her customers scattered in the presence of law enforcement. If the Lafayette Police Department wanted to bust her for openly operating an illegal gambling operation from a coffee shop, they would have done so years ago. Landry leaned down to give her a kiss on the cheek before grabbing a seat at her table.

"I was in the neighborhood this Sunday. Thought I'd stop by to see how you've been since you found Sterling."

"Terrible," said Glory, closing her blue gambling ledger. It was one thing to brazenly run a gambling operation in the open, as if she was selling Girl Scout cookies, but flaunting a ledger of gambling debts in front of a police officer was a bit theatrical, even for Glory. "Now I've got his widow trailing me like some lost puppy dog, expecting me to find the killer. I know I've done it once before, but that was for Amity, my dearest and oldest friend in the world. And that was only because the police did such a shabby job. No offense, of course."

He scratched the right side of his face, which brought Glory's attention to a couple of outliers about the man. First, he was at least a week deep into stubble, if not more. If he kept at this pace another week, he'd have the thin coating of a beard. Second, his nails had been chewed down to the nub. He was the kind of law enforcement officer who looked squared away at all times, but not now.

"That's also what I came to talk to you about," he said, running the top of his ragged nails against his jeans, using them as a file. "I wanted to let you know that I'm on the case."

Glory shoved her blue book into the leather tote bag that hung over his chair. "Well, good for you. I really do hope you find the murderer soon, so I can return to my regularly scheduled life. The good version, the one without my dead ex-husband's mistress in it."

Landry rubbed his reddened eyes. "I know that telling you to leave this to professional law enforcement is going to be a waste of time . . . but just promise me that you'll flag anything noteworthy my way?"

"I will wave a flag at the slightest clue," she said, holding her hand in the air like she was taking an oath. "Hey, are you okay? If I'm being honest, you look like you've been wrestling with an armadillo. And lost."

A weary smile struggled across his face. "It's just everything with Kerry and the girls. I'm sure Delphine filled you in."

As usual, there was a lot that Delphine had not filled her in on. "No, she hasn't said a word."

"Kerry and I are getting a divorce. I get the girls every other weekend and select holidays, according to a rotating schedule being hammered out by our lawyers."

"I'm so sorry to hear that, Landry. I really am."

He caught a glimpse of himself in the windows of the coffee shop and did a double take. "Wow, I really do look like shit, don't I? Note to self: stop looking like such a sad sack of a human being and pull myself together."

"Hey, don't you talk to my friend like that. That kind of negative self-talk is not going to help one bit. You're an outstanding father, that's not going to change. And you'll have a dozen women circling around you in no time when you're ready. Unless you're already . . ." Glory arched her eyebrows.

"No, nothing like that," he said. "Just trying to get through this divorce and minimize the blast radius to my girls."

"Listen, if I know one thing about you, it's that you're an excellent father." She paused. Memories of being a single mother, after Sterling walked out, stirred inside her. Glory wished she could cut herself loose from those old emotions, but she couldn't. At the time, the affair had broken her. And just when she thought she was healed, the old injury would act up from time to time. "I remember those days, how impossible it felt. And don't even get me started on the betrayal. Makes you feel like your whole life is a lie, like you were living out an entirely different version of events. It's crazy-making stuff, is what it is."

"Are you trying to make me feel better, because I'm not sure it's helping."

"Listen, you know I'm not going to feed you the same bullcrap everyone else does. This is going to hurt, and for a long time. I remember those days, being alone in that house, wondering how I was ever going to make it. Lean on your people. Keep your girls close. Don't retreat as a father."

He looked down at his phone. "Speaking of, I need to pick the girls up from dance and take them to their mom's. She's got them during the week, words I never thought I'd say about my own children. But you'll let me know if you hear anything that might help with the case?"

"Promise," she swore. He gave a smile that looked more like an anguished wince and headed out the door. There were maybe two dozen good men in Lafayette and Landry had always been one of them. She wondered if Delphine would ever have the good sense to lay claim.

Glory took the last sip of her *proprietary* coffee and was readying to leave when she saw Constance Wheeler waltz through the door. And it's not an exaggeration to say she waltzed. The hemline of her blue, silk-blend dress swiveled around her legs as she made her way toward Glory. Once she reached Glory's table, she plunked down a large plastic tote bag onto the floor.

"I thought I'd find you here after church, though I guess the entire town knows where to find you on Sunday afternoons, don't they?"

"I hardly recognized you without a clipboard glued to your chest. Normally you just show up unannounced at my home and rifle through my belongings. Did the court grant you permission to take your harassment campaign on the road?"

Constance pulled out a seat and joined Glory at her table. "This isn't court business. It's Mardi Gras business, which is much more serious if you ask me."

"Oh no, not here. I am too tired for this right now."

"I believe you're the one that pleaded for help. We have several decisions to make to keep this train on the tracks. Or would you rather be at the helm of the shabbiest Mardi Gras ever produced by St. Agnes, and the shame that comes with that?"

Glory leaned back in her chair, resigned. "Alright, what crucial decisions must we make today?"

Noah walked over and placed two coffee cups on the table, and also cleared Glory's empty one. "Hello, ladies, we're sampling some new drinks. I'd sure like your feedback."

Glory nodded to Constance. "Go ahead, it's good."

Constance took a sip, and her face lit up with approval. "Oh my, this is delicious. What do you call this?"

Noah puffed his chest. "We're still working on names, but you can look for this on our spring menu."

He walked off and Constance dipped her chin toward her chest and pursed her lips. "My, my. You mean to tell me you come here every Sunday and haven't put that fine specimen of a man on *your* spring menu?" No one seemed to understand that Glory liked being alone. It had taken some time to reach this place, but she didn't want any man living in her house ever again, inspecting her purchases or second-guessing her design choices. Some birds are meant to fly solo.

Glory pointed at the bag. "What's in there?"

"Items for discussion." Constance leaned down and plucked out various items from the bag. "First, we need to talk about beads for the parade. Now, I went down to Bead City today and this is the assortment that we can still order by the cutoff date." She pulled out a series of purple-, green-, and gold-beaded necklaces. Some strands were skinny and long. Others were chunkier with novelty shapes like crowns and fish.

Glory was overwhelmed. "I guess the skinny ones."

"The skinny ones are good for the Queen Evangeline's Parade to Cajun Field, but we need some of the substantial ones for the St. Agnes gala. Do you have a piece of paper so I can write that down?"

Glory reached into her bag and ripped a piece of paper from her gambling ledger.

Constance extended her neck like a turtle, trying to steal a glance at the book. "Any chance you scribbled my husband's name in that book recently?" Constance asked.

Since Constance was essentially saving her hide when it came to Mardi Gras, she didn't exactly want to rub her face in the truth. "You know I can't tell you that, on the grounds of client confidentiality."

Constance huffed. "There's HIPAA for gamblers?" She untangled the beads from the table and stuffed them back in the bag. "I'll take that to mean that he's still frittering away his money. *Our* money."

Constance pulled one tchotchke after the other from the plastic bag for nearly an hour—everything from cocktail napkins embossed with fleur-de-lis emblems to plastic champagne glasses to T-shirts and masks festooned with glitter and feathers. She was annoying as hell, but Glory had to confess that she was actually helpful.

"I guess I should thank you," said Glory. It was the best she could do given their contentious history.

"I guess you should," said Constance, her voice heavy with a kind of exhausted authority. "And make sure you get a hair appointment now for the big gala. Don't wait till the last minute or you'll be doing your color yourself. I can already see your roots need a touch-up." Constance could give as good as she got.

"Where do you get your hair done these days?" asked Glory. "I normally do a box color, but maybe I can splash out a little for Mardi Gras."

"I've been going to The New Woman Salon down on Johnston Street," she said. "Hey, wait, isn't that Valerie LeBlanc's salon, the woman who Sterling . . ."

"Yup, that's the one. I won't be seeing her for reasons I'm sure you understand. Box color is good enough for me."

"I don't see Valerie. I see another gal in her salon if that makes you feel any better." It did not make Glory feel any better. "But the gal who does my color said she's looking for a new salon. From what I hear, Valerie is behind on her mortgage."

The part of Glory's brain that calculated her gambling lines began to work double-time. "Mortgage? I thought she rented that little building."

"No, she owns it, and from what I hear she's two shakes away from foreclosure. That's why my colorist is looking for a new salon . . . doesn't have the luxury to see how things work out when you've got bills of your own." She gathered all the cheap swag on the table and stuffed it in the bag. "Alright, good work today. I better see you at the king cake testing, and please be early. The members are going to flip once they hear we missed the Gambino's cutoff. We've been doing Gambino's for the king cake since . . . forever!"

"I'll be there," said Glory, but her focus had already moved on. She may be underwater on her Mardi Gras duties, but she was more concerned with a little salon that may or may not be underwater on its mortgage.

8

The automatic doors of the casino slid open, and an air-conditioned chill hit Glory's face. She hadn't stepped inside a casino in over a decade, but she was on a mission to find Grady Williams, who signed his name in Sterling's funeral guest book in handwriting so tight that the letters overlapped one another. From the instant she saw his name, she made a note to follow up with him personally, and when Noah mentioned he now worked at the casino, she knew she was on the right path.

Glory first met Grady at the grocery store where they worked. He worked in the meat department, and all Glory could remember of the man was that he was slow and unimpressive. But it appeared that he knew Sterling well enough to show up at his funeral, and she suspected he might know something about Sterling's final days, his discontent with the casino, and how he ended up cold and dead on his kitchen floor.

She stepped inside. The dingy casino she knew from yesteryear had been fully renovated. Rows of gaudy chandeliers dangled over the slot machines, trying their best to make gamblers feel like they were in Monaco instead of Lafayette. They weren't fooling anyone with all this artifice. Glory's supportive shoes brushed over the kaleidoscope carpet, which had so many colors and designs you couldn't pick out any distinctive features. Any food or item dropped on it would simply be camouflaged within the chaos, which was no doubt the point.

Glory may have been involved in the dark arts of gambling, but casinos had never been her thing. Truth be told, she was a little intimidated by them. All the lights and booze and dealers in their little vests. It all felt like too much. And cameras pointed in every direction, like the eye of God. No thank you, she was happy at her little coffee shop with her blue book and taking prop bets on the Alabama game.

She inspected rows of slot machines, whirring and ringing with cartoon-like sounds that floated in the air. There's a certain breed of person that comes to a casino on a weeknight. A few of them seemed to be retirees, people for whom there was no such thing as a weeknight. Then there's the tribe of sad-souled people with a tinge of craziness in their eyes. Glory could almost hear the gnashing of their teeth as they attempted to claw back their losses, one quarter at a time. She knew this breed well. Some people need the action of gambling, damn the fallout.

She pushed through the slot machines, finding herself on the border of the buffet. A glistening ham at the carving station caught her eye, and it didn't look half bad. Maybe Noah was right about the Thanksgiving buffet. Who needs to be cooking for one on a holiday? But she reminded herself of her priorities—get to the bottom of Sterling's death so she could get Valerie LeBlanc out of her life. She wasn't here for a meal. But when she caught a worker putting a fresh tray of dinner rolls under a heating lamp, she figured that a little snack wouldn't hurt. Just a little something to tide her over, she told herself. She walked up to the rolls, looked in each direction, and tore one off from the pack with her fingers. The yeasty sides separated slowly from the others, and she savored the buttery roll while walking by the gift shop window.

The shelves of the shop were filled with tacky items like shot glasses with glittery alligators, oversized novelty bottles of Tabasco sauce, and boot-shaped pillows in the shape of Louisiana. Glory shook her head and took another bite of her dinner roll, wondering why anyone would waste their money on such ugly things. After passing the gift shop, she saw a sign on a black easel advertising an upcoming show for The Commodores. She stared at it for a while, wondering if The Commodores were truly The Commodores without Lionel Richie. Still, she took out her camera and snapped a picture of the sign, just in case.

"Excuse me, ma'am," said a burly security guard with gray hair. "No photographs on the casino floor."

Glory eyed the man from top to bottom. He was a large man, about her age, stuffed into a security uniform. His right leg was stiff from top to bottom, which forced him to hike his hip up when he walked, for clearance. Glory surmised that he probably needed a hip replacement and couldn't afford it. Hell, that kind of surgery with "good insurance" would still cost thousands of dollars, and most folks around there didn't have that kind of money lying around. His dark skin was mostly unlined and his facial features handsome. Glory inspected his face rapidly, like she knew him. Turns out, she did.

"Grady Williams, is that you?"

His stern face suddenly relaxed. "Glory Broussard? Never thought I'd see you here . . . I heard you done took over Sterling's book . . . but you know you can't do that here," he warned.

"Oh please, I know my place. Let me stay in my little coffee shop where I'm happy," she said. "I didn't know you were working here?" she added, even though he was the very reason why she had come.

"Started here not long after you left Adrien's." They had both been employed at Adrien's Food Market on West Congress. Glory worked in the produce department for twenty-five years, managing pallets of cantaloupes and cutting and arranging fruit on party platters—many of those years alongside Grady, who eventually ran the meat department.

"I had to get out of that meat refrigerator. Not good for arthritis or the hip," he explained.

"I hear you. We need warmth to keep the joints lubricated at this age," she said, hiding the last morsel of the dinner roll behind her back. "Hey . . . that must mean you worked with Sterling."

"Sure did, Mr. Big Time. I was just a lowly peasant compared to him. Anyway, sure gonna miss working with him. He was a good guy."

Glory had been getting an earful lately about what a good guy Sterling was and frankly found it tiresome. It didn't surprise her, though. She had been witness to his charms for many years, but there are only so many lies and excuses a woman can tolerate before the blinders come off.

She put her own white-hot feelings of betrayal aside and focused on Grady, remembering why she came here in the first place. "Hey, you ever heard or seen anything funny pertaining to Sterling? Anyone who had an issue with him, or anyone he crossed that would want to seek revenge by impaling a sharp blade in his chest?"

His eyes darted back and forth. "Wh . . . what have you heard, exactly?"

His shifty demeanor sparked a memory, an episode that happened at Adrien's, years ago. A cashier had noticed expensive cuts of meat coming through her checkout line. Porterhouse steaks for five dollars a pound, filet mignon even cheaper. When the manager started digging around to see who was responsible for this suspicious pricing, Grady, sweat pouring off his brow, informed the owner that the meat manager had held those cuts aside for friends and family, leading to the termination of his boss. Grady couldn't even pretend to lie. The flop sweat beading his brow had betrayed him, and he crumbled.

"Grady," she said, pulling on the thread she suspected was unwinding inside of him, "if you know something, or even suspect something, I need you to come clean. There's a murderer running amok in the streets of Lafayette Parish. Is that what you want?"

"Ugh, I got a lunch break in about twenty minutes. Meet you over there," he said, pointing to the buffet. Beads of sweat dotted his forehead.

She might as well eat. Glory inspected the buffet, which was not her preferred way of dining, but Noah had sparked her curiosity. Items in a buffet always approximate the real thing, but always compromise in some way, like the quality of ingredients or care of preparation. Buffet gumbo was likely to be thin and watery without the slow heat needed for a homemade roux. Glory could see that the exterior of the prime rib under the heating lamp lacked the savory crust it deserved. She grabbed a melamine tray and silverware, contemplating the options, before ladling steaming crawfish étouffée over a mound of rice. Crispy rounds of fried okra and another dinner roll beckoned her.

Glory spooned the crawfish étouffée into her mouth, surprised to detect subtle flavors of tomato, green onion, and cayenne. It needed a little more seasoning, but she was impressed. Someone in the kitchen had fussed a little bit over this étouffée, she could tell. She then bit into the okra. The mild, grassy flavor contrasted nicely with the crispy, salty exterior and she nodded to no one in particular. Someone had put their foot in this okra, as they say in the South, and that was a good thing. She rinsed everything down with perfectly prepared sweet tea, which was neither bitter nor cavity-inducing, and vowed to come back. The server refilled her tea as Grady appeared in the dining area.

"Go ahead and fix a plate," encouraged Glory. "It's on me."

"That's alright," he said, cracking his knuckles. There was no smile or even a bend in his face. In the few minutes since she last saw him, he had hardened. "I'm gonna make this quick. Sterling might have been in trouble here at work. I'm not sure."

"What kind of trouble?" asked Glory. A group of tourists interrupted, asking Grady to take a picture. A family stood in front of the dessert section while Grady snapped with their cell phone. Glory looked over her shoulder to see the entire family, the parents in matching T-shirts that read *Rajin' Cajun*.

After, Grady continued, "Sterling had something of a special job here in the casino." He went on to explain the rise of Sterling at Cypress Downs. At first, he applied for a job as manager of the slot machines, manning the floor and keeping an eye out for suspicious activity. Turns out he had an eye for suspicious activity throughout the entire casino, from shoplifters in the gift shop to people stealing desserts from the buffet. Glory swallowed hard but kept listening.

"The breakthrough moment was when he went to the sports book. He told T-Red that the lines in the sports bet were off and were losing the casino money. So, they tried his way out, informally at first, and turns out he was right. And then they changed over formally to Sterling's ways, and soon enough the sports book was bringing in an extra five percent, which may not seem like much, but it's a ton of money."

The sounds of a winning jackpot rang. The machine didn't dispense much, just a hundred dollars, but the tourist acted like she had just won Powerball with all that hooting and hollering. She was so distracted celebrating that her husband had to scoop it up in a green plastic cup.

"And who is T-Red?" asked Glory.

"Redmond Herbert. The junior." In Lafayette, *T* was a shortened form of *petit*, which could mean little or small, but usually meant junior. Every Louisiana family had a few T-somethings.

"I see," said Glory, inhaling another straw full of sweet tea. She was deeply suspicious of where the new betting lines really came from. "I can imagine Sterling was real celebrated after that."

"That was the weird thing," said Grady. "You'd think so, but around then was when he seemed to want to leave. Talking about starting a fishing business, you know, for tourists. He claims he was getting a license, but you know how Sterling was . . ."

"Claimed a lot of things . . ."

He nodded. "All I know is shortly after that, he talked about leaving the casino all the time, even though T-Red loved him. Seems like improving the betting odds had caused him more trouble than it was worth. The last time I saw him, we had drinks at the bar after hours. The only thing he talked about was how he wanted out, how he just wanted to support his family like a normal person."

Talking with Grady had peeled back something in her. Glory rummaged through her emotional thesaurus to try to name the feeling and, despite not wanting to go there, what she was feeling was empathy. Sterling had gotten himself in over his head, and for once it hadn't worked out in his favor. She hadn't cracked anything yet, but she suspected the answers resided somewhere in this casino.

9

You went to the casino without me and Valerie, even though we expressly agreed that we were going together?" Delphine was busy interrogating her mother at the kitchen table, where they were both shelling green beans. "I can't believe you're already excluding us."

"I'm not excluding no one," said Glory. "It's not exactly easy to walk around a casino arm-in-arm with two other people and not draw attention to yourself. No one wants to be questioned about sensitive matters in front of an audience. Plus, you don't know how to talk to people from around here. This ain't no deposition. You got to have a softer touch." Patti LaBelle slinked around the table and isolated a fallen green bean with her front paws. She batted it around and chased it into the laundry room.

"Did you just say that I don't know how to talk to people from *around here*?" asked Delphine, snapping a green bean with unnecessary force. "I'm from around here! I was literally born down the street."

But you've changed, is what Glory wanted to say. Delphine may have been from Lafayette, but she now inhabited another land far away, with different customs and values. The tension that sometimes surfaced between them was because Glory hadn't changed. It was painful to see your child become a different person, maybe one that looked down on everything she once was. That is what Glory was thinking but kept it to herself. The situation was already strained enough since Sterling's murder, and she didn't want to make things worse. Instead, the two continued to snap away at the beans and each other.

The vinyl-covered seat at her kitchen table squeaked under the weight of Glory's derriere. "Please look into Valerie's mortgage for me. We still don't have any idea who would want Sterling dead or why, and a life insurance policy for a mortgage in trouble is one fine motivation, if you ask me."

"Mom, just because Dad had an affair and you don't like Valerie doesn't make her a killer. She's not the killing kind."

"You think sociopaths just walk around snapping animal's necks and discussing their murderous blueprints in their beauty salon? I need to know how much the mortgage is for, the monthly payments, and how far in arrears her property is."

Delphine leaned forward in her chair to protest, but Glory cut her off. "You wanted me to lead the investigation, right? Sometimes that means I make decisions for the best of the search . . ."

Delphine backed down. "Just promise me you won't go back to the casino alone again."

Glory still wasn't sure if that was a good idea. She blended in more easily, especially now that Delphine had that fake hair stretching down to her backside and a nose ring, which she had thankfully removed for the funeral and had not reinserted. Yet.

She was thinking about all the ways in which Delphine had changed when she noticed a burgundy SUV in the driveway. Glory peered above her reading glasses to try to catch a glimpse. Driving into a stranger's driveway down here without a good reason was an act of hostility. In Louisiana, strangers get shot for less. "Damn out-of-towners," Glory complained. "Ever since Hurricane Katrina people from all over moved up here. Twenty years later and none of them ever figured out how to get around town." Glory waited for the SUV to make a three-point turn, but it didn't. Instead, the driver pulled up further, turned the engine off, and exited the car.

"I wonder who that is," said Glory, who put down her bowl of green beans and walked out of the kitchen to intercept the woman. Delphine swiveled in her chair and gulped when she saw who it was. The doorbell rang.

Glory opened the front door, leaving the glass storm door between them shut. This door was what Glory called her "security system." It kept strangers from busting into her house, although it had done little to keep the storm that was Constance Wheeler at bay.

"Can I help you?" asked Glory, who surveyed this person up and down. She had huge almond eyes, high cheekbones, and her hair shaved into a low fade on the side, the kind a man might get at a barbershop. On top of her head were braids styled neatly in a bun. Her earlobes were punctured with half a dozen holes. She had cuffed the short sleeves of her colorful, printed shirt as well as the bottom of her baggy jeans.

The woman behind the storm door answered. "I was wondering if Delphine Broussard was here? If this was the right address for her?"

Glory turned to see her daughter hurry from the kitchen, nearly sliding in her socks along the way.

"Oh hey! I'm surprised to see you. What brings you down here?" Delphine asked. Glory smiled, splitting her focus between her daughter and the woman.

"Remember? I told you I was *staging* as a guest chef down at Pierre's in New Orleans." Glory registered the searching look in the woman's face. "You know, never mind, I see I caught you at a bad time."

"This is your friend, Delphine? Why didn't you tell me you had a friend in town?" Glory unlocked the storm door, and without knowing it, let the winds of change breeze into her home. "What's your name?" Glory extended a hand.

"My name is Justine, but everyone calls me Justice."

"Well, that's an unusual name," said Glory, who had only asked the woman's name and was now confronted with an onslaught of information. "I'm sure your mama would prefer that we use your government name, but I'll give it a try. Come on in . . ."

"Thank you, Mrs. Broussard."

"You just call me Glory." She led Justice through the foyer and into the living room, where everyone took a seat. Delphine put her hands in her lap but then tucked them under her legs instead. She seemed to be looking at everything except Justice, or Glory.

"Delphine, you didn't tell me you had a friend who's a chef in Louisiana. What brings you down here, specifically?"

"*Justice* is actually a renowned chef. She's a James Beard Rising Star Chef of the Year," said Delphine.

"Well, maybe one day I'll be famous. Right now, I'm just getting a little bit of attention," said Justice, who seemed a little embarrassed to be introduced in such grand fashion. "I'm *staging* at a restaurant in New Orleans this month. Just thought I'd come down early to see how Delphine was doing with . . . her dad and all."

"*Stodging*? I'm afraid I don't know what that is," said Glory.

Realizing that most people didn't necessarily understand the jargon of professional chefs, Justice offered a bit more explanation.

"Oh, *staging* . . . that's just a French term, it means observing and working in a restaurant kitchen that's not yours. It's how we learn new techniques and get ideas for our menu, as well as the operations of kitchen staff and all that stuff."

"I had no idea that was a thing," said Glory, fascinated by this brief and tiny insight into the world of restaurant kitchens. "Do you want to *stodge* in my kitchen? We're making pork chops with green beans right now."

Justice either didn't see or ignored Delphine's strained face. "I'd love to."

♣♦♥♠

"Oh, I thought you keep the pork chops in refrigeration as long as possible, what with salmonella and all," said Glory, delighted to have a real-life professional chef in her own kitchen. She loved watching cooking shows on the Food Network, and don't even get her started on Ina Garten. She didn't even know half the food Ina made and always rolled her eyes whenever Ina called for "best-quality" olive oil or whatever she was demanding. But it didn't matter, she loved Ina anyway, and especially that big old fancy house somewhere in New York. Delphine had told her about the town Ina lived in, and she couldn't remember the name of it, but apparently it was filled with all sorts of rich people like Ina who ate truffles, which Glory had never tried but was curious about.

With pinched fingers high in the air, Justice sprinkled salt in a steady stream on the meat. "What you're going to do with most meat is bring it up to room temperature before you cook it. It's called tempering the meat." She wiped her hands against a borrowed kitchen towel that read *Laissez Les Bon Temps Rouler*. "It helps the meat cook more evenly. Otherwise, it gets charred on the outside and raw in the middle. Pepper?"

Glory handed over a tall orange pepper mill. Justice gave it a few twists and got back to her cooking lesson. "I'm going to let this pan get good and hot, and all this salt and pepper is going to create a gorgeous crust on the outside. You done prepping those green beans, D?"

Delphine rinsed the green beans in the colander, gave it a good shake to expel as much water as possible, and handed it over to Justice.

"Well, I must say I quite enjoy having my own personal chef. What a treat," said Glory, watching Justice as she sliced some shallots that Glory had dug up from the back of her refrigerator. "Remind me, how do you two know each other?" she asked, standing over Justice's shoulder as she carved the shallots into paper-thin slices with the speed of a ninja.

Justice turned away from her shallots toward Delphine and with a wicked smile said, "Remind me, how did we meet?" Glory couldn't quite put her finger on it, but it seemed like there was some kind of inside joke between her daughter and this stranger in her home.

"Yes, it was a while ago, wasn't it, at the . . . law associates' dinner," said Delphine. Justice raised an eyebrow. "We had a team-building day at the law firm to welcome the new associates and hired Justice to lead all the lawyers in a team-building exercise."

"How wonderful," said Glory. "So, walk me through what you're doing to the green beans."

Justice tore her eyes off Delphine long enough to explain the process of blanching. Quick boil of the green beans, then submerge in ice to prevent them from overcooking, also to keep their bright green color instead of going gray. Heat a sauté pan with a little olive oil;

cook the shallots for a minute or two, until they soften just a little. Toss the green beans in the pan for a quick minute and take them off the heat. Serve with slivered almonds and a squeeze of lemon.

"Lemon? With green beans? That's some real Barefoot Contessa stuff," Glory said, right before her cell phone rang. She looked at the number and winced. "Damn it, I forgot that I agreed to call Constance Wheeler tonight to review the budget for the Mardi Gras festivities. This woman is all over me like Tabasco on grits. Give me fifteen minutes—and don't start dinner without me! Looking forward to my first James-Beard-or-whatever-you-call-it meal." Walking to her bedroom, she answered her phone and held it to her ear. "Yes, I know I was supposed to call but I have unexpected company . . ." She closed her bedroom door behind her.

♣ ♦ ♥ ♠

Justice turned to Delphine, "A *team-building* exercise?" spat Justice.

"That's the truth—it's what happened!"

"I suppose you conveniently forgot to mention how we flirted all night. Or how we went out for bourbon afterward and I walked you home in the rain and kissed you under your apartment building's awning."

Delphine's face, which had been stern all night, finally softened . . . became pleading, in fact. "You just showed up here unannounced. What did you want me to say?"

Justice pinched the pork chops with tongs and seared one side in a sizzling pan. "I don't know . . . you could have mentioned that you're in a loving relationship with a woman who cares about you? That I practically live with you and cook all your meals and coax you to eat more vegetables? I don't know, it really doesn't seem that controversial to me . . ." She turned her back to Delphine and seared the other side of the pork chop. Droplets of fat jumped from the cast-iron pan.

Delphine stood up from the table and wrapped her arms around Justice's waist. "Babe, I'm so sorry. I was just unprepared for you to show up at my childhood home at a time when I'm furious with my mother and trying to figure out who might have wanted my father dead. But I'm glad to see you, I really am."

Justice twisted her head around to give Delphine a kiss that was short, but full of intensity and definitely not platonic. Delphine inched away, mindful that her mother was in the house and pork chops were still cooking on the stove. "If I can just ask . . . do me a teensy favor and continue to tell my mother that we're friends."

"What?"

"For me?"

Justice was as heated as that cast-iron pan. "You want me to tell your mother that we're just friends when . . ." She looked down the hallway to make sure Glory was nowhere within earshot, then lowered her voice. ". . . when I've seen the mole on your inner left thigh? No, I am not about to go undercover as you little *friend*."

"You know how my mother is," countered Delphine.

Justice cut a knob of butter and flicked it into the pan. "No, I don't. I know what you *tell* me about her, and I know what you *think* about her. But now that I've met her myself and seen her with my own eyes, I don't know, she seems kind of cool. She doesn't seem as narrow-minded and judgmental as you make her out to be. Maybe the one who is narrow-minded and judgmental is you."

"Me?"

"You keep saying that your mother won't like you dating a woman, but maybe *you're* the one who can't come to terms with it. I've seen it before . . . you're not the first self-hating straight woman I've dated."

Delphine's abrasive laugh could have scraped up the bits stuck on the bottom of that pan. "So how many of these women have you . . ."

♣♦♥♠

Glory's voice could be heard traveling from the hallway, ". . . and no, I haven't forgotten about the king cake . . . Well, they're going to have to get over it . . . Yes, see you then." She reappeared in the living room and ambled her way into the kitchen. "Let me tell you what, be careful what you ask for, because I thought I wanted to be chair of that Mardi Gras committee. Now I'm pretty sure it's going to cost me at least two years off the back end of my life." She closed her eyes and inhaled deeply. "My kitchen ain't ever smelled so good. What are you doing with that pork chop, bathing it in butter?"

Justice laughed, her wrist working overtime to spoon butter over the pork chops. "Ever wonder why restaurant food tastes better than home cooking? It's because we finish everything off in *way* more butter than you'd ever use at home."

"Well, I can't be eating like this every day, but I suppose I can make a special exception for a friend of Delphine's who happens to be a famous chef." She looked around, and then her face lit up as if she'd had a brilliant idea. "You know what, I'm going to pull out the good china for this. Come help me, Delphine."

The two went to the dining room to rifle through the china hutch, which was stuffed from bottom to top with assorted china, earthenware, and bric-a-brac purchased at various garage sales, estate sales, and thrift shops. Constance Wheeler always complained that she ought to sort through it once and for all, but Constance didn't appreciate fine things. Glory knew this because Constance had stayed married to that good-for-nothing man all these years, never once having second-guessed that decision. Glory pulled out a set of coordinating blue-and-white dinner plates and serving bowls. She had paid a hundred dollars for the set, more than usual, but later went on eBay and realized it was worth far more. Don't ever tell anyone that Glory Broussard doesn't know quality when she sees it. People discard things all the time, unable to see them anew.

They returned to the kitchen, piles of dishes trembling in their hands. "Whoa, let me help you with that," said Justice, who had just lifted the meat out of the pan with tongs and let it rest on a plate covered with paper towels. She lifted the plates in Glory's arms and rested them on the table.

"You're mighty strong. Guess that comes with working in a kitchen, huh?" said Glory, trying hard not to gape at Justice's muscular biceps, or the tattoos running up and down them. "How long are you in Louisiana, anyway?"

"A month, but I have another week til my stint officially starts. Guess I'll be headed down to New Orleans tomorrow and looking for a place to stay."

Glory clapped her hands excitedly. "You could stay here!" Delphine looked as if she had just seen a car crash in her own home. "We have a guest room, well, it's technically my office but it has a little foldout sofa that has never been slept on. You'd be the first!"

"I couldn't . . ." said Justice.

Glory was undeterred. "And even though I know you're on vacation, I promise we won't make you cook every meal. But maybe you could teach me a few tricks for the kitchen, help me raise my game. Wait, do you make sweets? Because if you're one of those pastry chefs, too, I may have to take that back and ask for a couple of treats."

"You know, maybe I will take you up on your guest room offer. And no, I'm not a pastry chef but I do make a mean crème brûlée."

Justice transferred the deeply green, perfectly cooked green beans into the fancy blue-and-white bowl, which Glory commented was the perfect bowl for that dish. She then plated the pork chops, their perfect salt-and-pepper exteriors glistening with butter and topped with a tiny sprig of thyme that Glory managed to snip from her neighbor's herb pots.

Nights like this were the reason Glory had accumulated all that china, and seeing it back in use warmed her heart and made her think of Sterling and the good times they had shared. She only wished there had been more of them.

10

In downtown Lafayette you could see the past and the future within three short blocks. Boarded-up buildings mingled alongside restaurants with entrées that cost thirty-six dollars and came with no sides. Recently, the viable businesses in downtown had organized, trying to give folks a reason to visit, other than the courthouse. As luck would have it, a food truck festival coincided with Delphine's trip to Lagniappe Records, which was a must-visit for Delphine each time she was in town. Glory and Justice were up late exchanging cooking tips and recipes, and, as a result, were still asleep. Delphine decided she could use the alone time, given the bomb that dropped into her life, and into her mother's house, overnight. She snaked her way through trucks selling po'boys and boudin balls—the smell of vats of grease coming to frying temperature filling her nose—before making her way into the store.

The bell on the door jingled as she walked into the record store. Scratchy zydeco music pulsed on the speakers, maybe Clifton Chenier, if she had to guess. In the front corner was a small rack of vintage clothing and a sign that said New to You. Behind the cash register was a collage of stickers: the Sub Pop label, giant eyes and ears, and a poster of Prince in a purple bikini brief. Two rescue dogs scrambled through an aisle of records and wagged their tails in her direction. She waved at Cora, the store owner, then lavished the dogs with scratches and pets until they tired of her attention. They wandered to the back of the store and where worn dog beds awaited them.

Delphine loved music because her father had loved music. When the house lights were turned off and everyone had gone to bed, Sterling could be found smoking a cigarette and lying on the floor, arms propped up in a triangle, reading album liner notes. His tastes were as complicated as he was. On the turntable could be Steely Dan or Earth, Wind & Fire. Lots of Sam Cooke and even more jazz like Keith Jarrett, Miles Davis, and Stan Brubeck. Delphine rifled through one section of vinyl called "Really Cheap Shit," then another called "Really Expensive Shit." She thumbed through the R&B section, stopping at a Donny Hathaway album.

"Mind if I play this?" she asked Cora.

"All yours . . ."

Judging by the sign over the record player, the store was now visited by a good share of Gen Z shoppers, assholes, or both. It read: IF UNSURE ABOUT HOW TO OPERATE, PLEASE ASK FOR ASSISTANCE. DO NOT SPIN THE PLATTER MANUALLY W/NEEDLE ON PLATE W/O A RECORD ON IT. YES, SOMEONE HAS DONE THAT.

Delphine dropped the needle onto the album and the store filled with Donny Hathaway's live cover of "What's Going On." She collected a few albums in her arms, enjoying this brief moment of solitude. Glory had been acting as if trying to find her father's killer was an imposition, which felt cruel, even for her mother. She was worn down by her mother's eye rolling, pouting, and complaining. She hadn't meant to debut the braids and nose ring to her mother, but there was no time to revert back to Glory Broussard's Respectable Daughter before the funeral. And then there was the matter of her girlfriend showing up unannounced at her house. She hadn't meant to belittle or demean Justice by asking her to pretend they were just friends, but she wasn't ready to tell her mother about this side of herself, not because she was ashamed, but because it was so new.

Justice wasn't the only thing on her mind. There was the issue of Valerie's salon, rumored to be underwater. Upon hearing this rumor from her mother, Delphine's knee-jerk reaction was to dismiss it, chalk it up to the bored housewives and gossipy churchgoers of Lafayette, people who had never left this small town and had nothing better to do. But Delphine couldn't stop thinking about it, not to mention all the expensive furniture and high-end finishes she had observed while she was there. In addition to a mortgage, could there have also been a loan for a renovation? She hated that her mother had made her so suspicious, but when she woke up this morning she called her firm's investigator to see what he could find out.

Ever since she arrived in Louisiana, it felt like she was doing nothing but sinking. But when she saw Landry walk through the door of Lagniappe Records, she felt buoyed by his presence.

"Hey," he said, leaning in for a hug and pressing his body against hers, and the armful of vinyl she had found in the shop. "Never been here before . . . You have a record player?" She laughed. "I've been meaning to tell you I like the hair." He was wearing jeans, a form-fitting T-shirt and work boots. It created a silhouette that proved he had been putting that gym in the garage to use.

"A woman cannot live by streaming service alone. My music tastes cannot be contained by an algorithm." In the back of the store were two chairs, a coffee table, and a cockatoo in a silver cage. She motioned for him to follow her. "What was so secretive that you wanted to meet in person and couldn't talk on the phone?"

"So, I have some bad news." They both sat at the coffee table. "Remember when we were having lunch at Spoonbill? And I put my hand on top of yours? Well, turns out a colleague was walking by and happened to see me. He's now claiming that we're on too 'intimate' terms for me to be working on this case. He forced me to recuse myself, which I did."

"That's absurd. I'm so sorry. We should have been more careful."

"We did nothing wrong," he said, flashing back to that night months ago. "And it has nothing to do with you, and everything to do with the fact that he's in the pocket of the Benoit family. He thinks he's doing them some kind of favor coming down on me, which he's been doing ever since Kerry and I separated."

"I object on your behalf," Delphine said. "You have more integrity than anyone I know, and of course you would never be influenced by the fact that I'm involved."

He scratched his head. "Except now, I have nothing to lose . . ." Delphine felt a divider between them fall.

"What do you mean?"

"I may not be on the case anymore, but I still want to find whoever did that awful thing to your dad." One of the shop dogs moseyed its way to the sofas. Landry mussed up its ears and nuzzled its face for a minute, then said, "I wouldn't call it a lead exactly, but we interviewed that Marguerite Dunlop woman and something's not quite adding up with her."

"She's the woman that lived on the top floor of his duplex. My mom, Valerie, and I already interviewed her."

He shook his head in disbelief. "I really wish you'd let the police do our job, but of course you did," he said. "She said she was working overnight with the horses when your father was murdered, but there's not a clear consensus on whether she was there that night. Apparently, it was real hectic moving the horses and cleaning the stalls. No one wants to definitively vouch for her whereabouts. I can't work this case anymore, but I figured that was information you and your mama could use."

"I don't want you doing this. I don't want you getting into trouble at your job," said Delphine firmly. "And besides, we already talked with her. I don't know, she seems to check out. My dad helped to get her clean, even gave her a place to stay at his duplex. Maybe she doesn't have the most airtight story, but I don't know, I have a hard time believing it. And she's so petite. It's hard for me to imagine her overpowering my dad."

"She's setting off my cop alarm, if you know what I mean. Something about her ain't adding up."

Delphine scrunched her face, a sign that she was letting his suspicion register. "Alright, we'll keep a close eye on her."

"And one more thing . . . the knife. It's not a regular knife. First of all, it's very high quality. The blade is sharp, and still sharp after, you know," he refrained from sharing any of the grisly details of her father's murder. "And the handle, it has all these unique carvings on it. I'm a hunter. I've been to a lot of hunting shows, seen a lot of knives. And I've never seen anything like this knife. My guess is that it's handmade, and by someone who knows what they're doing."

"Okay . . . how would you go about finding the maker?"

"There's a lot of folks here in Louisiana that make their own weapons and blades. I'd try a few hunting shows, for starters."

Delphine nodded her head, having a hard time imagining herself in the company of a bunch of hunting enthusiasts. Plus, how many of these shows existed in Louisiana? She didn't know the answer, but probably a lot.

Landry wrung his hands, like there was something else that was burdening his soul. "Hey . . . want to grab something to eat from the food trucks?"

Delphine paid her for records and gave the dogs a final pet before heading outside with Landry.

The street fair was now in full swing. Terrance Simien and the Zydeco Experience, a well-known local band, were warming up. The charismatic lead singer ran through the opening of "Tee Nah Nah," with the keyboardist harmonizing along. The folks of Lafayette were beginning to turn out. The crowds were as thick as an okra stew, and the air was scented with the flavors and seasonings of a dozen food trucks. Delphine and Landry did a lap to map out a plan of culinary attack.

"Want to share a muffuletta?" asked Landry.

"I was afraid you were going to suggest that. It's about a week's worth of salt so yes, I absolutely want one of those. Except we're also going to need one of those raspberry kolaches to pair it with. We need just as much sugar as salt to balance the palate."

They each grabbed a pale ale from the Parish Brewing kegs on tap and found a bench. "So, tell me . . . what's going on with you in New York. Work, life, give me an update," said Landry, apparently excavating for information.

"Oh, you know . . . work is work. I haven't told my mom yet because it's not one hundred percent official, but it looks like I'm set to make partner at the law firm."

"What? That's amazing," he said, tearing into his muffuletta and chomping at the chewy bread. "I always knew you were going to make it in the big city, so I'm not surprised. It feels right on time, doesn't it?"

She sipped her beer and wiped away a light layer of foam from her upper lip. "That's nice of you to say. You know, when I first moved to New York I walked into a leasing office to rent an apartment. There was a big sign—three intersecting circles. One circle said price, another said location, and the last one said size of the apartment. Underneath it was a statement: *You can only have two of the three*. That's kinda how I feel about my life, you know? Just when I finally straighten out my professional life, everything else is crumbling."

Straightening out her professional life had been her top priority in recent months, after she had been placed on a mandatory leave of absence for shenanigans that involved her married coworker and activities everyone had agreed to—except his wife. The affair had been spectacularly unveiled at the firm's summer party when the wife imprinted her palm on Delphine's cheek. But law firms are capitalistic organizations. Bring in new clients and keep your billable hours unreasonably high, and all is forgiven. Delphine had done both. And it was good therapy because Delphine had no interest in dwelling on her recent divorce. She found that she could distract herself by working a hundred hours a week. Except, when Justice led the cooking class for the summer associates, she found herself smiling for the first time in months, in a genuine way. There was a warmth to Justice that made her forget about work, about all the past troubles. When Justice proposed lingering at the bar across the street after the dinner, she surprised herself by saying yes.

Landry touched her shoulder, snapping her out of her brief memory spiraling. "Anyway, I'm fine. Just working hard . . . and a lot of change with the divorce and everything."

He rubbed her knee. "I can appreciate that," he said.

"Sorry, I'm such an idiot. Of course you have your own bullshit that you're working through." She dabbed the filling of the kolach with her finger, tasting the raspberry jam inside.

"You've got a few months ahead of me on divorce. When exactly does it feel like you're not a boneheaded idiot for missing every sign and clue that your marriage was falling apart?"

"Good question. For me it was a little different. I happened to be the wrecking ball in my marriage, so I guess you can say I knew it was coming. Do you know when I got married, I remember walking down the aisle of that fancy hotel, looking at my ex and thinking, *Alright . . . I can make this work for a while.* Not exactly the inner dialogue a person should have on their wedding day. So, I guess you could say I knew from the beginning."

He took a long swig of his beer. Time-honored liquid courage. "Do you ever feel like things are happening for a reason? Your divorce, my divorce. Maybe we shouldn't be looking at this as our lives falling apart. Maybe it's our lives finally coming together." It was a big swing.

She looked at him, wordlessly, and inhaled. She would have been lying if she said she hadn't had the same thought over the past few days, especially once she learned of his divorce. But she didn't want to admit it. For one, it was too easy. Things that seem too good to be true usually are. Two, there was a woman currently stashed in her mother's guest room who was masquerading as her friend and whose body she had folded into, after Glory had fallen asleep. And now she was questioning everything.

Delphine was grateful when his police radio chattered. The voice on the other end barked out a series of codes and letters and Landry immediately began gathering himself. "Gotta run," he said. "Ten-car collision on the I-10 and they're requesting extra units."

Delphine was starting to feel like her personal life was going to be a ten-car collision when all was said and done.

"I'll let you finish off all this food," said Landry.

"Yes, great, thanks. I'll be ten pounds heavier the next time you see me." The radio chattered again. "Go on, go rescue the people like the big handsome hero you are. Go . . ." He cracked a smile, turned around, and hurried toward the garage where he had parked his car.

Once he was out of eyesight, Delphine surrendered to the impulse every modern woman has when suddenly alone—she checked her phone. She was eager to see what the law firm's investigator had been able to dig up about Valerie's finances and clicked an email titled "Valerie LeBlanc Financial Summary." The investigator had attached several documents, which Delphine would review later on her computer, but she was slack-jawed at the summary in the body of the email.

> *Ms. LeBlanc has a high level of debt relative to her reported income. In addition to $137,350 in personal loans, she has a $250,000 loan attached to The New Woman Salon, LLC on Johnston Street, Lafayette, Louisiana. She is more than five months in arrears on this commercial loan and will enter into foreclosure proceedings for this business within thirty days.*

11

That afternoon, Glory escaped Delphine and Justice by telling them both that she was going to an estate sale. Justice half wanted to go, but Delphine had convinced her that it was nothing but a bunch of sad old homes that smelled of mothballs. That seemed to convince her otherwise.

Glory walked into Cypress Downs wearing a pair of champagne-colored palazzo pants and a gauzy, diaphanous blouse of the same color, embellished with crystals around the collar. If it were up to her, she'd have worn a pair of matching heels that she had stashed in the closet, but these days, her swollen feet made the final decision, and they had objected at the mere glimpse of those old shoes. Instead, she went with the less flattering black patent leather pumps with a block heel. They dragged the outfit down a little bit, but at least she could walk without her feet hollering with each step. She had a single goal for the evening: learn something, *anything*, about why Sterling had soured on working at the casino.

The seafood buffet was calling her—crab pistolettes in a hollandaise sauce and blackened oysters, and that was just to start—but it was going to have to wait. She did her best to ignore the savory fragrance coming from the buffet cutting board and decided to try out a little gambling, which was her trade—not something she did for personal enjoyment. That said, if forced to play, blackjack was her choice.

She eyed a table, one with a woman her age as dealer, and waited for her moment. As soon as there was a break in the game she sat down and nodded to be dealt in. A middle-aged man in a button-down shirt and khakis bristled at her presence. Glory was not surprised. A Black woman who has done some living is used to people letting her know she doesn't belong. It's not always obvious. She noticed the tense upturn of his smile at her arrival. It might as well have said . . . *Look at this woman. Such a fool that she doesn't even know she doesn't belong here.*

Dispensing of the man became her focus, and she would enjoy it. She bet conservatively at first, wanting to get a feel for the game before she made bigger wagers. Glory could dial into a game of blackjack the way people who had migraines knew rain was on the way—by feel. Well, maybe it was more than just a feeling. It all came down to what cards were being thrown down and where they were landing. She had developed this instinct from countless Friday nights of playing blackjack at parties Sterling had hosted at the house. Over time she came to observe that when the dealer had cards of higher value, the dealer won. When she, as a player, had higher cards, she won. Her memory was so sharp that she could remember the exact color shirt Sterling wore when he came home at 3 A.M. (green) and the brand of perfume that lingered on said shirt (Charlie, by Revlon). She could sort of keep track of the cards and roughly how many high cards might be left after just a few hands. Someone once said that playing this way had a name, and that she could get kicked out of casinos for it, but it didn't matter. Glory didn't play in casinos and had no desire. Tonight was business.

After about four hands, she could feel things starting to click. Starting off slow, she wagered five dollars on her first hand, which she won. The man playing alongside her gave an irritated smile. He'd allow her this one game. That's what his face said, anyway. Feeling confident that she was locked into the flow, she bet ten dollars on the next hand, which again played out in her favor. He sniffed and rubbed his nose. After Glory won a twenty-five dollar hand, the man threw his cards down a little harder than was necessary, stood up, and walked away from the table—not before hiking his pants up aggressively to underscore that while he may be down, he was still very much a man.

The dealer gave Glory a respectful nod. "I can see you know how to play this game. One thing I've learned working in this casino all these years is that it's always the unassuming types that know what they're doing. What's your name?"

"Glory Broussard. And you?"

"Bonnie." She pointed to a cocktail waitress with cleavage up to her chin and a hemline that wasn't much longer. "I see you've caught the attention of the house. You're welcome to order anything from the kitchen or the bar."

"It's complimentary," said the cocktail waitress, smacking her gum with vigor. "That means it's free." Glory, who wasn't sure if catching the attention of the house was a good or bad thing, placed an order for a rum and Coke and French fries.

"I have a question for you," asked Bonnie. "How did you learn to play like this? Is it a course you take or something else?"

"Nah, nothing like that. I just pay closer attention than most people do."

The server returned with her rum and Coke. "Your fries are coming up in a second."

Glory thanked her, then returned her focus to Bonnie. "Am I allowed to ask you a question or is that against the house rules?"

"You can ask. Doesn't mean I can answer, but I do try to be cordial," she said, without any bite whatsoever.

"I assume you knew Sterling Broussard, the man that passed away last week?" asked Glory.

Bonnie nodded slowly, seemingly making a connection between Sterling and why the woman in front of her played blackjack like the devil. "I knew *of* him, mostly," she said. "Didn't have a lot of direct interaction with him."

Glory's fries arrived in a silver cup, standing vertically inside a ring of parchment paper. She could get used to this, she mused. For the first time since she found Sterling's body, it felt like the universe was on her side. "Is there any reason anyone at the casino would have wanted him out of the picture?"

Bonnie turned over her cards and respectfully tipped her head to Glory, who had just won another hand. "Not that I can think of, but I'm real low on the org chart, if you know what I mean. The casino bosses aren't spilling their secrets to a fifteen-dollar-an-hour dealer."

A tall man in a loud burgundy suit with broad shoulders and shoes polished to a high sheen walked to the table. Of note, he was the rare Black man with red hair and freckles. His smile showed so many teeth, God must have given him more than the standard issue. Glory assumed the worst, that this would be the moment when she would be kicked out of the casino for winning. She remembered that the way she played, called "card counting" by the casinos, wasn't illegal, but that didn't mean the casino had to put up with it. They're private property and they can kick you out for any reason they want.

Bonnie and Glory locked eyes, as if they both suspected the same thing was coming.

He reached across the table. "Good evening. My name is Redmond Herbert, the manager of VIP-client services here at Cypress Downs. We couldn't help but notice your talent for blackjack. We see that you're a student of the game, and appreciate that some of our more skilled clients may enjoy playing in a more discreet environment. If you like, we would be happy to invite you to our lounge."

Bonnie beamed, as if Glory was her pupil who had graduated magna cum laude. Glory had a strong BS detector, and she felt itchy just looking at this cheap suit. But it was an opportunity to see more of the casino. Corruption was part of the DNA of Louisiana, and Glory knew that real power moved in the shadows, away from the harsh lights. The story of whoever turned on Sterling was more likely to be found in the VIP lounge, not on the casino floor.

"Why not? Just let me take my fries with me."

The first thing that Glory noticed, once the elevator doors opened, was the quiet. Unlike the floor downstairs, the slot machines weren't chirping. A silent hush enveloped the room, from the thick, chocolate brown carpeting to the burgundy velvet drapes. There was no bar, but drinks appeared from curtained-off areas. Cocktail waitresses looked more like secretaries in clingy dresses, high heels, and more tasteful cleavage.

"Fifty dollars per hand is the minimum in the Sassafras Lounge," said Mr. Herbert, her escort. "Will that be a problem?"

Glory gulped. She had been lulled by flattery into the lounge, but now it was clear that she was the mark. She should have seen it coming—free drinks, endless fries, a little flattery, and now she was in a so-called VIP situation that would cost her fifty dollars a hand. Damn those fries. It would take her four or five hands, at least, to situate herself within the game. She may have been an expert at blackjack, but frittering away this kind of money was what her clients did; she was smarter than that. Usually.

A few gamblers lifted their heads to contemplate Glory's presence. She could tell that they found her curious. Hell, she found her presence curious, too. But she loved nothing more than pushing buttons.

The woman at the cashier's cage had caught Glory's eye, with a warm and appealing way about her. Glory had noticed the sheen of thick support hose on the woman, underneath the table, when she walked in, which helped Glory to peg her to be around the same age as she was. It also meant she had probably worked on her feet her entire life. Support hose aren't a sign of surrender, like some people think. They're a sign of resilience.

"Do I know you?" Glory asked.

The woman smiled, as if she was waiting for a sign that would puncture the stuffy formality of the Sassafras Lounge. "You do. Odille Clemons. I didn't want to say anything, because we are trained to be discreet, but I grew up down the street from you on Delhomme Street. I was one of your mama's cousin's neighbors." Odille smoothed Glory's money and then dropped it into a machine, which made quick and accurate business of counting it.

In Louisiana there's your next of kin, and then there's adjacency. You may not be directly related to someone, but you might be in the vicinity of someone who is related to them, and that's a proxy for family. In most cases, it's good enough.

A fresh rum and Coke appeared by one of the sleekly dressed women, seemingly out of nowhere. Glory took it. "I thought you looked familiar. How'd you get a job working up in this fancy high-roller place anyhow?"

"I was a bank teller for thirty years at Bayou Federal Credit Union. Most of that time on my feet, working drive-through deposits. I was more than happy to take a job here where at least I get to sit down."

Glory identified with this woman the moment she saw her. She looked around the room, and the man with the tacky suit was not far behind. "Girl, I'm so happy they gave you a seat this time." They laughed together, because they both knew the residual pain of working on your feet, as well as the lack of opportunity to do anything else in Lafayette. "I have a question for you. Who is that man in the tacky suit and shiny shoes who is keeping his eyes on me?"

"Oh, that's T-Red. What did you do to have him following you around like this? Must have been something real good, or something real bad."

How could she not have connected the dots until now? Redmond, with the red hair and freckles. This was the T-Red that Grady had warned her about. The one that had plucked Sterling out of unglamorous slot machine duty and onto "special services" and betting lines. Grady had made it sound like Sterling was happy enough working at Cypress Downs, until he became enmeshed with this T-Red.

But why was he casing her? She hadn't won much money, by casino standards. Was it because she seemed like the kind of woman who might overplay her hand, and her pocketbook, in exchange for a couple free drinks? Or did he know something more? Judging by the lines deepening between his eyebrows, he seemed troubled by the conversation she was having with the cashier.

He looked at his watch, then back at the cashier. When he caught Glory glancing at him, he flashed that smile again, and all ninety teeth.

"I figure you must know something about Sterling," Glory said to the woman, suspecting that the gossip spread fast around these parts. "I got about sixty seconds before T-Red comes over here and drags me out by the ear. If you knew someone was investigating this place for a secret no one wanted to get out, where would you start?"

Odille pushed a pile of chips Glory's way. "The casino is a pretty tight ship—by the book. Regulators are in and out all the time. But the horses? It's the horses you've got to look into. You know that saying, 'Follow the money'? Here, you follow the horses."

T-Red's pants even sounded cheap. Glory could hear them rubbing against each other and getting closer to her. She thanked Odille for the counsel and allowed T-Red to escort her to one of the fifty-dollar blackjack tables. It looked like she'd be heading back to the stables at Opelousas again . . . but not until she played a few hands.

A gambler must have a line that cannot be crossed. A limit. Glory may have had a couple of cocktails, but she was strategic and clear-eyed enough to take advantage of the opportunity in front of her, playing until the early hours of the evening and earning $3,000.

12

Follow the casino. Follow the horses. Glory thought about this all night long and couldn't help but feel like she was getting the ol' runaround. But there was something about the way the cashier shared information with her. She was a woman like Glory, who no one really saw, and yet was all seeing. In another place and time, her skills might be valued. The House always wins, but people like her never seemed to come out on top. Glory could relate. She had a hunch the woman would not intentionally steer her wrong.

Over a breakfast of toast and tea at the house, Delphine and Glory caught each other up on their separate investigations. Delphine had to summon the patience of the entire order of Discalced Carmelite nuns when Glory shared that she went to the casino alone, again. But she managed to listen intently when Glory shared that the casino regulators had been streaming in and out on a regular basis, not to mention the possibility of the stables being the heart of illicit activity.

Then, Delphine reluctantly shared the news about Valerie being behind on her mortgage. "And I know what you're thinking, but that doesn't make her a killer."

Declaring *I told you so* would have been a little too obvious, but if Glory had a love language, it was being right, and she was thrilled to have that hunch validated by inscrutable outside sources. That said, if she was giving full credit, Constance Wheeler deserved fair credit for leading her in this direction in the first place.

"And I met up with Landry at the record store," said Delphine. "He recommended that we look into the knife more, which he said was unique and well-made. And also Marguerite, who I told him we already spoke to. I can't find anything about the knife," she said, stopping herself. "Oh wait, I actually have a work call I need to do today."

Glory dropped a sugar cube into her tea. "Damn, what's the point of working a high-powered job if they can't even give you proper bereavement leave when your father is murdered?"

"You're not wrong about that. I got a text last night pleading with me to join this call, followed by, *We understand if you can't.* They obviously didn't understand, or they wouldn't have asked. I caved. We can go to the stable again tomorrow, right?"

"Sure, we can go tomorrow." Glory stood up. "Want anything at CC's?" She gathered her belongings and prepared to head out. She would have stopped by CC's if Delphine wanted anything, but since she didn't, she happened to take a forty-mile detour to Jennings, and Sterling's duplex.

♣♦♥♠

Sterling's duplex was in a working-class neighborhood with front yards that contained small fishing boats and rusty basketball hoops without nets. Glory slowed down and tried to figure out if Marguerite was home or not. The reason she had traveled to the duplex? She couldn't conduct an investigation at the stable if the woman was there.

She eyed a filthy Toyota Tacoma parked on the side of the road with a bumper sticker that had drawings of a horse's rear end and warned *Keep off my Tail.* With caked mud clinging to the side and the horsey warning, Glory felt pretty confident that this was her truck. Marguerite was home, at least for now, so Glory had a small window to make her way to the Opelousas Stable.

But there was another car parked in the driveway. Parking in the driveway meant that you had a claim, and Glory wondered who would make such a claim at Sterling's house. From the side door, the same one Glory walked through on that dark day when she found Sterling with his chest split open, walked Valerie. Glory was about to flex her ankle and speed the hell away from this street, but a small child on a tricycle pedaled across her path.

The delay gave Valerie enough time to teeter over to her car in heels, jeans, and a tight turtleneck. Did she ever wear stretchy pants and a sweatshirt and sneakers, like an ordinary person? On top of that, Valerie was smiling at Glory, like they were actual friends. Glory lowered her window as the child pedaled out of her path—about five seconds too late.

"Hey! What are you doing out here?" Valerie asked. Her highlights looked expensive, like Constance's. Maybe Glory should go see that woman who worked in her salon before Mardi Gras, she thought. Glory racked her brain for a lie that would be sufficient, but then it occurred to her that Valerie might actually be useful at the stable. She recalled how those jockeys and trainers nearly fell over themselves to talk to her the last time they were there. Maybe it made sense to bring her.

"Hey! What are you doing out here?" Valerie asked. Glory had the same question for Valerie, but given that Sterling owned the place, it was likely Valerie's problem to deal with now. Valerie's highlights shimmered in the low sun and looked expensive, like Constance's. Glory squinted at the low sun and smacked her gum. "Listen, someone said that I ought to spend some more time at the stable to see if there's a connection to Sterling's death."

"What kind of connection?" Valerie's eyes widened like a little girl and Glory had to suppress the urge to roll her eyes.

"I'm not entirely sure, but from the sound of it, that horseshit isn't the only manure they're shoveling down at the track. Whaddya say? You in?"

"I'm in," Valerie responded. She didn't walk as much as balance on those heels. She teetered herself right over to the passenger side of Glory's car and let herself in. The nerve. Valerie peppered her with questions along the way. *Who told you to follow the horses? You mentioned you had a source? Is the source someone I know? Someone Delphine knows?*

"Oh, you know how people down here talk. You just have to give them the opportunity," said Glory, a ring of dismissiveness in her tone. It was enough to quiet Valerie for the rest of the ride.

Glory had just enough time for a quick chat with the Lord.

> *You are really testing me today with this one. I swear, if this woman makes one wisecrack or one wrong move, I will see to it that she mysteriously washes up in Grenovilliers Swamp. Oh, you don't think I will? Try me . . . I care less about the afterlife than you think I do.*

♣♦♥♠

Not long after, Glory pulled off the highway. Before them was an endless stretch of industrial, oil-based businesses with equipment stored under giant carports. Acadiana Exploration Company, Boudreaux Oil & Gas, Livingston Engineering, Mattex Energy Co., and on and on. That eventually gave way to more and more grass, until they were enveloped in lush, knee-high grasses and the soothing sound of late afternoon crickets.

"Do me a favor and open that gate," said Glory, pointing to a gate of galvanized steel, powder-coated green to blend in and connected to two sturdy posts.

"Are we going to get into trouble for this?" asked Valerie suspiciously.

"If you are going to participate in this investigation, you are going to have to develop some gumption. You can't go around skulking and looking over your shoulder like you don't belong, because it's going to give us both away."

Valerie nodded, like she was screwing up the courage.

"Let me put it another way. Being undercover means not asking for permission. Taking liberties." Something Valerie could relate to, Glory knew.

Valerie bit her lip, as if she needed to physically hold back what she had really wanted to say to Glory. With a newfound determination, she opened the car door, swung open the gates, and made a dramatic "come on in" gesture to Glory, who drove her car toward the line of trucks and trailers parked along the back of the stable. Valerie trudged behind her, her heels sinking deeper into the soft ground with each step.

If Glory was kinder, she could have driven closer to the gate. Valerie really didn't need to walk that far. Glory shrugged. That Woman didn't need to sleep with her husband, either. Maybe one day they'd be even.

Valerie got back into the car and slammed the door. "So, what exactly is the plan, Glory? Or did you bring me out here to just humiliate me in front of half of Opelousas?"

"Half of Opelousas? That's a little dramatic, don't you think? There's about thirty people here and we're outnumbered by horses five-to-one," said Glory. She made a face that could have been caused by two irritants: the smell of horse manure wafting into her car or listening to Valerie complain. If she felt a sliver of indignity, it was nothing close to the sting Glory felt when she realized Sterling was spending his nights at her home.

"Oh, go ahead and admit it, you like seeing me covered in horseshit, with my best heels caked with Lord knows what."

It pleased Glory to no end, but she couldn't give Valerie that satisfaction. "Girl, please. I can tell that you're proud of those flimsy little shoes dangling off your feet, but do you really think I care?" asked Glory, nodding at a man leading a horse through the maze of cars by its reins. She turned to Valerie. "Now listen here, I ain't got time for your hysteria. Not today. Smells like a cesspool up in here."

Valerie smacked her hands against her lap in sheer frustration. "That's why I asked you what the plan was."

Glory took in the lay of the land from the driver's side of her Honda-CRV. To the left was the stable where they had previously visited Marguerite. Even farther left, beyond the stable, were a quadrant of tracks where horses trained.

"Okay, here's what we're going to do. I'm going to walk around the stalls looking out for anything that's unusual. You're going to trail behind me, ready to intercept and distract anyone who gets in my way or looks at me suspiciously. I need you to create a buffer, some space, so I can snoop around just a little."

"I can do that." Valerie nodded in a determined way. "We need a safe word. Something I can say that means that we're in trouble."

"That's not a bad idea. Got any ideas?"

Another horse was led in front of the car. Its mane was wrapped in an intricate braid. It seemed to give Valerie an idea. "I do hair, right? I'll just say that I'm the braider and ask if any of the horses need a touch-up."

Oh Lord, did horses get touch-ups? Glory knew nothing about horses and was all but certain that wasn't the lingo used, but it wasn't a terrible idea. At any rate, she was tired of sitting in this car with Valerie LeBlanc and her shoes that were making Glory's car smell even worse. "Okay, fine, but we need to get started. If Marguerite reports to work, our cover is blown. Plus, I have other responsibilities in my life, including serving as chair of the Red Hat Society Mardi Gras committee. I can't be hanging out in the stable all day."

Glory grabbed hold of a bag in the back seat of the car. She stepped out of the car and pulled a drab jumpsuit on over her clothes. When Valerie finally had an opportunity to see her entire outfit, she stopped, put both hands on her hips and quietly giggled.

"What the hell you laughing at?" asked Glory.

Valerie wiped her eyes and caught her breath after the outburst of laughter. It wasn't the overalls that Glory was wearing that made her laugh uncontrollably. It was the large, oversized patch stitched under her right clavicle that read *Singletary Car Care* that did it.

"Where did you get that from? Are you moonlighting from your job as a bookie doing oil changes? Or is your specialty brake pads and tune-ups?"

Glory wanted to slap That Woman upside her head, but she trudged forward. "See, I knew I should have left your narrow ass at home. At least I look like I could have some kind of job here. This is why I'm leading this investigation and you're not."

Two men stood at the front doors of the stable. They smoked cigars, inhaling greedily and exhaling foul-smelling stench into the air. Glory remembered Marguerite snatching the cigarette out of Valerie's hand, as if it was common knowledge that you don't have anything flammable around a stable. From the thick cigars to the dress shoes and the crisp white shirts, Glory did not take them to be regulars. They looked like special company. The men and their cigars entered the stable. Glory stalked from behind.

"Do you need me to distract them?" asked Valerie.

Glory suppressed a sigh. She thought it would be a good idea to have a partner in this outing, but now she had some ninny following her like some helpless orphan animal. "No, not yet." She spied a row of rubber boots lined up against a wall. She turned to Valerie and pointed, "Put a pair of these boots on, so you don't stand out like a Baptist on Good Friday."

Next to the boots were a wheelbarrow, shovel, and rake. Glory steered the wheelbarrow out from the corner and set the other tools on top. She trailed far enough behind the men to not draw attention but kept them in her field of vision. The clothes the men wore were quiet, but expensive. That's the thing about rich people. They communicate in a frequency only other rich people can hear.

The wheelbarrow was turning out to be heavier and more awkward than Glory anticipated. She gripped the handles tightly while somehow managing to balance the rake and shovel across it. There must have been a better way to do it, but if there was, Glory could not figure out how. She continued to struggle with the wheelbarrow, several paces behind the men. She stopped and placed the wheelbarrow's airborne wheel down on the cement bricks of the herringbone floor. The rake crashed down, startling the men. They turned around and shot Glory a menacing look.

Glory gave a wave before she picked up the rake and started mucking the stall. They say that you get used to the smell of horses, and even come to like it, but Glory could not understand how that was possible. It was the worst kind of stink. The last time she was there, the scent had permeated her hair and haunted her dreams.

A chestnut-colored horse with hair knotted into braids stared her down. "Don't you even try it," said Glory under her breath. "I don't like this any more than you do." She entered the stall and separated the damp straw from the dry straw, impaling it with her pitchfork, and loading it into the wheelbarrow. The horse heeded her warning.

The men, convinced that Glory was nothing more than a lowly stable hand who dealt in manure, carried on. Glory stood in the corner of the stall, opposite the horse who was breathing hard and making plenty of noise, but thankfully leaving Glory alone. She stabbed the hay mindlessly while standing on the tips of her toes to keep an eye out. The men entered one stall after another, each for a couple minutes. After they had made their rounds to every stall in the stable, they entered the tack room.

"*Psssst.*"

Glory's heart galloped like a racehorse in her chest until she realized that it was Valerie. "Girl, don't scare me like that," she said, clutching her chest as if she had just suffered a cardiac event.

"I'm just checking to see if you need me to do anything."

"I don't know," Glory said. "Just stay out of the way and stay nearby. Do you think you can manage that?"

Irritation streaked across Valerie's face, and even Glory could tell she had probably pushed it too far. Valerie disappeared out the stable's side door, her rubber boots squeaking with each step.

After several more minutes, the men emerged, smoking cigars and chatting like it was a casual outing. It was possible that they were veterinarians, but wouldn't a vet that tended to horses know better than to smoke in a barn? Glory knew from her own gambling operation that men with the most confidence knew the least, and judging by how those two walked around the stable liked they owned it, she had plenty of reason to peg them as amateurs. They disappeared down another row of stalls and Glory seized the opportunity. She was wholly unprepared for what she saw in the tack room.

The walls were lined with shiny wood. Bronze hooks organized an array of equipment, like mahogany saddles polished to a sheen, reins and bridles without a speck of dirt, and assorted other equipment like riding crops and helmets, all in perfect order. At the bottom of the wall were storage drawers. Glory searched each one, rummaging through fly masks, tins of polish, and stacks of wool blankets. While searching between the folds of a blanket, she felt something sharp penetrate her skin. She yelped and yanked back her hand. A single droplet of blood pooled on the tip of her index finger.

Carefully, she reached back in and saw the offending needle. Next to it were small bottles of liquid with a name that she had never heard of written on the labels. She was trying to commit the name to memory when the men's voices suddenly grew louder. The sound of squeaking boots, walking quickly, intercepted them at the door.

"Let me ask you something," asked Valerie to the men. "What kind of plaits do you prefer on a racehorse? I'm here braiding today and well, you two look like men who know a thing or two about horses."

It was just enough time for Glory to shove the needle and the vials back inside the blankets and crack the door open a little so she could watch Valerie at work.

The men looked at each other, confused. "We don't know much about braiding," one said, sucking his cigar so hard his cheeks hollowed themselves out.

"There's a lot of different styles, you know," said Valerie, bending at the waist ever so slightly, which had the effect of making her low-cut blouse even lower. "You've got straight braids, running braids, button braids, though I'm partial to the continental braid, if you ask me."

Glory continued to watch from behind the door of the tack room. If she didn't despise the woman, she might have admired Valerie for the show she was putting on.

"Where are you two from, anyway?" she asked.

The talkative one took another inhale of his cigar, and judging by the look on his face, he must have been also thinking about inhaling her. "We're from Kentucky, just taking stock of the fine horses you have here at Opelousas."

"I should have known you weren't from around here, handsome as you are. In Louisiana, distinguished men are a lot like good wine—imported from out of state."

Valerie chatted up the men and put on a show for another ten minutes, long enough for Glory to snap a picture of the medicine vials and return to her pretend stable hand duties, taking her wheelbarrow right past the men and Valerie.

Once the men were gone, Valerie found Glory. "How'd I do?" she asked. Glory heard her talk, but the voice sounded faraway, as if she was in a tunnel. She took a left turn with the wheelbarrow and ran smack into the wall. The wheelbarrow and Glory came crashing down.

Valerie helped her up. "Are you okay? The color just drained from your face."

Glory leaned against the stable wall, trying to keep herself upright. "I got pricked with whatever that horse medicine is. I guess horse medicine and human medicine ain't the same thing."

"My God, let's get you back into the car and get you home." Glory trudged through the mud; her arm slung over Valerie's shoulder. Valerie opened the passenger door and Glory protested.

"I don't let people drive my car. A light on my dashboard always comes on when someone else drives it."

"You can barely stand up on your own power, let alone drive in a straight line. Now quit making all that noise and give me your keys so we can get home."

Glory barely remembered giving the woman her keys. Next thing she remembered, she was headed down I-49 South. She felt like she was flying.

13

Glory woke up the next morning, her head pounding and heavy. She was so disoriented that she didn't have the chance to research what got hold of her at the stable, but now that she had her wits about her, she had to know what nearly landed her on her ass. She looked at the picture of the vials on her phone for the name, and then looked it up online. She wasn't surprised at all by what she found.

After the day she had at Opelousas, Glory was pleased to wake up not with the harsh ringing of the alarm, but with the warming aroma of bacon. It had to be Justice. Delphine wouldn't be cooking, and if she was, she'd make some kind of bird food like granola and yogurt, not anything hearty to stick to your ribs.

Somehow during the night, she managed to sink a foot deep into her mattress. It took a gargantuan amount of effort to even lift herself out of the bed. Once she was upright, she staggered around the room a bit, the drugs apparently still lingering in her system. This went on for a couple of minutes until she was able to steady herself.

She wrapped herself in her yellow robe, tugging at its belt, and knotting it up. The smell of bacon dragged her down the hall and to the kitchen. As she thought, Justice was at the stove, her shirtsleeves pushed beyond her elbows revealing more tattoos that Glory had not yet seen. One of Glory's gingham dish towels rested on her shoulder. Delphine sipped some green drink from a mug.

"My goodness, I could get used to this. It's about time someone made a meal for *me* for a change." said Glory, winking at her daughter and leaning on the counter, eyeing Justice's prep station. "You got my kitchen looking like a real restaurant. What you cooking in here?"

Justice walked Glory through her breakfast configuration. Eggs were coming to room temperature before being poached, lemon juice was already squeezed, and cayenne pepper was on the side for a hollandaise sauce. Crawfish was courtesy of Herbert's Specialty Meats, in exchange for all the free labor she had provided over the past couple of days, learning the culinary secrets of southwest Louisiana. Justice baked the English muffins from scratch, using the tops of Glory's mason jars as a form.

"You baked these English muffins? Thought they only existed in that little cardboard box from Thomas'."

"Aww, it's not that hard," said Justice, monitoring a handful of lazy bubbles emerging from the water in a saucepan. She broke an egg into a mug, then gently submerged the mug in the water, letting the yolk and whites slip into the pan. "I don't leave town without my starter. With a starter you can make just about any bread. I call her Weezy." She opened the lid of a plastic container and thrust it into Glory's face.

Glory's eyebrows quivered at the smell. "I don't know about this Weezy, but I feel like she might clear my arteries and strip the oil from my garage floor. That is something, girl." Justice laughed and returned to poaching the eggs, treating each one like it was in a spa.

"What did you two get into last night?" asked Glory.

"Oh, nothing much. Justice worked late at Herbert's, stuffing turkeys inside of ducks inside of chickens. No wait, do I have that order right? I suppose you can't stuff a turkey inside of a duck."

"I was prepping turduckens for Mardi Gras," laughed Justice.

Glory made a face. "Once again I ask: *Why are people doing too damn much?* It used to be that having a ham or a turkey was good enough. Now people got to have three meats in one carcass. It's indulgent. I blame that TikTok app. I saw a segment on the TV about how people make this nasty food on purpose, purely to go viral. A waste of good food."

"Now I agree with that," said Justice, lifting the eggs out of the simmering water with a slotted spoon she had found in a crock of utensils. She grabbed a mound of parsley and separated the leaves from the stem with the edge of her knife.

"What else did you get into last night?"

Justice raised an eyebrow, like she was curious to hear how Delphine would respond. She used the knife to gather the parsley into the center of the cutting board and began to mince the curly leaves.

"Not much, just watched some TV before going to bed."

Justice seemed to take Delphine's response out on the parsley, pulverizing it with the large knife. By the time she was done it looked like it had been through a blender, not hand-chopped.

"Damn girl, you're going after that parsley like you're mad," observed Glory. She leaned against the counter, amused to watch all this cooking happen in her own kitchen. "You've been so busy *stodging* or volunteering or whatever you call it that I've barely seen you, though I do appreciate this feast you're preparing this morning.

Tell me more about your life in New York. What do you do when you're not slaving away in the kitchen? Any hobbies? And are you dating someone?"

With that question, Justice forgot where the parsley ended and her finger began. She cursed, suctioning the side of her finger with her mouth.

"Dear Lord, I'm sorry, I can see that I distracted you and now you've gone and cut yourself," said Glory. "Let me run and get you a bandage."

Justice pulled several lengths of paper towel off the roll and wrapped her finger, "Not the first time I've been cut deep, and it won't be the last," she said, aiming the comment squarely at Delphine.

"Goodness gracious. I think I bought a first aid kit at the dollar store a few years ago . . . lemme check the garage. I'll be right back." Glory opened the door that led to the garage and shut it behind her.

Delphine shot out of her chair to inspect the finger. "I am so sorry. Are you okay?"

Justice flinched. She pulled the finger to her chest. "The finger is going to be fine. My pride? Not sure."

"I know this is terrible, but I'm not ready to go there with my mom yet. You know how she is . . ."

"Delphine, this isn't middle school. It's time you act like a grown woman and stop blaming your mother. This isn't about her. It's about you. And your mother? She's not so naïve . . ."

Delphine was stunned. She had never been slapped before, but imagined this is what it felt like.

Glory came back toting a first aid kit with the price tag still attached. "See, I knew I had a little something. I also found some hydrogen peroxide. Might have expired in 2003 but that's just a suggestion, right?" She put her new found supplies on the counter, led Justice to the sink, and poured the disinfectant over her finger. White bubbles foamed up from the cut. "See? That stuff never goes bad. I suspect you're going to be as good as new in about a week or so."

With the wound cleaned and bandaged, Glory snapped her fingers and changed the subject abruptly. "That reminds me, I found out something about the stable yesterday that was interesting."

Delphine put her mug on the kitchen table with a thud. "I figured that's where you were when you went to CC's and didn't come back for three hours. You should really text someone if you're going alone."

"I wasn't alone. I was with Valerie."

Confusion clouded Delphine's face.

"It's a long story, but yes, Valerie was there, and she was rather helpful, actually. Turns out she has a talent for distracting people," said Glory, having witnessed firsthand the talent that had ended her marriage. "Anyway, did I tell you how I ended up playing blackjack in the Sassafras Lounge at Cypress Downs? And that the cashier grew up on Delhomme Street and told me to 'follow the horses'? Well, I did, and I think she may have been onto something."

"My, my, looks like you've been keeping a lot of secrets," said Delphine. Justice let out a single, ironic laugh. Glory saw her daughter wince and for a nanosecond wondered what that was all about. "I just thought we were doing this together," Delphine said in a way that sounded more tacked on than real outrage.

"We are, but you had that work call. Anyway, Valerie and I headed down to the stables again after I got that tip, and I saw the strangest thing." She told Delphine and Justice about the two cigar-smoking men from Kentucky who did not seem like veterinarians but visited each stall, and about finding the drugs in the tack room. "And then I looked up that drug, and it's a banned substance, apparently." She decided against telling them about pricking her finger, and how she felt afterward. Her daughter would turn it into a referendum against her techniques, and she didn't have the patience for it.

"Whoa, it's amazing you figured that all out," said Justice, high-fiving Glory with her good hand.

"It's good work, Mom," piped Delphine. "But I just don't understand what the connection is to Dad. How do we know that *he* was involved with this?"

This was why her daughter was a good lawyer, and not a good investigator. Following a lead requires honoring the sensation in your bones that quivers when something is amiss, even if there's no evidence. Though it would have been nice to have a full-throated endorsement from her daughter for a change.

"I just have a feeling that your father was involved in this, and I don't see how any kind of involvement in doping up racehorses can be a good thing. You should have seen those men yesterday. They were so jumpy, like folks that know they're up to no good."

Justice had returned to the stove and was plating her crawfish eggs Benedict, ladling the rich hollandaise sauce over her creation. "Are they your only suspects?" she asked.

Glory stuck her finger in the pot of hollandaise for a taste and swooned before filling Justice in on her list of suspects. "Obviously, I have a lot of questions about what's happening with those horses down in Opelousas. There must've been a reason that gal at the casino suggested I visit. And then there's Valerie herself."

"Let it go, Mom."

"Roll your eyes all you want, but that pending foreclosure is motivation to kill someone, for sure. I want to know how Sterling's death may have benefited her financially. Can I have a little bit more of that sauce? It goes so well with these eggs," said Glory. Justice spooned more hollandaise over Glory's breakfast.

Justice's muscled arm was now up close to Glory's face. She couldn't resist. "You sure do have a lot of tattoos."

"Mom . . ."

Justice, full of coffee and good will, shut Delphine down. "It's okay. You asked about my hobbies before? I guess you could say tattoos are one of them. Decided to take some of my favorite things and turn them into art." She rested the small saucepan on a trivet, pulled up her sleeve and entertained Glory. "First off, I love oysters. The brinier, the better. Just a slurp of heaven, so that was my first tattoo. And then I have some of my kitchen favorites. Diamond kosher salt because it's the gold standard." She pointed at Glory's countertop. "I got some for your kitchen, Glory, so you can try it for yourself."

"What's so special about it?" asked Glory.

"It's really about the shape and the texture. It's not flat, but has a triangular shape, which gives it a lot of crunch. And then I have a Pyrex measuring cup, because is anything better than this? You can find a million measuring cups, but do any of them perform better than a Pyrex?"

Glory finished chewing her eggs so she could chime in. "Girl, that's what I'm always trying to tell Delphine. You don't always need the latest and the greatest. Classics are classics for a reason." Delphine scrunched her mouth but kept silent.

Justice pivoted her body to display the ink on her other arm. And that's when Glory choked on her coffee.

Justice poured a glass of water for her and bent over. "You okay, Glory?" Within the sea of tattoos on the other side of her arm—a stick of Land O'Lakes butter, the shape of a chef's hat, and a bagel—was a knife.

"This knife. Why did you get this specific knife tattooed on your arm?" asked Glory. Delphine leaned in to view it more clearly, trying to understand why her mother had been so curious about it.

"This? This is the knife I aspire to own one day. It's handmade by renowned blade master Cleotus Farmington. His knives are the most coveted in the chef world. A blend of flexibility and strength. And each design is different. Some of his most famous knives have celestial markings, like the one on my arm. No one knows why he uses these designs because he refuses to do any media interviews. Adds to his mystique. I have it on my arm because it's my goal to be a good enough chef to own one of his blades."

Glory put on her reading glasses and sat in stunned silence. She traced the outline of the tattoo with her fingers. "That's the same kind of knife that was used to kill your father."

Justice and Delphine looked at each other, their eyes stretched open with this unexpected news.

"When I found your father, I noticed that the knife handle looked different. I couldn't figure out why."

Delphine stood up. "Oh shoot, this is what Landry was talking about . . ." She trailed off, recalling their conversation at Lagniappe Records.

The volume of the pounding in Glory's head turned up even higher. She gulped her coffee. "Justice, you mean to tell me each one's unique? That means if we can find this knife maker and have him identify the knife, we might find the killer?" Glory stated these facts out loud.

"Yes, no two knives are the same." Justice ran her fingers through the shaved side of her head. "Man, I never thought I'd be in the middle of a murder investigation. I don't know how to feel about this." She paced the kitchen with nervous energy.

"Child, you should be feeling real good. It's our first real break."

"It's fantastic," echoed Delphine. "So, all we need to do now is get a picture of this knife, call this guy up, and ask him if he remembers who he made the knife for."

Justice stopped her. "No, it's not that simple. There's a single phone number where you leave a voicemail, and if you're lucky, he might return your call in a month. Then, if he decides that you're worthy of one of his knives, you pay, and then you get the knife when he's done. Could be six months, sometimes longer. Apparently, Eric Ripert had to wait a whole year to get his knife. *Eric Ripert.*"

"Child, you say that like I'm supposed to know who that man is," said Glory.

"He's a very famous chef in . . ." Delphine started to explain.

"You know, just because I don't know something doesn't mean I can't *infer*," snapped Glory. It was exhausting to get a Wikipedia explanation from her daughter no matter how big or small the matter. "We need to find a different way to reach him. Directly."

Delphine was already busy calling someone on the phone. "Calling my assistant. On it."

Glory moved the runny yolk of her eggs around with her knife, wondering what other secrets Sterling harbored, and how she could puncture the truth.

14

The knife. The Mardi Gras committee. Delphine and her nose ring. The Lord would understand if she needed a night away from it all.

Since it was a special occasion, Glory had decided on a special outfit. She waltzed into the Sassafras Lounge wearing a navy velvet dress that draped a little at the neckline for a slightly dramatic look. Because she was a proper Southern woman, she had purchased the matching shawl to go with it. The skin on her upper arms had transformed into a crepe-like texture, which she had long ago accepted. Unlike other women with no sense, she didn't need to go parading her bare arms around for the world to see. It was a covenant between her and God, and would stay that way. She had even sprung for a pair of heels with a wedge—wearable for about four hours—which was all the time she needed to play a few hands of blackjack and catch The Commodores live, in concert.

On her last visit, T-Red had given Glory his cell phone number and had told her to reach out whenever she wanted to "enjoy a hospitality experience like no other." She was about to take him up on that offer. Add The Commodores concert into the mix, and she was getting excited, for a change.

Her first order of business as she entered the Sassafras Lounge was a rum and Coke. Over the years she had seen how alcohol and gambling formed a reckless team, but a night on the town was a rare event for Glory. And it's not like she acted the fool, like other people—she had proper house-training and was a God-fearing woman, after all. She had decided she would make the most of it. On this night, a jazz trio tinkered in the corner. Somehow even the drummer managed to be quiet, caressing that drum with a little broom. She liked the vibe. It was a casino, not a drum circle, and no one wanted to come down with tinnitus on account of an overzealous band.

Glory sat at the bar in the lounge for a moment to relax her feet. The bartender shook her rum and Coke in a silver tumbler, poured it into a double-walled glass, and topped it with a boozy cherry. Glory sucked the liquid through the tiny straw so fast it might as well have been injected into a vein instead. *Slow down*, she admonished herself. She took another sip, more slowly, and scanned the room with her eyes. Opposite the jazz band was Odille, the cashier she'd met before, the one who knew her mother. She must have been dispatched to dealing blackjack in the lounge for the evening. She walked over and got dealt into the game.

Glory played double Dutch when she was a girl, and blackjack had a lot in common with it. First you got a sense of the speed of the ropes. Once you had a sense of the speed, you jumped right in and kept time. Just as she did last time, she wagered low amounts at first, until she got into the rhythm of the cards. Within five or so hands she was in the groove, just like when she was a girl, dancing and jumping between the ropes. At fifty dollars a hand, her winning tally was growing fast, and after another three hands an Asian businessman dressed in a suit and a scowl dashed out a cigarette in a crystal ashtray and sulked away in defeat.

"That didn't take long," said Odille.

Wisps of smoke circled the ashtray. Glory pushed it to the edge of the table, as far from her as possible. "In blackjack you play against the house, not the people sitting next to you. Rule number one of gambling—understand your opponent. How are you supposed to win when you don't understand who your real opponent is?"

"Spoken like a real gambler."

"I wouldn't call myself a real gambler. Just a student."

Odille gathered the cards and ran them through the shuffling machine. Glory took another sip of her drink, looked carefully around her to see if there was anyone who could overhear their conversation, and leaned in closely. "So, I went down to Opelousas and met a few folks. Let's just say I met some people who looked like they didn't belong, doing things that may or may not be of interest to the Horseracing Integrity and Safety Authority."

Odille cut the deck in half. "Looks like you're a student of a lot of things."

"Game recognizes game," said Glory. "I can tell you're a lot like me. You see everything. A sharp eye for what transpires around here. But what I'm trying to piece together at the moment is how—and why—someone who works in the rarefied Sassafras Lounge would know the goings-on of what happens behind closed doors at a stable more than twenty miles away?"

A cocktail waitress came with an offering of another rum and Coke for Glory. She decided to take it for later.

Odille dealt two cards to Glory and two cards to herself. "When you think of the word *home*, what do you think? A place where you're loved, right? Or at least respected. Let's just say that this house has a lot of cracks in its foundation, so I don't feel too attached to it."

Glory wondered what these so-called cracks were, and whether they led to Sterling growing so discontent. "If Sterling was unhappy in his final days here, why might that be?"

"Who said that?" said Odille.

"Oh, you know, just something one of the horses whispered in my ear at the stable . . ."

Glory lifted her cards to her chest and took another gulp. A large Black man in a purple suit and a black turtleneck appeared from the shadows. He fiddled with something in his ear, and from what Glory was seeing, was talking to someone in the palm of his hand. A Black man with a dark red afro was always a jarring thing to see, especially in Louisiana. Damn if T-Red wasn't the perfect name for the man.

"I didn't know you were working tonight, T-Red," said Odille. "You've been pulling some overtime this week," she added.

"I'm just doing my best to help out around here, as always," he said, before turning to Glory. "I saw your name on the guest list for The Commodores' show tonight. The show is starting in about half an hour. We upgraded your tickets to the front row, which is being seated now. Why don't you cash out and take a seat?" It was phrased as a question, but it was an order. Glory had worn out her welcome in the Sassafras Lounge. She gave Odille three black chips, each worth one hundred dollars, and walked to the cash-out area. Don't ever say Black women don't tip.

T-Red followed a few lengths behind but kept a watchful distance. Glory stuffed a slim stash of bills in her wallet and turned around to find T-Red sucking on a toothpick, smiling at her. He was making his presence known, even delighting a bit in intimidating her. Or so he thought. It would take a lot more to scare Glory. She knew about monsters and had tangled with a few before. At any rate, she might as well get ready for the concert. Gambling and greed don't mix, and she was grateful for what she had. The elevator doors slowly opened and Glory stepped inside, leaving T-Red and his sparkling pinky ring on the other side.

When the doors opened again, it was a shock to Glory's system. In the brief time she'd been upstairs, she had forgotten about the riffraff of humanity that gambled in a pit of chaos. Kids whose faces were smeared in chocolate played tag around slot machines and busloads of wide, pasty people from Arkansas spilled onto the gambling floor. Glory pushed her way around the tourists and through curtains of air, hazy with cigarette smoke and sweat. She turned the corner and found herself in the performance area.

To Glory's surprise it wasn't a theater, but just a stage squeezed into a corner of the casino with chairs lined up. A worker scanned the barcode on her paper ticket and let her into the area. The seats were beginning to fill up with older women, mostly Black, in loose-fitting clothing and comfortable shoes. Glory was shocked to find herself in the same room. The only thing more shocking than finding yourself in a room of old women is realizing you're one of them. It wasn't as if Glory wasn't acutely aware of her age. It's just that when she looked in the mirror, she could still see the remnants of a young, attractive woman, even if no one else could.

Another rum and Coke kept her company until the band came on stage. How many had she had? She had lost count . . . at least three, though she wasn't certain. The drinks continued to be free, and she was in a casino. What was she supposed to drink, lemonade? It's not like she ever came to casinos, anyway. The only reason why she was here in the first place was Sterling. She'd slow down just a little now, she cautioned herself, so that she could drive home.

By now, a flock of women who could remember both the Civil Rights Movement and the launch of Soul Train filled their seats. The lights dimmed and a roar rose from the room. Glory felt a lightness she hadn't felt in months, and certainly not since she discovered her ex-husband dead on the floor of his kitchen. Maybe she should come to the casino more often. The buffet was good, and the drinks were free—she had a right to entertainment.

The opening notes of "Lady" played on a synthesizer, and Glory joined the rest of her peers with a scream of approval. She set her purse on the floor, stood up, and danced for most of the concert. *That Lionel Richie can write a song that stands the test of time*, she thought. And what a pity that he left the group.

She saw a woman in a loose black dress and a gray braid. Instantly, she recognized her as Felice Phelps, who called herself a spiritual intuit but had scammed Glory out of a few hundred dollars last year. Even more annoying, she was the one who had convinced her that there was a curse placed upon her, though given the body count Glory was racking up, maybe it was time to admit that Felice was right. Two wasn't a lot, in theory, but you try finding a murder victim and see how you feel about that. Felice was also the reason Glory had decided to take in Patti LaBelle, who had turned out to be a nice enough cat, but Glory didn't approve of this trickery. She had half a mind to ask Felice to predict which song was going to be next, to test if she was truly psychic, but you can't let her destroy your night, Glory decided.

It turns out that The Commodores were halfway decent without Lionel. The lead singer sounded soulful and smooth, whoever he was. Glory stood the entire concert, even during the ballads. "Still," about a lover vowing to be there for his one true love even though she's moved on, was a song that one ought to sit down for. Even the lead singer sat on a stool for "Sail On," one of Glory's favorites. Yet Glory remained standing for everything.

"Sit down," sniped a woman behind her.

"Don't you tell me what to do," said Glory. "I bought my ticket just like you did."

She quickly made an enemy of the audience. "Sit down!" said the chorus of angry voices.

"Oh, that's my song!" screamed Glory, moving her head to the opening bassline of "Brick House." Now *this* singer was the original, not some sad substitute for Lionel Richie. She bucked her head left and right, spilling her drink onto her seatmates. They dabbed their dresses and gave her menacing looks. She danced a little two-step, which should have been easy enough to pull off, but her coordination faltered. She twisted her ankle and found herself in the lap of a stranger. *Damn these wedge shoes*, regretted Glory.

"None of us can see the concert with a BRICK WALL in front of us."

"Y'all need to turn the volume up on the band," she screamed. Why was the band playing so softly that she couldn't hear it? "You hear me? Turn it up!"

A young Black man walked down the aisle toward Glory. "Ma'am, you're causing a disturbance. We're going to need you to settle down so that the show can go on," he stated.

"It's not me that's causing a disturbance," she slurred. "Blame it on LIONEL RICHIE!"

"There's always one," said a woman, tsking straight at Glory just like those Red Hat women used to.

One thing was clear. Glory was disturbing the peace at a concert featuring The Commodores, and the mild-mannered women behind her were fed up. "Ma'am, we're going to have to ask you to leave."

Her head, once light, now felt unbearably heavy, like a stone resting on her shoulders. Her vision went sideways and then diagonal. Then she couldn't see at all.

15

Glory struggled to open her eyes. The insides of her eyelids felt like a sponge that had hardened and dried out. Once open, the sun shone through pink drapes that fluttered from the morning breeze. Glory found herself swaddled in a pink, ruffled comforter in a room that was painted the same color. *I must be in hell*, she concluded.

A doorknob rattled and Glory startled. *Oh lord, this is it.* She'd been kidnapped and now she'd have to fight for her life. She scrambled out of bed, removed the shade from a bedside lamp, and gripped the base in her fist. She knew she'd lose in a battle of hand-to-hand combat, but at least the autopsy would reveal defensive wounds. Glory Broussard would not go down without a fight, and there would be proof.

"What on earth are you doing with my lamp?" asked Valerie, who didn't look afraid, but did seem annoyed. "Put my lamp down and get back into bed before you fall down." Valerie entered the room with a wicker tray, a mug of steaming coffee, a bottle of Kentwood Springs water and two pieces of dry toast.

Glory looked at Valerie, and then the room, as if she had woken up on Mars. "What did you do to me? And how did I get here?"

"I had a feeling you'd wake up this morning without remembering a thing, given the pitiful state you were in when I picked you up."

Glory sat on the edge of the bed and gripped her head with both hands. "I . . . I . . ." Somehow just thinking made the pulsing in her head worse. "I have no idea what you're talking about."

"Let me refresh your memory," said Valerie. The pink carpeting puffed up around her bare toes as she set the tray down on a bedside table. "You got absolutely blackout drunk at that Commodores' concert last night, so much that you assaulted a security guard. They had to stop the concert because of you."

Confusion contorted Glory's face. "Why would they stop the show because of me?"

"I wasn't there, but I was told that you requested 'All Night Long' by Lionel Richie and when they explained that that wasn't a Commodores' song, you began to rant about how the band wasn't shit without Lionel. And maybe something about how they'd been cruising commercially off of his songs for decades, when Lionel was the real artist."

Glory did not recall any of this, but she had to admit that this was an astute assessment. *Whoever said it.* Glory leaned back against the floral-patterned headboard, letting the spinning of the room slow down before she spoke again. "I'm afraid to ask, but how exactly did I get here?"

"Ah, good question." She explained to Glory that, after she was detained and taken into casino custody, security had called the Lafayette Police Department to haul her away. "But I guess that cute detective got wind of it and he tried Delphine, and then me, to come and get you. If it wasn't for him, and me, they would have hauled you and this velvet tent dress off to the drunk tank."

"You mean . . . Lieutenant Beau Landry?"

"Yes, him. Word has it he's getting a divorce. Delphine should try to lock that man down. He's clearly in love with her. Anyway, he couldn't get you because apparently he had his kids and couldn't drag them into a casino to pick up a drunken elderly woman. So, he begged me to grab you. And that is the tale of what happens when a retiree consumes too much alcohol and doesn't know her limits. Damn, Glory, did you at least eat something at the buffet? You gotta put down a proper foundation if you're going to pour all that alcohol down your throat." She laughed and clapped her hands hard, like a sonic exclamation point.

"Geez, will you stop carrying on like that? My head isn't about to explode in a thousand pieces."

Valerie leaned into the doorframe. "A 'thank you' for my efforts would be nice. Or maybe I should have let them arrest you for disorderly conduct?"

Glory took a sip of water and swallowed her pride. "Thanks. I appreciate it." She lowered her head in her hands, hoping it might help with the pounding.

"Towels are under the sink in the bathroom down the hall. Eat your toast and take a shower. You smell like you licked an ashtray. I'll drive you back to the casino to get your car, once you've sobered up. And take some of these." She reached into her cardigan pocket and tossed a bottle of Tylenol in her direction. Glory lifted her hands just in time to avoid it hitting her face, but not with the dexterity to catch it. It tumbled to the floor and Valerie shut the door behind her.

Glory emerged an hour later, her hair still damp, and the casino film steamed off her skin. The residue of cigarettes, rum, and the buffet carving station could still be detected on last night's clothing, but it was the best that she could do, for now. Glory walked slowly through the hallway with a towel around her neck and a hand running the length of the wall to steady herself.

Valerie's house was more updated than Glory's. The living room was decorated with a tasteful gray sofa with matching gray chairs and coordinating throw pillows. This may have been the current style, but there was something antiseptic about it, as if all the furniture arrived on the same day, from the same store, off the same truck. Glory's house may have been a bit more chaotic, but it was a *delightful* chaos. Something with a bit of personality. At least that's what she told the judge who tried to get her on hoarding charges last year, to no avail.

When she walked into the kitchen, she noticed that there was nothing on the kitchen counter except vitamins. Judging by the empty countertops, the only cooking that happened in this house was in the bedroom.

Valerie inspected Glory, who immediately recognized that she was being scrutinized.

"I'm sure I look a mess right now. You'll have a grand old time gossiping about my situation at the beauty salon. The hens will be cackling for months, I'm sure . . ." She took a seat at Valerie's kitchen table.

"Anyone who takes a seat in my chair is assured complete confidentiality. The same is true of my home." She placed breakfast dishes in the sink and walked over to where Glory was sitting. "And speaking of my salon, I was looking at your hair the day we drove out to Jennings. It looks to be in good condition, but I can tell it's thinning. Totally normal for a woman your age. You should let me cut it a little shorter. I know that sounds counterintuitive, but it'll thicken it right up. You'll see. Mind if I take a closer look?"

"Yes, I mind. And my hair is fine. I'm not letting you take your rusty Weedwacker to my head."

"I see you're back to your old self," observed Valerie, eating yogurt out of a plastic container.

"You know, I keep thinking about the things I said last night, *allegedly*, and I'm starting to think someone slipped something into my drink. A roofie or something. One minute, I was winning a lot of money . . . and the next I was escorted out of the VIP lounge. It's pretty clear that the casino was tired of losing and wasn't about to lose no more."

"How much money did you win?"

"$1,500"

"Did they really kick you out of the VIP lounge?"

"Sure did," said Glory, taking another sip of much-needed coffee. Maybe the caffeine would repair whatever damage might have been done on a cellular level last night. "And they kept following me around like I was some kind of common criminal. What they should have been worried about was all those damn children, running around unsupervised in a casino. Whatever happened to casinos being for adults only?"

There was something familiar about how Glory felt last night. She was tempted to tell Valerie that how she felt at the casino was a lot like how she felt when she pricked herself at the stables, except twice as dizzy. Could that be just a coincidence?

"It is a bit strange that they wanted you to stop playing blackjack, but slipping a Mickey into your drink? That sounds a bit outlandish."

Why is everyone so dismissive? thought Glory. Did she not very recently solve a murder that made the paper in town? Every TV station? Apparently, it was going to kill folks to give her a little respect.

"And just assume you're right, that I wasn't drugged. That casino should have known better than to ply a woman my age with all that liquor. They didn't even offer me a glass of water. I have a mind to report them for overserving unsuspecting women like myself. It's not right, and it's not Catholic."

"Report them for what? Because you got greedy and inhaled too many free rum and Cokes?" Glory's face clenched from Valerie's snide remark, and the sunlight.

"I don't know why I would expect any sympathy from *you*."

Valerie stood up and threw her yogurt container in the trash. "Yes, no reason to expect any sympathy from me—the person who woke up at midnight to drive more than an hour to keep your butt out of jail. Not to mention the ride back, where you babbled on about all sorts of nonsense, like how Beyoncé's daughter needs to get her little butt off that stage and back to the classroom when school is in session. It would have been amusing if my car didn't smell like a distillery."

Glory winced. "I said thank you, just . . . lower your voice already. I already got enough rattling going on up there without you making more racket."

Valerie refilled Glory's coffee and joined her. "I am not your enemy. Remember, I asked for *your* help."

If Glory could go back in time, she would have declined—and firmly. She might have started out on this journey for her daughter, but just one week later, she had found herself gallivanting with horses, plied with alcohol, possibly drugged, and gambling in the Sassafras Lounge. However, she did have to confess that winning $1,500 wasn't too shabby.

"Can I ask you a question?" asked Glory, rubbing her forehead with the tips of her fingers.

"I don't like the sound of this, but sure, I'll play along. Shoot."

"How do you really expect me to feel in this situation? You slept with my husband for years. You expect me to just brush that aside, like it didn't happen? I hope you know the reason I'm doing this is because of my daughter. After that, I intend to be through with you once and for all."

Valerie closed her eyes, gathered her thoughts, and said, "I regret what happened, too. Even more so, I regret *how* it happened. But, Glory, you had to know your marriage was over, didn't you? He told me how you two barely spoke anymore, slept in separate bedrooms, all that. He also acknowledged that a lot of it was probably his fault, on account of the early years, all that drinking and cavorting. He was an unreliable person back then. From the way he told it, and he had a lot of shame about that. But I agree, we could have done things differently."

"And I never got an apology. From either of you."

A tiny head appeared in the kitchen window, followed by a knock on the kitchen door. In Louisiana, a knock on the side door is from a visitor that knows you. The front door is for the exterminator, or someone trying to sell you something.

"Oh, that's old Mrs. Roubichoux from down the street," Valerie said. "I told her I'd cut her hair at my house because she can't drive anymore. And now she just shows up whenever my car is in the driveway. Let me send her away."

"Go on and cut her hair. I can call a taxi to take me back to the casino so I can get my car," said Glory, grateful to have a wad of cash in her purse for the exorbitant fare. "Thanks again for picking me up."

Valerie opened the door to let Mrs. Roubichoux inside. There was a gentle lecture about not just showing up any old time, and how she didn't want to chemically relax her fragile hair anymore. *Why not wear it natural? It's more modern. And you have such beautiful hair!*

While Valerie was busy with the old woman, Glory gave herself a tour of the living room. Everything was tidy and organized. It seemed that when Sterling went in search of a new life, he wanted the exact opposite of Glory, in every conceivable way. A bookshelf had mostly trinkets and a few books but was weighed down with picture frames. There was a picture of Valerie, many years younger, holding a certificate of graduation from the Grand Coteau School of Cosmetology. Another picture of her cutting the ribbon in front of her salon. Then another with Sterling. She wore a tight white dress and clutched a bouquet of pink dahlias. He wore his good navy suit, the one Glory had bought for him, for what Glory assumed was their wedding portrait.

She froze when she saw a picture, unframed, tucked into the corner of another frame. Delphine, Sterling, and Valerie, cheek to cheek, grinning for the camera. The fact that everyone looked so relaxed, like *family*, felt like a fist tightening around her heart. Delphine had the same braids in the pictures as she did now. *When was this taken?* she wondered. Two men stood behind them, deep in conversation. Glory didn't need to rack her brain to figure out who one of them was. She had just had an encounter with T-Red last night.

16

Glory tipped the Uber driver thirty dollars in the parking lot of Cypress Downs. He had said nothing about her appearance on the long drive, and he ought to be rewarded for that. Her feet were so swollen from alcohol and sodium from the night before that she couldn't get her shoes on. She held them in one hand, with her keys in the other, as she walked barefoot to her car, the asphalt digging into the soles of her feet. A feeling of gratitude washed over her when she locked herself inside her Honda-CRV. She may not have been home, but she was on her turf.

Thank God she found a pair of old gas station sunglasses in the glove compartment, because her eyes rejected the sunlight. Various thoughts jammed her brain while she was driving. According to Valerie, and what she was told at the casino, she had had too many drinks. That may have been true, but Glory felt so physically demolished that it had to be more than just alcohol. She couldn't stop wondering if someone had slipped something into her drink. In fact, the only sensation that came close to how she had felt the night before was when she pricked herself at Opelousas. It could not have been a coincidence.

Then there was the matter of Delphine's chummy picture with her dad, Valerie, and T-Red. Glory knew that she occasionally saw her father, but usually only when she came down to visit her. Delphine would meet him for dinner or coffee, but to Glory's knowledge she was not hanging out with Valerie. They'd only met a handful of times, or at least that's what Glory thought, but everyone looked pretty cozy in that picture, more than meeting a handful of times might suggest.

When she stepped into her home, she found Delphine and Justice working away in the kitchen. Mary J. Blige singing about real love pumped through speakers, while they cleaned and trimmed figs for canning. The upbeat atmosphere inside the kitchen made her head pulse even more. Glory kept her sunglasses on, like a shield.

"Well, well, look what the cat dragged in, and I'm not talking about Patti LaBelle," said Delphine. Justice smacked her on the arm. "I don't know what's more surprising—that you'd stan so passionately for Lionel Richie, or that rum and Coke is your drink of choice? I really pictured you as a mai tai kind of woman."

Glory ignored them as acids roiled in her stomach. She saw a piece of bacon atop a grease-soaked paper towel and her stomach flopped in revolt. "I see you heard all the details. I would expect no less from Valerie, who will no doubt buy a page in the *Advertiser* about my misfortune by the end of the week."

"Oh, come on," said Delphine, walking back the sarcasm. "She only texted me late last night to let me know what had happened and that you were safe and sleeping it off at her house. That was awfully kind of her."

"She would have never gotten involved, had you picked up your phone. Where were you?"

"We were down at the Blue Moon Saloon until about midnight, listening to Terrance Simien and his band play. It was so loud that I couldn't hear the phone ring when the casino called."

"Can't even rely on your own children anymore," Glory groused. She couldn't stop thinking about the picture she found of her daughter at Valerie's house. She'd have to figure out how to best approach this, but given the condition she was in, now was not the time.

"Are you hungry, Mrs. Broussard? I'd be happy to fix something for you," offered Justice. "How about my sourdough pancakes? I've made them for many a hungover person, including your daughter here, and there's not one person who hasn't felt eighty percent better after eating them. I think it has something to do with all the active organisms restoring balance to the gut microbiome.

"I appreciate that, Justice. At least one person in this house is trying to help, instead of snickering at my misfortune. All I want to do is peel these smoky clothes off, lie down in my own bed, and rest." Her phone rang, which it seldom did anymore. Just about everyone texted unless it was an emergency these days.

She looked at her phone, her face registering instant frustration. "Damn it." She steadied herself, then answered. "Hey, Constance, what's up?" Last night's misadventures had deepened her voice to a gravel-like tone. "That's today? Oh, it's now. No . . . I didn't forget, I just . . . Fine. I forgot. Okay, yes. I *understand*, Constance, I do. Yes, I know you pulled a lot of strings. I'll be there in fifteen minutes . . . I'm leaving right now . . ."

"What was that all about, Mama?"

"I apparently forgot that the king cake tasting was scheduled for today. Right now, matter of fact. I also forgot to place orders at Gambino's before the cutoff, so now we have to find a new vendor. This is the worst possible timing." She looked at Justice, who was plunging jars of figs into a vat of hot water until the lids were sealed. An idea simmered to the surface. "Justice, why don't you come with me? I hate king cake, and it sure would be nice to have a professional chef with me to help narrow it down. Everyone's going to be mad enough that it's not from Gambino's. I can't mess this up, and to be honest, I do not exactly feel like sampling a bunch of sugary cake with frosting and cream cheese at this particular moment."

"Why don't you go," urged Delphine. "You already showed me how to get the seal on these figs. I can finish up. She could use a sober companion about now . . . help keep her out of trouble." Delphine's chest heaved in silent laughter.

"Okay. . . but I'm driving," said Justice.

The Red Hat Society of Acadiana held its monthly meeting at St. Agnes, in its largest rec room with its ceiling panels, fluorescent tube lighting, industrial carpeting, folding chairs, and card tables. Committee members Constance Wheeler, Millie Broward, and a handful of other women mowed Glory down with their eyes as soon as she walked in, more than an hour late for the tasting. They sat in a row behind a long table, like a parole board.

Justice and Glory walked toward the tables. In a hushed tone that was only audible to Glory, Justice added, "Ohhhh, these women are furious with you. I can smell the rage from here."

"Yeah, well, it's not the first time. Won't be the last. Don't let them get to you."

"Me? I thought I'm just here to be a part of the tasting panel?" questioned Justice, with a quizzical look on her face.

Constance intercepted them. "We've been waiting nearly an hour for you to grace us with your presence."

"I know, and I'm real sorry about that. I had an unexpected situation. You see, I was canning some figs and dropped one of the jars into the hot water. Got all up in my eyes and I had to run to urgent care, which is why I'm wearing these here sunglasses. Anyway, I'm here and I have a *surprise* . . ." Glory swooped an open arm toward Justice, who could not hide her amusement. "This here is Justice Harris, one of New York City's most accomplished chefs and a James Beard Rising Star Chef of the Year . . . which is a very famous food award that you probably don't know about . . ."

Constance interrupted, "*Of course* I know what the James Beard award is."

Glory continued, "She's going to be a guest chef at Pierre's in New Orleans for a few weeks, but today she is here to bring a trained and sophisticated palate to our proceedings." The women oohed and ahhed just a little, impressed to be in such distinguished company.

"Nice to meet you all," said Justice, just a little taken back by this side of Glory but getting into the swing of things. "Have you started?"

"No, we've been waiting for Glory to arrive," said Constance. "But now that she's here we can *finally* begin."

Justice and Glory took a seat at the long table. Boxes from Lafayette's most well-known bakeries were placed in a line and numbered. Before each number was a smattering of plates with small pieces of cake on them. "Let's start with cake number one," said Constance. She passed out the tiny bits of cake with green and purple icing, dusted with gold glitter.

Justice ate her piece and grimaced. She was barely able to swallow it. "This is incredibly sweet."

Millie Broward objected. "I like a donut king cake. A king cake should be sweet."

"I agree with the chef. A cake should be sweet, yes, but shouldn't give you a cavity on contact," said Glory. "And let's be real. It's a donut smeared with icing. It's nothing special, and it's the ugliest of the bunch."

Millie and Glory eyed each other warily. Constance kept the meeting moving. "Next up, Breaux Brothers bakery."

Glory's stomach was stabilizing. Turns out she needed a little something to eat after all. She sunk her teeth into the layers of dough and then clutched the side of her mouth. Something was not exactly right with the cake, and she spit it into a napkin. She was furious when her tongue scraped up against the sharp edge of a jagged tooth. She inspected the contents of her king cake in the napkin and screamed. "What the hell is this?" Among the wet, chewed up dough was a tiny plastic baby, covered in cream cheese and icing.

"If your piece of king cake has a baby, it's a sign of good luck for the year," said Constance.

"It's supposed to symbolize baby Jesus," agreed Millie.

"This ain't Jesus. It's a white, plastic baby wearing a diaper, and I just chipped my tooth on it!" said Glory.

"Do not speak ill of Jesus in the house of the Lord," snapped Millie.

"Is Jesus going to pay for my dental visit? Or the crown I probably need to fix this tooth?"

"I'm sorry you chipped your tooth, Glory, but surely you know there's a baby in every king cake. You have to chew *carefully*. It was probably time for that tooth to be looked at anyway. Let's stay focused on the cake for now," said Constance, trying to rein in the tasting.

Furious, Glory looked at Justice. "What do you think of the cakes we've sampled so far?

"These cakes are all fine—except that big, giant donut cake—but if you want something truly special, I'd suggest doing things a little bit different."

"How so?" asked Millie, who was cutting herself a second, larger piece of the donut cake.

"First, these doughs are all too heavy and sweet, in my opinion. I'd start with a *pâte à choux* base for the pastry. It'll give the cake a nice, light texture without being overly sweet. I would pipe that into a circle, cut it in half, lengthwise, then fill it with a whipped cream, which we can dye purple or gold, if you insist, and then do a light-purple luster sprinkle across the top."

"That sounds good, but where are we going to get that around here?" asked Constance. "And on this time frame? It's only one week until Mardi Gras."

Glory looked at Justice with her puppy dog eyes. "What do you say?"

Justice opened her eyes wide. Then, with the demeanor of a football coach, she assumed a wide-legged posture and pushed up her sleeves. "Okay, listen. I'm not a pastry chef, but I think I can pull this off if I can have a couple of assistants the day of the event."

"I volunteer," said Glory. She could see the rest of the women would need some convincing. "I don't know about the rest of you, but I am going to speak the truth: these king cakes are terrible. And even Gambino's is not all it's cracked up to be. We have the opportunity to have all of Lafayette talking, or at least all of St. Agnes. Personally, I'd like to try to do something a bit more special, a bit more elevated, especially since y'all insisted on raising the price of the tickets. We need to show the parishioners what we can do."

Constance nodded her head. "Okay fine, I'll volunteer. But if this doesn't work out, I'm blaming you, Glory Broussard, not this young chef. It's your fault we are in this predicament, and I am not going to point fingers at someone who is merely trying to help."

"Thank you, I guess?" said Justice, trying to keep pace with the petty rationale of the members.

Millie cut yet another piece of the donut king cake and sat down while the other women cleaned. "Don't look at me, you know I can't stand long with my rheumatism, but I do support this decision." Constance tossed the rest of the donut king cake away, and the two women began to fuss over the trashed cake.

"Meeting adjourned," declared Glory, pushing the bridge of her sunglasses up closer to her face. The women milled about, alternately cleaning the room, whispering, and looking at Glory and Justice with beady suspicion.

Justice was half terrified, half amused. "Wow. This is . . . a lot."

"Imagine how I feel." Glory wiped the table down with a paper towel. "Between all the meals you've fed me, the lead on the knife, and now this, I owe you big time."

"Aw, you don't owe me anything, Mrs. Broussard. I'm happy to help."

"Speaking of the knife, you and Delphine get any leads on that knife maker . . . or what do you call him?"

"Blade master," said Justice. "And no, not yet. Delphine is looking into it and so far, it's just a bunch of LLCs and no-name legal entities, and nothing more than a phone number that Delphine is trying to track down an address for. But I'm on it, and I'm working my restaurant contacts as well, in the off chance any of them visited his studio."

"Good girl, good girl," said Glory. A folding chair leaning against the wall fell, causing Glory to clutch the top of her still-pounding head. Her tongue poked at her broken tooth. It must have been Sterling, taunting her from the grave.

17

CC's Coffee House was a totally different scene on a weekday versus Sundays. It was quiet, with no expectations from the customers that Glory was there to work. Sometimes Glory liked to go to clear her head, enjoy the leisurely pace. After the disaster at the casino, and nearly dropping the ball on her Mardi Gras duties, she needed to regroup. The good news was that her hangover had finally subsided. She vowed never to touch that devil's tonic again. Whether she was drugged or not, rum and Coke had been the vehicle. That was on her.

She was surprised to see a uniformed police officer walking through the doors of CC's, his face as sunburned and prickly as a cactus. Glory tried to remember where she had seen this man before, and remembered it was at the police station, right after she had found Sterling's body split open. He had taken her to the station and complained when she had asked for Landry to take her back home.

He sauntered into the coffee shop with an air of arrogance and put-on authority and sat down at her table. "Glory Broussard, isn't it? Glad to see you here."

It was widely known within Lafayette Parish that Glory could be found at CC's Coffee House on Sundays, but this was an off day, and not a day she would ordinarily be here. Either Noah Singleton was a snitch, or they had been following her this morning. Glory knew for certain that Noah would always have her back.

Glory kept her face as expressionless as possible, and her tone cool. "Why yes, I am Glory Broussard, but I suspect you knew that already. How can I help you?"

He took off his police-issued hat, the one that made him look like a cartoon park ranger instead of a real cop, and placed it on the table. "I just came to check in on your investigation into Sterling Broussard's murder. You got us real good by solving the murder of that nun last time, embarrassing the entire Lafayette Police Department. We're not about to let that happen again."

She pushed her shoulders back. "I see what you mean, but there would only be cause to be embarrassed if y'all had been investigating. You signed off on a suicide and called it a day." She regretted her words immediately; she should have held her powder.

The officer flung a low-key snarl at Noah, who was behind the counter working on his proprietary coffee drink but keeping a close eye on the conversation. Glory knew this was a wasted gesture. Noah had served in Vietnam during the fall of Hanoi. He was as solid as they came.

A couple of Lafayette's stay-at-home moms trickled in for drinks, dressed in pink and purple hues. "Yes, I am trying to figure out what happened to my ex-husband, which I've made no secret of," said Glory. "And if you're wondering what I've found, the answer is very little."

"I'm not sure whether to believe you or not," he said. She noticed the length of his ears, which seemed to stretch down to his chin.

"You want to hear what I've found out? I'm happy to tell you." The moms giggled a few tables away, and for once Glory wanted to join them. "I learned Sterling worked at the casino. Some people say he loved working there. Other people say he hated it. The gumbo at the casino buffet is pretty good; you can tell they make their roux fresh, from scratch. And I was probably drugged at that same casino, so maybe take a look at the surveillance system and see who was responsible for that, if you're looking for a crime that's easy to solve."

"Yes, I did hear that," he said. "Truth be told, I didn't hear about any drugging. What I did hear is that you caused a real scene . . ."

Glory groaned and interrupted. "That is the very proof that I was *drugged*! I would never act like that under normal circumstances. Anyway, that's all I know."

A baby in a stroller made the tiniest cry, causing one of the moms to put her drink aside and glide the stroller gently.

The man tugged on one of his droopy earlobes and scratched his nose. "I don't know whether you're telling me the truth or not, but it sure would be helpful to your future freedom if you shared whatever information you had. That's all—"

"Freedom? I'm going to need you to clarify what you mean by that threatening remark."

He looked at Glory as if she was some kind of prey. "As I see it, you were first on the scene at the murder of your husband. That's awfully suspicious."

"Ex-husband," she corrected, with a note of defiance in her voice. "And you don't have one thread of evidence or a motive, because there ain't one."

He nodded his head. "True, not yet at least. At the minimum we've got you on operating an illegal gambling operation. I suspect some of your customers are from out of state, so maybe we also get you on some interstate crimes, which could be a federal offense. Though I'd have to ask my buddies at the FBI."

Eventually, Glory knew it might come to this. How long did she really expect that they'd allow her to openly work as a bookie the way she did? She knew that solving the murder of Amity Gay would be a blemish on the record of the Lafayette Police Department. Just a couple weeks ago she saw on KLFY that the chief of police shot himself in his own foot during target practice. He even had the nerve to do a press conference about it from a wheelchair. It was hard to outdo the shame that they brought on themselves.

But in Louisiana, dirty cops make the state run. If bad cops are just one bad apple, then Louisiana grew them by the bushel. She felt compelled to depict herself as a woman who might want to comply.

"Well, there is one thing I'm looking at," she said, stirring her coffee with a spoon for extra emphasis.

He couldn't help but lean forward, a little too eager. "Go on, what is it? You gotta speak up, now, you hear me?"

He took the bait, as Glory thought he would. "In my view you should be looking at the knife," said Glory, which was the truth. "That knife was real different."

"And how do you even know about the knife that was used," he asked.

"If you recall, I am the very person who found the knife impaled in his chest. I saw it firsthand." He backed down. "And it wasn't an ordinary knife. There was something about it that looked homemade."

He looked around the coffee shop. Disapproval seeped from his pores. "That's all you have? About half the men in Louisiana are probably tinkering with some kind of homemade knife in their garage. This is a state of duck hunters."

"Details matter in a murder investigation, you know that," countered Glory. She could tell that he was probably better suited for a desk job rather than detective work.

He stood up. "You better not be leading me astray, because I will surely see to it that this little business of yours is ruined. Not to mention your life, you hear me?"

"You have a good day, now." It was a goodbye and a mic drop. But when the Lafayette Police Department knows your whereabouts, it is best to be polite.

She had only agreed to help find Sterling's murderer because of her daughter, but now she was starting to see things more clearly. Delphine had been right—it was in her best interest to solve this crime, and quickly. She had an idea who might be able to help her do so.

18

Glory, and her tires, were so worn out by all this driving, she had half a mind to bill Valerie for mileage and gas. If Glory was going to make yet another trek, she'd make sure that it was not in vain. In that effort, she read the online instructions for visitation carefully. She did not intend to get turned back on a technicality. The rules for clothing included: women must wear pants; blue or black, not clingy. Blouses must be up to the neck; no V-necks or anything revealing. Shoes must be flat, no laces. All bags would be inspected. No gifts allowed.

Fortunately, abiding by most of these rules would not be an issue. She was not about to show up at the Louisiana State Penitentiary with a short skirt, high heels, and her cleavage on display. Unlike Valerie, Glory could appreciate dressing for the occasion. Context matters. The only problem was the shoes, which could not have laces. Most of the pairs she wore were orthopedic, lace-up shoes, something between a loafer and a sneaker. They were stable, with a thick sole that insulated the painful bones of her feet against the sidewalk.

She reached into her closet and found a pair of flat ballet shoes that Delphine had bought her, to help her look more "chic." Glory had never worn them. Delphine didn't know what it was like to have feet that felt like they might crack with each step. But rules are rules, and Glory wasn't about to have some prison guard chastising her and staring at her feet. She tossed them into the back seat and drove an exhausting two hours to the most notorious prison in the state.

Who even knew if Milton Knowles would agree to see her, after everything that had happened over the past few months. Maybe a peace offering would help get him talking. It wasn't like she was responsible for him being in jail. He was there because one of the pit bulls he used in his dogfighting ring had escaped the kennel and attacked his neighbor; events she had nothing to do with. But she suspected that he felt a certain kind of way toward her, on account of her showing up unannounced at his home and place of employment, such that it was, in the months prior. She had also accused him of murdering her friend, which he had nothing to do with. Let's just say Milton Knowles was a complicated man and there were extenuating circumstances.

She arrived at the prison. Everything was inspected—her bag, her shoes, even her hair. If they wanted to inspect anything more, Glory would have to up and leave. Because she was an unannounced visitor, there was a long wait in which Milton would be told of his guest and given the opportunity to decide if he wanted company. But the time didn't bother Glory, because she honestly could have stayed in that waiting room all day and people watched. It was a circus of humanity. Small children were dressed and pressed, presumably to see family members they didn't get to see often. Women rouged their faces to show the best version of themselves to their men behind bars. Glory had been a little nervous going in, because she was a proper Catholic woman and had never been to prison. But she could tell that everyone was in good spirits, happy to see each other, and making the most of their visitations.

Would Milton feel the same way about her? Probably not, but maybe a special treat might thaw the tension. Glory made her selection from the vending machine and tried to pay, but couldn't figure out where to insert her card. A young woman, whose skin was graffitied from head to toe, grabbed her card. "Excuse me," said Glory, snatching her card back. "That's mighty bold of you, stealing in a *prison*. I should ask if they can just toss you inside immediately."

"I'm *helping* you, not stealing your card," said the woman. She snatched it again—the nerve!—and waved it in front of the machine. "It's contactless," she said. Out came the pepperoni Hot Pocket and Dr Pepper that she had punched in. Truly, eighteen dollars was exorbitant for a Hot Pocket and a can of soda. She had seen something about how prison services had been outsourced to private companies, and she had a mind to talk to someone about the price gouging happening in prisons these days, but someone else would have to take up the cause. Glory thanked the woman and microwaved the Hot Pocket. Shortly after, her name was called for visitation.

Milton Knowles's biceps were even bigger than she remembered. He must have been busy in "the yard," as Glory had heard it called once, lifting weights and such. His neck was thickened and rising from his shoulders were slabs of muscle that looked like they had been bolted on. He was in a black-and-white striped jumpsuit like the old days, which was still standard issue in Louisiana. Glory knew better than to comment. He sat down on a chair. They were separated by thick plexiglass that had been etched on by previous visitors, with initials and hearts. They picked up their respective phones and began talking.

"Thank you for seeing me today," said Glory, trying to start out on a positive note.

"Don't get many visitors. I guess you could say that curiosity got the cat."

She gave the guard her peace offering from the vending machine, which he brought to Milton on the other side of the glass. "Well, well, to what do I owe the honor of this processed, microwaved snack and a cold Dr Pepper?" he asked, opening the soda and taking a long glug. He drank greedily, probably half the can in one sip.

"You might have heard that my ex-husband Sterling was murdered."

He wiped his mouth with his hand. "I did hear that."

"And why would that be discussed in this jail?" A woman cradling a crying infant sat in the station beside Glory's.

He took another sip of his soda. "I don't have anything to do with Sterling's murder, if that's why you're here. I barely knew the guy, but he was always nice enough to me."

"Then how do you know he died?" asked Glory, mistrustful, but hopeful their conversation might have some light to shed.

He bit into his Hot Pocket and fanned his mouth once he took a bite. "Damn, Glory, how long did you put this in the microwave for? It's so hot it's going to melt my esophagus."

"Then don't be so damn greedy. You could wait a minute before you inhale it," she said, knowing she shouldn't have responded with such sass when Milton was finally talking, but also, who cares? She and Milton had a good read on each other at this point. Their understanding of each other was formed by their innate survival instincts and outsider status. They may not have liked each other, but a certain amount of mutual respect existed between them.

He took another swig of soda to cool his throat. "You like church gossip, right? You and those old ninnies sit around, talking about whose husband is stepping out on who, who needs to lose twenty pounds, who needs to stop making that fruitcake?" Glory did not want to validate this surface-level, petty analysis of the goings-on of the Red Hat Society, but damn if he wasn't right. "Well, those of us who inhabit the underbelly of Lafayette like to gossip too, about our own. Except I must admit that I was surprised to hear about Sterling. He seemed to leave the real properly a few years ago. I guess the game catches up with you, one way or another."

"You have any ideas who might be involved?" asked Glory, speaking in hushed tones into the phone's receiver.

"I have some theories, but why would I tell you?"

The baby next to Glory continued to cry, irritating her. The mother was cooing over the baby while trying to balance the prison phone between her ear and shoulder.

He scratched his head, and she noticed him fixing his gaze on the vending machine beyond her. "That'll cost you one Hostess HoneyBun." Sometimes old players want justice; sometimes they want a little bit of icing. She stood up and walked back over to the machine, waved her card over the contactless reader, and watched the HoneyBun tumble to the bottom of the machine. She handed it to the same guard who arched an eyebrow. "He's really milking this, I see."

Glory picked up the receiver again and took her seat. "Okay, what have you got?" asked Glory.

"Tell me about what you've found out thus far, in your investigations." He said *investigations* almost like it was a joke. Glory ignored the slight and told him everything. She told him about Odille, who told her to follow the horses. And Marguerite, who told her to check out the casino. And T-Red, in his flashy suits that sounded cheap, as well as Grady and his sweaty brow. And the alleged public drunkenness at the concert and what she thought really happened.

"Now on that I agree with you one hundred percent," he said, stuffing the HoneyBun into his mouth. "The Commodores ain't shit without Lionel Richie. I don't think they even had a top ten hit without Lionel."

The baby continued to cry, and Glory had had enough. "Hold on a minute."

She put the phone receiver down and walked over to the flustered mom and crying baby. "You can't hold a baby all willy-nilly like that. You have to hold a baby like you mean it, with some firmness. That's why she's crying like that. She doesn't trust that flimsy grip." Glory took the infant and cradled it in her arms, with authority. Finally, the baby quieted, and Glory returned the child to its mother.

"Impressive," said Milton. "It's been what, ninety-two years since you had a baby of your own?"

"Haha, very funny," she said, adjusting the phone receiver to a more comfortable position. "No one teaches you how to be a mother. I imagine the same is true for criminals. You have to learn on the job."

"Very true."

"Ten minutes left of visitation," said the prison guard.

"Okay," said Milton, finally dispensing with the chitchat. "I knew T-Red well, back in the day. He's as crooked as a crocodile, but smart. Whatever he's involved with, it ain't legal. But you see how he dresses, all shiny and clean? He's not about to get his hands dirty.

He'll have someone else doing his dirty work. My guess is that it was Sterling when he was alive. The question you need to be asking yourself is this—who's playing Sterling's role now?"

Glory couldn't deny the logic to his thinking. "Okay, so step one: figure out who T-Red's enforcer is now. But I have a question. Why would some folks be telling me to check out the casino, and others telling me to check out the stables?"

"So, I used to wrestle, back when I was a kid. There's this move in wrestling called the Irish Whip," he said. "It's when one wrestler grabs his opponent's shoulder, then runs them in a circle until they're dizzy and disoriented, and then drop-kicks them. That's what Cypress Downs is doing to you . . . the casino, the stables, everyone. They're throwing you off the scent, or trying to."

"And do you think I was drugged?"

"Possibly . . . though it does sound like you drank one too many rum and Cokes if you ask me. Anyway, my guess is that the casino and the stables are dirty, both of them. And now here comes an old woman in sequins nosing around, the one who helped solve a murder and was on every TV set in Lafayette, and they're not too thrilled with it. If I were you, I'd get some help. Someone other criminals can relate to, unlike yourself. You're not going to be able to do this on your own."

"I can see that." The guard pointed at his watch. Visitation was over. "And rumor has it there's a lifetime ban against me at the casino anyway."

Milton laughed so hard he nearly spit his Dr Pepper all over the plexiglass separator. Glory stood up and readied herself to leave.

His face sagged a little. He seemed kind of sad to see her go so soon. "Uh, do me a favor on your way out and put some money on my commissary?" he asked, with pleading eyes. "You know how it is. Everyone says they're gonna take care of you when you go away. Ain't heard from nobody."

She stood up and slung her purse over her shoulder. "I'll think about it." It seemed to be good enough for him. When she left, she stopped by the commissary office and deposited one hundred dollars into his commissary account. She also bought him a fresh package of socks and underwear. Did she care about him as a person? Not really. He was a menace. But now, all she could see was another Black man in prison. Maybe a full commissary would keep him going until he came home.

19

Glory's tooth was becoming more jagged and pointy with each passing day. She hated to think of how much money it was going to cost her. Nothing infuriated her more than going to the dentist because dental insurance is a scam. She once needed a root canal and the pain that preceded it was second only to childbirth, and it had cost over $1,000. Turns out teeth were luxury bones—only for rich people.

She turned left into Magnolia Medical Center, a series of identical one-story doctor's offices arranged around a parking lot. Glory had been seeing Dr. Filbert for twenty years and sat in the waiting room until he called her name.

"What brings you in today, Glory? You aren't due for a cleaning for another three months." A local radio station playing "Iko Iko" was piped in throughout the office.

"I am chairing the Mardi Gras committee at St. Agnes this year and there was a king cake tasting. Someone without a brain put a plastic baby in the cake, even though it was just a tasting. I bit down on it and broke my tooth."

"Ah yes, the old chipped tooth. I get about a dozen of these king cake emergencies every Mardi Gras. You're the first this year," he said. "You're not just having a tasting now, are you? That's awfully late if you want a cake from Gambino's . . ."

Everyone had an opinion. "Will you just take a look at my tooth and patch me up?" She missed the good old days when people knew how to keep some things to themselves. She bore down on the bite-wings, nearly gagging in the process. *They can send a man to the moon, but we can't figure out a better way to take dental X-rays?* Dr. Filbert pointed the arm of an X-ray machine at her mouth and then delicately removed the cardboard that Glory had been biting down on.

Glory rinsed with a tiny cup of mouthwash while the dentist looked at the X-rays. "Looks like you bit off more than you could chew with that plastic baby," he said, amusing himself. Glory spit in the sink. "You bit the entire corner off. You're going to need a crown."

"Oh Lord, I was afraid of that. Not only is that going to cost a fortune, I'm going to have two or three appointments and I ain't got time for that. Not right now."

Dr. Filbert interrupted her. "I can do the crown today if you have an hour. Got this new machine," he said, pointing at an unassuming white box in the corner of his office. "I can make a crown in about an hour."

"Not if that's going to cost me more. Otherwise, you can just send it out to the lab," said Glory, swinging her legs over to the side of the chair and reaching for her purse.

"The only thing it costs is time."

"In that case . . ." She settled back into the chair.

He moved a little computer on wheels over to her, detached a wand from the side, and took about a hundred pictures of her mouth.

Once he was satisfied, he sent the image over to the computer. "You're free to go for about an hour while it creates your crown from a square piece of porcelain. Once it's done, I'll install it, give it a little polish, and then you can go home."

"Well, I'll be damned. That's some science fiction stuff right there." Dr. Filbert offered a needed forearm, which Glory used to steady herself and lift herself from the chair. "While you whip up my made-to-order tooth, I'm gonna go get me a po'boy down at Champagne's Grocery."

"No, you won't," Dr. Filbert chided, wiping his hands against his embroidered smock. "I just took precise measurements of your mouth and a crown to fit around that break. If you chip it any further, we'll have to start all over again. And you'll have to pay for yet another crown. If I were you, I'd get the soup. Sip lightly."

Glory walked out with a scowl on her face. *That damn plastic Mardi Gras baby*, thought Glory. *See what happens when you try to do a good deed? You break a tooth, wind up spending $1,000 on a crown, and sipping on some goddamn soup.* So much for her casino winnings. Between this crown and the cab money she spent schlepping back to the casino to get her car, it was now all gone. She trudged through the Magnolia Medical Center on her way to the grocery store, hoping to find a food source that wouldn't require yet another crown.

She headed toward the grocery store, but reversed course when she remembered that her friend Georgette Pruitt worked at the reception desk of a physical therapy office about eight places down. She headed there to pay Georgette a visit and was surprised to see Valerie exiting an office.

Valerie straightened herself up and walked toward Glory. "Good morning. Didn't expect to see you here, although I guess I should have known that it was a matter of time before you'd start surveilling me."

"I'm not . . ."

"I'll spare you the speculation," she said, dabbing her eyes in a determined way, like she didn't care if Glory saw her crying. "Dr. Deborah Jones, whose office we are standing in front of, is the top fertility specialist in Lafayette. Sterling and I were trying to have a baby. Or rather, *I* was trying to have a baby. Sterling wasn't fond of the idea, given his age and what he described as his own poor performance the first time around with Delphine, but I wanted a child. More than you'll ever understand."

"That's something I can understand," said Glory.

"And each round of IVF was over $10,000, and we've had . . . a few rounds. I've got nothing to show for it now except bills, bills, bills." She paused and looked around the parking lot. "Anyway, I'm sure that will give you and Delphine plenty of ammo to gossip about."

"For what it's worth, Delphine's been defending you this entire time," said Glory.

"Yes, well, she's a good person. And reasonable," Valerie said, her frustration dissipating slightly.

Glory figured this was as good a time as any to ask about the photos. "I have a question I've been meaning to ask you. At your house, there was a picture with you, Sterling, and Delphine, and in the back of the picture are Grady and T-Red. When was that taken?"

Valerie took out a cigarette and lit it. "Oh, that was over Christmas. Sterling was always making a big pot of something—jambalaya, chili—and inviting coworkers over." Glory knew this to be true.

"And did T-Red come over often?"

"Yes, he's my cousin. He comes to all my BBQs and parties. He's a very friendly, extroverted person." She took a puff of her cigarette.

"Don't you go getting any ideas, Glory. T-Red had nothing to do with Sterling or his death. He was the one who got Sterling promoted at that job. He relied on him. He was torn up when he found out about Sterling's death, so you can take that line of questioning somewhere else."

At last, Glory could see Valerie's fatal flaw—not accepting the truth that was right in front of her face. Sterling had spent most of his marriage to Glory tomcatting around with other women, leaving both Glory and Delphine alone to fend for themselves more often than not. And T-Red was clearly the mastermind of whatever was going on at that casino and the stables, including whatever cruel thing was happening to those horses, but Valerie still couldn't see straight. Glory knew a thing or two about blinders. Sometimes, it's called love.

"Glory, I've got to go. I have to work out a payment plan for a baby that never materialized, and figure out how to somehow scrounge up the rest. So, you can stop chasing me and my cousin because I've told you the truth."

20

The rental commercial kitchen on Jefferson Street had no decorative touches. It was a container of stainless steel . . . nothing but gas stoves, induction stove tops, towering bakers' racks, and stainless steel workstations for the culinary hustlers of Lafayette.

Delphine watched as Justice poured cream into a heavy-duty mixer. "I can't believe my mother convinced you to do this," said Delphine, as dots of cream splattered across both their aprons.

Justice stopped the machine, installed its shield, and restarted it. "I'm not exactly a pastry chef," she said, dabbing the cream off her apron with a damp towel. "But I can't say she dragged me into it, exactly. Those church ladies were giving her a workout over missing that deadline. I could see things were about to get out of hand. I like your mom. I didn't want it to devolve into some kind of angry church lady lore. You know, *'remember that one year when Glory didn't get the king cake order on time'* . . . so I stepped in to help. I figured as long as I didn't have to whip something up under pressure, I'd be okay."

Delphine ran her finger along the inner rim of the bowl filled with cream.

"Oh no, you can't do that here. This is a professional kitchen, not your mama's house," said Justice, who then took Delphine's hand and put her finger in her own mouth. This move roused the feelings Delphine had for Justice, and made her wish she was back in New York where she could properly act on them.

"But it's okay for you to do?" teased Delphine.

"Yes, I'm the chef, and you . . . my lowly assistant." Justice smacked Delphine's butt with a towel.

A group of attorneys, probably from the nearby courthouse, walked by the large kitchen windows.

"I don't even know why my mom hangs out with these Red Hat women. They don't treat her well. They don't really like her, and they barely respect her."

"I don't know if that's exactly true," said Justice. "There was tension around the king cake, but Constance seems to like your mother. She supported the new vision for the cake. Those two seem to be getting on. And besides, if anyone hasn't been treating your mother well lately, I'd say it's you . . ."

Delphine jumped off the stainless steel countertop, her feet landing with a heavy thud. "What do you mean? I love my mother."

"No one is denying that you love your mother." Justice turned off the machine, the spin of the bowl slowing. "It just seems like there's a lot of tension, and it seems to go beyond normal mother-daughter stuff . . . like there's something unaddressed between the two of you."

"Oh, please, there's an ocean full of things said and secrets kept between the two of us. That's perfectly normal! We're mother and daughter. "

"And why do you think that is?" Justice opened the commercial refrigerator and pulled out a tray of pastry dough she had made the night before. She placed the rectangles of dough and plastic wrap on the countertop to warm up.

"It's because of her," said Delphine, with total assuredness.

"Okay . . ." Delphine sprinkled the countertops with flour. "I'm still not understanding. She's been perfectly nice to me."

"She's nice to you because you're a stranger, and my friend."

"I already told you, I'm not your little friend . . ." Justice snapped.

"You know what I mean. She's been chipping away at me for decades now. *I like your hair this way. Don't wear that dress. I sure would love to have a lawyer in the family.* I got so worn down by it that by the time I was a teenager, I had to go to NYU. Literally had to leave the state and get a clean break. I'm still recovering from the henpecking. And on top of that . . . she's just so embarrassing sometimes, walking around town in her red hats, gambling from the coffee shop. I would have preferred to have had a normal mother."

"Ah yes, I too know what it feels like when someone you love is embarrassed by your presence. I would prefer to have a girlfriend who isn't ashamed to tell her mother that she's dating a woman, one who cares for her very much, but here we are."

Delphine groaned, walked across the room and touched Justice's face. "I know, I'm terrible. And I'm absolutely sorry about all of this. But may I also add, without a trace of sarcasm or defensiveness, that you showed up here unannounced."

"I showed up unannounced because I was concerned about my girlfriend. Because your father was murdered."

Girlfriend. Was this the first time that Delphine was hearing this word? It must have been because the hairs inside of her ears suddenly felt aflame. For the past couple of months, she had enjoyed spending time with Justice, but assumed it was casual. Now that Justice had rushed down to Lafayette, it was starting to solidify into something else. The word "girlfriend" felt like a complication.

"Just promise me you'll think about talking to your mom," added Justice. "It doesn't even have to be about me. Just about . . . this thing that you're going through right now."

"Fine. I will think about it."

Justice nuzzled herself into Delphine's neck, giving it a short, sweet kiss. "Now, let me get back to these king cakes or else those church ladies are going to sentence your mama to eternal damnation."

Delphine turned around and looked at the window facing the street. The glass was fogged, on account of two children's noses pressed against the glass. Behind the children was Landry, looking at her as if he was stricken.

Justice looked at them and then Delphine. "Do you know those people?" she asked.

Before she could figure out what to say, the doors flung open, causing bells placed above the door to chime. They awakened Delphine from her brief stupor. "Landry, hi . . ."

The girls, one around eight and the other just slightly older, stormed the bakery like ants. "What's this?" one said, pointing at everything at once. "Do you have a cookie?" asked another, in a tone that sounded more like a hostage demand.

Justice smiled, confused and charmed. "No, I don't have a cookie. But do you like cake? Because I'm trying out a new cake recipe for Mardi Gras if you'd like to try it."

Without hesitation, the girls began to jump up and down and chant in unison, "Cake! Cake! Cake! Cake!"

Landry followed close behind them. "Girls, that's not how we behave in a store. You know better than that."

Justice disappeared into the walk-in refrigerator and pulled out her previous samples and plated them. Glory had loved this version of the recipe, but Justice found it to still be a bit too sweet, all that sugar masking the subtle flavors of rum and vanilla. "Let me know what you think," she said to the girls and to Landry.

Between Justice and Landry were two worlds of secret hookups and feelings that Delphine tried hard to compartmentalize. Except now both worlds were colliding. Before anyone caught on, she snapped out of it. "Justice, meet Lieutenant Beau Landry, a longtime friend." Maybe she was making it up, but he seemed to flinch at that introduction. This he had in common with Justice—two friends who were anything but.

"Nice to meet you," he said, extending his thick forearm and shaking Justice's hand. "Do we know each other? Northside High School?"

"I know Delphine from New York. Just here because . . ." Now it was Justice's time to find the right words. If words were a battlefield, this conversation was filled with mines. "I'm a chef, observing at Pierre's down in New Orleans. Thought I'd stop by here and see what Delphine and her mama are up to, learn some of the Creole culinary traditions." Justice offered him a small plate with the pastry and a fork.

"No, thank you . . . I'm sure this is delicious but I'm not a dessert guy," he said. He looked at Delphine, his eyes brimming with pain.

"Justice, would you mind giving these girls a cooking lesson while we catch up about my father's situation."

"Yes, of course," she responded. She turned to the girls. "Who wants to see all the desserts in the walk-in refrigerator?" They scrambled behind her.

Landry and Delphine walked out to Jefferson Street, cars whizzing by. When the door shut to the bakery, he started in on her. "It all makes sense now."

"What makes sense?" she asked, confused.

"This . . . *you* . . . you marry a rich man in New York City, then you show up here in a suit and heels like you're some high-society lady showing up for tea. And now you're dating women? A chef with tattoos and braids. You've got a nose ring and wearing your hair in braids and dressing like you're some bohemian going to a yoga retreat."

"That's not fair," shot Delphine. "You have no right to ridicule me because I'm dating a woman."

"No one is disparaging you because you're dating a woman. I'm just pointing out something I don't think you can see for yourself. You've lost track of who you are."

"Oh, come on . . ."

"No, it's true. You disappear into whoever you're dating. You're not the same person you used to be. Do you even remember who that is?"

Anger sizzled from her core. "Why don't you tell me who that is, since you apparently know me better than I know myself."

"You used to be someone audacious. You used to be someone who wore cool things from the thrift shop and paired them with an army jacket and combat boots. You used to care about other people. I thought you wanted to go to law school to do something good in the world. That's the person I remember."

"I'm still those things."

"I'm not so sure. I look at you now, and the only thing I see is someone who looks lost. You're adrift."

"Just because I'm not dating you doesn't mean I'm lost or adrift."

He looked beyond her, checking on his girls inside the store who were stuffing more sweets into their mouths. "I guess I was hoping that this might finally be our chance, especially with what happened between us a few months ago. But if that's not in the cards, I sure wish you'd stop trying on other people's personalities and making them your own. That'll end in nothing but another heartache for you, and I'd sure hate to see that."

His daughters burst through the doors, as if the scant amount of sugar they'd consumed in a few minutes were delivered intravenously. "Daddy, there's an entire REFRIGERATOR filled with cookies and pies and cakes and . . . sugar!"

"I might have let them have a Willy Wonka moment in the dessert refrigerator," said Justice. "Hope that's okay."

"Too late for that now, I suppose. About to drop them off to their mother. It'll be her problem now. Nice to meet you." He wrangled up the girls into his truck and drove off.

"Remind me who that was again?" Justice asked, dangling an arm around Delphine's shoulder.

"Just a friend."

21

Glory, Delphine, and Justice sat inside the car and were parked in the casino parking lot, waiting. Glory reached into the compartment between the two seats and pulled out a CD organizer. She flipped through the plastic sleeve, ultimately deciding on *The Best of Luther Vandross, Volume 1.* The CD player gobbled up the disc and Luther's "Glow of Love" filled the car.

"Ohhhh, that's some good music right there. Some real old-head stuff," said Justice cheerily from the back seat.

"I'm going to take that as a compliment," said Glory.

"You may be the last person I know with a CD player in their car," said Delphine.

"I'll tell you what. With a CD player you own your music, I don't have to pay for some satellites in the sky to listen to radio in the car, or some monthly subscription." Glory knew about online streaming services because she had one of those smart home speakers and Delphine had set it up with streaming music.

"Oh please, don't act like you don't like streaming music. Sometimes I'm home in Brooklyn and suddenly the music switches over to Teddy Pendergrass. I know you listen on my account."

"Ah yes, sometimes I forget I'm living under a surveillance state." Glory really ought not to be giving her a hard time about this. It was true that Delphine had rigged a bunch of so-called "smart" cameras and speakers in her home. And Delphine had occasionally used those speakers to "drop in" on her mother. When this happened, her daughter's voice was piped through the cylindrical speaker in her living room like the voice of God, stressing what little remained of Glory's pelvic floor. But it was also true that Delphine's so-called surveillance state had saved her life just a few months earlier when Delphine was able to track her down during a sticky patch while investigating the murder of Amity Gay. She turned down the volume on her complaining, for now.

Justice stared at the oversized watch on her wrist. "Okay, it looks like it's time. I'm not going to lie, I'm a little excited to have a mission of my own."

"Good girl," said Glory "And tell me, why are you touring the kitchen at Cypress Downs Casino today?"

Justice looked at them both, confused. "To see if anyone has a Cleotus Farmington knife?"

Glory shook her head, as if all the esteem she had for her favorite student had evaporated. "No, the official story."

"Oh, yeah, of course," said Justice, remembering the official line she gave to the kitchen when she spoke with them on the phone. "My name is Justice Harris and I'm a James Beard Rising Star Chef of the Year. I've received a number of offers to have a restaurant of my own in a casino. I'd love to observe your kitchen at work, to truly understand the rigors of working in a large-scale, commercial kitchen, as opposed to the smaller kitchens I'm more accustomed to."

"Exactly," said Glory. "I can see why the two of you became friends. You're both so smart. And don't forget to get a close-up look at the knives. Poke around, ask if they've ever had any knives from that Cleotus you keep talking about, or any connections to him."

"I got you," Justice said, slinging a backpack strap across one shoulder. "Wish me luck," she said. She exited the car and walked across the casino parking lot for her scheduled kitchen tour.

Glory and Delphine listened to Luther Vandross agonize about how a house is not a home, and how bad life had been since he lost his baby. At this point, Delphine was growing fidgety, searching the casino parking lot.

"Remind me . . . how do you know this man Franklin that we're waiting for?"

Glory was reluctant to tell her the truth, but she'd first met him years ago, when Glory worked at the Adrien's Food Market on West Congress. At six foot seven inches, he had been a promising freshman on the LSU basketball team when he tore his ACL. This was years ago, when that was a death sentence for any kind of basketball career, so he ended up working the floor at the supermarket.

One day Ms. Nanine came into the store. She was in her eighties with eyes cloudy from glaucoma, but she still inexplicably drove and shopped for her own groceries every two days. Some hooligans crossed over from the gas station to harass her when she was putting her groceries in her trunk. Franklin dashed out of the store, bashed their heads in with nothing more than his meaty knuckles, and then gave Ms. Nanine a ride home. It was around this time that Glory needed some muscle to enforce her strict payment schedule. Thus, a business partnership and friendship were born.

Just then, a man the size of a door walked toward the car. "That's him," said Glory. He was wearing navy slacks with a crease pressed down the center and a white shirt with a collar that stood at attention. Glory unlocked the car doors and Franklin slid into the back seat.

"Good morning, Miss Glory. Nice to see you." He turned to Delphine and looked at Glory impatiently, like she had failed to make the proper introductions. Another reason why she loved the man.

"I'm sorry, this is my daughter, Delphine."

"Wow, the last time I saw your daughter she was in high school, I think."

"Nice to meet you," said Delphine, swiveling in her seat and extending her arm toward the back seat for a handshake. "I hear you and I have a mission today."

"Yes, ma'am, that's what I heard, too." He leaned toward Glory. "How come you're not joining us? It's not like you to trust others with your business. I don't see why you can't go into the casino, at least play some slots or something. You'd blend right in."

"What do you mean, '*blend right in*'? I'm not one of those people, retired and lazy, wasting my days yanking away at those slot machines and eating stale buffet food," said Glory, who really could use one of those buffet rolls right about now.

"My bad," he said, in deference. "But for real though, why aren't you coming in? I need to know the full lay of the land before I go inside."

Delphine interrupted. "She was banned because of drunken and egregious behavior."

He raised his eyebrows.

She turned the volume of the Luther Vandross CD down, for emphasis. "I have said this before, and I'll say it again—I was drugged! I would never behave like that in public."

"Yes, that's what someone *would* say who had at least seven rum and Cokes in a couple hours," said Delphine.

"Who told you that?" snapped Glory.

"Valerie. That's how much the casino approximated that you drank that night, although they didn't actually review the footage to confirm the specific alcohol intake."

"That's enough," said Glory. She could see Delphine was enjoying this a little too much. It was time for her to refocus. "It is true that I cannot go into the casino. I have a mind to file an appeal one day, except for that I don't care enough about casinos to bother. So yes, that's why I need you today."

"You know I got you, Miss Glory. What's the assignment?"

"I have been told, between my memorable appearance at the casino and my reputation as Lafayette's most successful amateur sleuth, that my personal brand is not helpful to investigating at a casino. Did you ever cross paths with that T-Red that works here?"

"Not cross paths, exactly," he said. "But I know of him. A lot of bodybuilders at the gym I go to see him."

"T-Red with bodybuilders? With his bingo arms?"

"He's not a bodybuilder, but he's padding his pockets with the money he makes from them selling HGH." He must have noticed the bewilderment on their faces. "Human growth hormone. It's not exactly a steroid, but it's pretty close."

"Franklin Clottilde, I better not find out that you're injecting that poison into your body. I thought you were smarter than that!"

"Miss Glory, you know I'm a natural bodybuilder." He flexed a bicep as if it would prove his purity. "No, ma'am, no performance-enhancing drugs for me. You should know me better by now."

A casino security car, which had been traveling up and down each row of parked cars, inched its way past Glory's vehicle. She tightened her grip around the steering wheel, then relaxed as the guard drove past them.

"I'm sorry, you're absolutely right. You just never know these days. Feels like everyone in this world done lost their damn minds." She regrouped. "So, check him out if you can. He runs the casino."

"Anything else?" he asked.

"Yes. There's this woman named Bonnie. You play blackjack?" He shook his head. "Doesn't matter. Anyway, I didn't think much about it at the time, but she knew almost immediately that I can remember cards when I'm playing and predict what's next, but she didn't do anything about it. Shouldn't she have done something about it if she was a proper employee?"

"You know how to count cards, Miss Glory? Where'd you learn that?" he asked, astonished.

"Why does everyone say that like I'm some kind of degenerate? I just pay attention, that's all, son. Anyway, it's not allowed, because I guess they don't want anyone smart and observant in the casino. But she saw what I could do, and she didn't kick me out. Feels like T-Red might have cause to be upset with an employee who disregards the state of play. See what you can get out of her."

He nodded, sure of the game plan.

"Hey, how's your business coming along these days? Remind me what you're up to?"

"Industrial lubricants," he beamed. "Got three new contracts just last week, on account of my A+ rating with the Better Business Bureau. Eight accounts in total. If you hear of anyone having a problem with their gear box, you let me know."

"I'm real proud of you, son. Real proud."

♣♦♥♠

When the sliding doors of the casino opened, Franklin and Delphine were standing side by side. "Hey, why don't we separate? I'll do a lap and see if anything stands out. Why don't you see what's happening at the gift shop?" he said, gesturing to a display of extra-large bottles of hot sauce and plush pelican toys.

"Why? Is something going on in the gift shop? What should I be on the lookout for?"

He reached into his pocket and pulled out a hundred dollar bill. "No offense, but I tend to work better when I'm alone. I didn't want to say anything in front of your mama. You know how she can be sometimes."

"That I do." She paused. "Can I ask you something? What is it about me that screams that I don't fit in around here, or anywhere in Louisiana? Because this seems to be coming up a lot lately."

He eyed her up and down. "Well, if you really want to know the truth, it's a lot of things. The shiny Roger Vivier shoes with the buckles, and that bag . . . is that the Loewe Puzzle Bag?"

Coins fell from the mouth of a nearby slot machine as Delphine's mouth opened in disbelief.

"I read the *New York Times* Style section," he said, noting her surprise. "And that's another thing. Most people don't know the names of these fancy brands like I do, but that look of surprise you just gave me? The one that suggests you were shocked that I knew anything about fancy things? I don't mean no disrespect, but you kind of give that off. Your vibe. Not through anything you do, but people can smell it on you. The way a dog can smell fear, folks down here can sniff out that maybe you think you're a little better than anybody else."

A woman behind them scooped up her jackpot quarters with a plastic tumbler. "I know your heart is in the right place. But your mama hired me for a job and I'm just trying to deliver. Can't do that with you and your Van Cleef. That Alhambra necklace is sounding off like a dog whistle."

"Wow, I am somehow deeply offended but also have the utmost respect for that level of directness."

He smiled and cocked his head toward the gift shop. "Meet you there when I'm done. Shouldn't take more than an hour." She snatched the money.

Franklin lapped the casino, curling his lip like a tiger stalking in the evening hours. He couldn't necessarily articulate what he was looking for, but he'd know once he saw it. Illicit activities happen in the shadows, so he was on the lookout for any figures or movement happening offstage. Franklin had a knack for finding these kinds of guys because he was one of them, or rather, had been one of them. When his basketball career collapsed, he found himself desperate to make ends meet. He wasn't proud of the things he did during that time, but it did give him a skill set that was useful from time to time.

He passed the sunken den of slot machines with names like Zydeco Cha Cha, Rajin' Cajun, and Crocodile Rock, then passed the crap tables and the wheels of baccarat. What the hell was baccarat anyway? Sounded like something you played in France, not Lafayette. He had just entered the section of the floor with the poker tables when someone seemed to jump out of nowhere. Grady Williams.

"Franklin Clottilde. I haven't seen you in a minute," said Grady. They clasped hands and embraced the way men do. "What you up to these days? I heard you went legit and opened a business."

"Man, I'm trying, but they don't make it easy for a Black man, if you know what I mean."

"Ain't that the truth." Grady was as jumpy as a grasshopper. His eyes were unfocused as he looked everywhere at once. If Franklin was looking for something, or someone, operating in the shadows, he may have just found it. "So, you're all set? You make a living with this new business?"

"I make a little money, but I'm always open to opportunities, if you know what I mean," said Franklin. He suspected Grady would know exactly what he meant. "You have a job I should know about? Sure could use some freelance work."

Grady wiped his nose with his forearm and looked over his shoulder. "Yeah, I got something. But I can't talk about it here. People been nosing around asking questions."

Franklin cocked his head, involuntarily inhaling the aroma of fried shrimp from the buffet. "Asking questions? About what?"

"Man, this place has more investigators crawling around than cockroaches. And we have a lot of cockroaches."

Franklin made a mental note to skip the buffet.

"Do you happen to know that Glory Broussard, the one that solved that murder a few months ago? She was all over TV, even *The Advocate*."

Franklin pretended to contemplate the question. "Oh yeah, older lady? Overweight? Real churchy, right? I think she goes to church with my grandma."

"Well, she's real nosy. Solved one murder and thinks she's better than everyone. With her, Lafayette police, and the gaming commission, we haven't been able to operate the way we normally do, if you know what I mean. Anyway, I know of an opportunity, but I can't discuss it here."

"Gotcha, just let me know where and when. I'll be there."

"Monday night. Opelousas Stable."

Franklin wrote down the address, embraced Grady, and went back to the gift shop to check on Delphine. She had purchased an oversized bag of praline candy and a sampler of Tabasco. "See, I'm trying to fit in."

They exited the casino and huddled in Glory's car, where Justice had returned from a mission of her own.

Glory made quick introductions. "Franklin, meet Justice." They nodded. "So, the kitchen's clean, right?"

Justice looked as if she had just swallowed a pill. "I wouldn't exactly call it *clean*. If I ran that kitchen, the first thing I'd do is shut it down for the weekend and scrub it from top to bottom. I'd definitely call in a service to steam that vent over the stove. Those clogged-up traps are a grease fire waiting to happen. But if you mean did I see anything suspicious, or any Cleotus Farmington knives, the answer is no. I even poked around to see if anyone had even heard of him. They looked at me like I was crazy . . . seemed pretty clear to me that they had never even heard of him before." She reached into her backpack and pulled out a Styrofoam box. "But these beignets are pretty good. They just changed out the oil, so I figured it was safe. Anyone want one?"

Glory reached for one, but Franklin declined. "No thanks, I'm competing in the Mr. Acadiana bodybuilding contest next month. I need to lean out. Makes the abs pop. No sugar for me."

Glory shrugged and sunk her teeth into the beignet, sending an explosion of powdered sugar all over her blouse and the driver's seat. "Did you find out anything, Franklin?"

"Okay, remember Grady Williams from the grocery store? Turns out he works here, and it didn't take much for him to start talking," said Franklin with excitement.

"Grady?" said Glory. "I talked to him already and he seemed afraid of his own shadow. He was the first one to tell me that Sterling had soured on working at the casino, but didn't have anything more to add. You mean he's in on this?"

"He's in on something," replied Franklin. "He couldn't say what, so he asked me to meet him Monday night at the stables."

"So, it *is* the stables," said Delphine.

"Good work, Franklin, good work," said Glory. "We'll go together."

"Oh no, Miss Glory. I'm afraid not. First, you're banned by the casino, and they own the stables. And also, he said you've been nosing around the casino and something about 'too many eyes' on the joint. I'll tell you one thing, he seemed on edge."

"Okay fine, I won't go to the stables, but I do intend to get a full accounting the second you leave." It turns out Milton Knowles was right. Criminals are just like everyone else—they need someone to confide in. Grady hadn't trusted Glory, but he saw something in Franklin that he could relate to. She'd have to add another fifty bucks to Milton's commissary as a thank you, and in case she needed him again.

22

The next morning, annoyance was running high and patience running short with the women of the Red Hat Society of Acadiana. There were so many items that needed to be taken care of in the final days leading up to Mardi Gras that, coupled with their skepticism of Glory's ability to deliver, that the group made the unprecedented decision to skip Sunday Mass and use that time to grill Glory on every detail. They convened instead in their designated community room, while hymns floated in the air. The Lord would have to forgive them.

Glory was flanked to the left and right by the membership. They started first with an overview of The Pelican Club, Lafayette's toniest private club with grand, ornate ballrooms. Glory had gotten a close-up look at it last year, and though she knew it was not as grand as they made it out to be, it had the kind of artifice that would wow their guests. From there, she and Constance passed out photocopied menus and seating assignments. The masks had been ordered, she assured them, along with the beads. The tablecloths and napkins had been rented and would be ironed and crisp. She walked them through the music options. Terrance Simien and the Zydeco Experience would be headlining the evening, with DJ Big Shaun playing music in-between sets. And yes, she had been crystal clear with everyone that under no circumstances were they to play any songs with cursing, sexually explicit lyrics, or rap. Not even the clean versions.

In short, Glory was getting her hide roasted, mostly for show. All of the details were taken care of and in motion. She had Constance Wheeler to thank for that. For all her airs and that goddamn clipboard, Constance had proven herself the kind of woman that got things done. She was even tempted to tell Constance that, but she knew she'd never hear the end of it. There was still a part of her that would never forgive Constance for those so-called home inspections. In the moments when Glory could be logical, she knew the inspections were not Constance's fault. But as usual, Glory's default mode was vengeance. She felt more comfortable holding grudges until kingdom come. Maybe she'd get over it one day. Or maybe hell would freeze over.

There was only one point of contention at the regroup, which was the low volume of gala ticket sales. Glory was not surprised. When the organization had decided to raise the tickets from seventy-five to one hundred dollars, she knew it would be a deal-breaker for a lot of people in Lafayette. "*In this economy?*" she had challenged them. Much of the town was employed by the oil companies and related industries, and there had been uncharacteristic layoffs in an industry that was supposed to be recession-proof. Plus, maybe it was her years of work experience as a bookie, but she knew that one hundred dollars was a psychological barrier. Two figures are better than three figures, even if it just amounts to a few dollars' difference. But as a result, they had agreed to have a ticket drive in the coming days, and every member of the group was responsible for selling twenty additional tickets. She vowed never to chair the group again. It was a thankless job.

Glory was already exhausted when she dragged herself into CC's Coffee House and took a seat in her usual booth. Those women could have nitpicked for hours, fussing over Glory's weary bones like vultures circling over prey. But Glory never forgot where her income came from, and it was not these women. It was from gambling, mostly football, and mostly in January and February, and that was her priority.

Noah brought over a cappuccino. "Whew . . . I can tell just by the look of you that those women had you in the hot seat today," said Noah, giggling.

"I spent the whole morning getting fussed at," said Glory, taking a sip of coffee. "And you know what gets me, it's like they *want* to see me fail. They should be rooting for me to succeed. I tell you, it's Black-on-Black crime is what it is."

He joined her at the table. "So, there's some gossip I heard the other day. I couldn't believe it at first. People seem to think that you were acting up at that Commodores' concert at Cypress Downs." Glory stiffened. "Folks say that you're banned. Something about you screaming at the security guard about having hairs on your arm that were older and smarter than he was."

Did she say that? That was good, she'd have to remember that.

"You might as well know the truth. I may have had one too many rum and Cokes, but hand on my heart, I truly believe that someone slipped something into my drink. When have you ever known me to act the fool like that?"

"I'll plead the Fifth," he said, enjoying Glory's discomfort.

"How did you even hear about that?" asked Glory, wondering whose knees might need a bat swung to them. She had a guy for that, after all.

"My buddy works maintenance at the casino. I heard it from him, and then I heard it from Millie Broward from your little volunteer group," he said, practically wheezing from laughing so hard.

Glory groaned. "That must have been why those women interrogated me today like a felon. I was the *victim*. I didn't do anything wrong!"

"I agree with you there. If we prosecuted everyone in Louisiana that drank one too many free casino cocktails, half the state would be incarcerated." He was openly laughing now, throwing his head back and enjoying the moment. "Maybe I can add an alcoholic coffee drink to the menu, call it Glory Hallelujah." Noah always had a way of rubbing her nose in things at precisely the wrong moment. If she hadn't known him for thirty years, she might be tempted to ring the man's mama and have a word about her disrespectful son.

"If you'll excuse me, this is a busy season. I have clients waiting to see me, and buy your coffee, for some reason. You must have something else to do other than mock me."

He stood up. "I'm not mocking you. No, ma'am. Been sober for twenty years." He chuckled all the way back to the kitchen.

She was bedraggled in spirit and body but had to tend to her customers, who were doing their part. Ordering coffee, minding their business, and keeping a low profile until Glory summoned them. Envelopes were slid across the table, and Glory recorded wagers in her book. Occasionally, she reached into her handbag and slid an envelope toward a customer. Sometimes her customers win, and occasionally they win big. But Glory knew how to budget for surprises. She was never caught resting on her haunches when it came to business, and she knew that the house always wins in the end. In this case, the house was her.

A man, and not a regular customer, walked through the coffe shop doors and headed straight toward Glory, cutting her informal line. He wore a purple wool coat with matching shirt, navy pants, and a smirk. His red curls looked almost transparent in the harsh sunlight. T-Red.

He sidled up next to her, not at the seat across the table, but alongside her in the booth, like they were lovers who couldn't get enough of each other. Glory grabbed her purse straps tightly.

"You don't have to worry about that," he purred in her ear. "I'm no common criminal, and I have plenty of my own."

"How can I help you?" asked Glory.

"Thought I'd place a wager on the Tulane game. Heard you're the go-to gal around here for those kinds of things."

Suddenly, all she could think about were the horses galloping at Cypress Downs, because her heart thudded as loudly as those horses' hooves against the track. She took a slow, deep breath. She wasn't going to let this man get her blood pressure up. "Wagers are a privilege for my regular customers, of which you are not. I hear there is an entire book at that casino of yours. I suggest you return to your turf and place a bet with your own people, because you can't do that here."

"Rule number one: never work with strangers. I see Sterling taught you well," T-Red said.

Her heart sped up again. This was a man who knew her ex-husband, and from what she had heard, it was possible that Sterling had been afraid of him. The question was: What did he want with her?

"I don't need anyone to tell me to avoid entanglements with strangers. I've got sense of my own." She stirred her coffee, if only to have something to do with her hands. "I'm afraid there's nothing I can help you with."

"That's alright. I didn't come here needing anything from you," he said, meeting Noah's hard glance from behind the counter. "I came to deliver a message. Keep your nose out of casino business, and the stables, too. Ain't nothing happening over there that concerns you."

It wasn't that Glory was unafraid, but this wasn't the first time she had encountered a man puffing up his chest and telling her what she could and couldn't do. Maybe she just wasn't as afraid as she might once have been.

"I guess you don't have to worry about that, seeing that you already banned me from the casino. I assume your cameras and computers can recognize my face on sight, and that your security team would drag me out on the spot. So, what is it that you're really here to tell me?"

He gave a sour smile. "You are barking up the wrong magnolia tree, if you know what I mean. And I don't need you of all people, a professional busybody, in my business. The last thing I need is a nosy church lady, running an illegal side hustle, who recently solved a murder, and was on every television station in the parish, on my premises. Don't you go shining a light on things that should stay in the dark."

She inspected his face, his gaudy clothes, really took him in. "I'll keep that in mind. If you came all the way down here to scare an old woman like me, I assume that means I'm on the right track. I may not be able to enter your casino, but I have my ways."

He removed a piece of lint from his purple shirt, then stood up, smoothed his pants, and hovered over her. "Really a shame we can't be friends. I've been studying your odds on games. I have no idea how you do it, but you're better than my own casino, and we invest in a service of professional statisticians or some bullshit. We send someone here every week and adjust our lines based on your odds. So, I guess I really should say thank you."

Grady had mentioned that the betting lines had improved with Sterling at the helm, and this confirmed what Glory had suspected from that moment forward. Turning the casino onto Glory's special algorithm had been one of Sterling's final acts of betrayal. Dying the way he did, and leaving the mess to Glory, had been his last.

"Do me a favor before you leave," she said, pulling a stack of gala tickets out of her purse. "The least you can do is buy a few tickets to the St. Agnes Mardi Gras gala, on account of disrupting my day. Goes to a real good cause. A hundred dollars apiece."

He cracked a smile, pulled the money out of his wallet, and slapped it down on the table.

"Thank you," said Glory.

"Where're my tickets at?"

She counted the wad of money—$3,000. Glory handed over a stack of tickets. "I only have twenty tickets on me, but I can guarantee the rest will be spent wisely at the St. Agnes Food Pantry to support food-insecure individuals and families."

He took his tickets, stored them in the silk lining of his coat, and strutted out of the coffee shop. She watched as he walked out the door, angry that the casino was stealing her money lines, but glad that someone had finally appreciated the craft behind her work.

23

After being grilled like a chicken on a spit at church, and the run-in with T-Red, Glory decamped straight to her bedroom. There was a third circumstance weighing on her mind, and one which she could not share with anyone. Today was the anniversary of her wedding to Sterling. That milestone didn't mean much most years, just another day for the history book that was her life, but on the heels of his murder, she couldn't help but reflect.

Sterling had been the greatest storm of her life, and as anyone in Louisiana can tell you, the storm is bad—but beware the surge. She had quickly learned to weather the whipping winds and snapped trees that he seemed to leave in his wake. That was the drinking, the nights when he was volatile and unpredictable. No matter what, these moments would pass and be replaced with sunshine for good stretches of time. But the surge was another matter altogether. The deluge came later, women knocking on their front door, announcing that they had slept with her husband like it was something Glory had never heard before, like they were the first. Glory promptly sent them marching, with stern words to never darken her doorway again. Most of the women were so shaken by Glory's ferocity that they never bothered her again. Glory had tried to keep the surge out of her life, deploying emotional sandbags that kept it at bay. But sometimes the tides were so astronomical, rising so fast, that there was nothing she could do. The fallout eventually washed over her and Delphine, leaving them underwater and breathless.

But as much as Glory had despised the storm, who would she be without it? Hadn't it taught her things that the younger version of herself never thought possible, like how to survive? How to be resilient, no matter the conditions around you? Storm after storm had forged her into something new, a woman who did not need a man to survive. In fact, it was exactly *because* of Sterling that she had learned how to endure.

After she found Sterling cold as a fish on his kitchen floor, she had come home and rifled through some of her photos and found a picture of their wedding day. Sterling wore a bow tie and a big grin, and Glory wore a short dress with a shoulder-skimming veil. He had been dashing and confident. She was enthralled by the tall, handsome man with curly hair that played the trombone and could dance the zydeco like his feet were possessed. They began to linger at the dance halls, and then the back seat of his car. Nine months later, Delphine arrived.

In hindsight, they were too young, and Sterling too wrapped up in the life. Glory wanted the trappings of the middle class and Sterling wanted the trappings of a big shot. While Glory was busy diapering a baby, he was busy cooing *baby, baby* into the unsuspecting ears of other women.

Glory hung on. She convinced herself that if she fixed his dinner this way, or arranged the house that way, he'd come to realize what good he had in her. If he couldn't do that, maybe he'd come to realize what good he had in Delphine. But ultimately, none of it mattered. This is all to say that, if Glory didn't initially dive into the investigation of his death with enthusiasm, there was a reason. To some, it might have looked like anger. For Glory, it was disappointment.

Laughter erupted from the living room. Justice seemed like a nice enough woman, and Lord knows Glory was grateful for her work on the king cake, but the closeness of the two of them did not go unnoticed. She decided to stick a pin in this for now, because she needed to focus on Sterling's murder. There were only so many investigations Glory could manage at once. She turned off her bedside lamp and went to sleep.

♣♦♥♠

"There's three of you?" asked Franklin, eyeing Glory, Valerie, and Delphine, who were lined up against the inside of Glory's garage. Delphine had invited Valerie to join—to Glory's consternation.

"We all loved Sterling, so we are all going to help find his killer," said Valerie.

Glory let out a puff of air. Yes, she knew that Sterling was Valerie's husband and the woman was upset. That was reasonable. But why must Valerie be so melodramatic about everything, all the time, and test Glory's fraying nerves?

Valerie had had enough of Glory's eye-rolling. "You know what?" said Valerie, pivoting on her heel and inching toward Glory's face. "I have tried to be nice to you, I really have. I even dragged your butt from the casino when you were prattling off Lionel Richie trivia. Sitting up at the casino talking about '*Did you know Lionel's grandfather was a Tuskegee airman?*' in the middle of "Brick House," disturbing the whole show. And I was happy to do it because you were supposed to be helping. But I've done nothing wrong, and I'm tired of being treated like a criminal. I should have done this on my own."

"Ha, you wish you could do this on your own! You need me," spat Glory. "You wouldn't have gotten half as far without me."

"And where are we, exactly? We still don't have any strong leads . . . just a bunch of shady individuals circling around the drain of that casino, which just sounds like another day in Lafayette, if you ask me."

Franklin stepped between the two warring women. "I'm going to need you both to settle down, you hear me?" He had the countenance and the authority of a first-grade teacher, getting the class in line after an outburst. "Now, if you two can't get along, I'd recommend you both stay here and out of my hair."

"Oh, ain't no way in hell I'm staying home. I'm the one who got us this far," said Glory.

"And once more, remind me where we are again?" asked Valerie.

Delphine, who had been quiet until now, stepped up. "I do not know how many times I'm going to have to separate the two of you. It's like a cage match, just two hens determined to peck away at each other until there's nothing left of either one of you!" She turned to Franklin. "Why don't you take your own car? I'll follow behind and manage these two, so you don't have to."

He nodded wearily. "Dang, Miss Glory, I don't even know why you need me to collect any money. All you have to do is run your mouth. You can wear people down with the sound of your voice."

"Boy, you better mind your manners and remember who put that start-up money in your pocket before you go fussing me like you just did."

Delphine corralled the two women into Glory's Honda-CRV and followed Franklin all the way to the Opelousas Stable.

Delphine drove, mostly silent. Glory sat shotgun, periodically shooting hard glances at Valerie, who pouted in the back seat like a child, and turned her head every time her eyes connected with Glory's. When Franklin's Lexus pulled into the parking lot of a Shell gas station, Delphine followed and parked beside him.

Franklin got out of his car and joined Valerie in the back seat. "So, am I just supposed to see where events take me and report back, or do you have some other plan?" he asked. All occupants of the car turned to Glory.

It was real funny, she thought, how everyone liked to tell Glory everything she was always doing stuff wrong, but when it came down to having actual solutions, they turned *to* her. *Ain't that a blip?* If Glory was the kind of person who kept receipts, she would . . . well, she was the kind of person that kept receipts. She had learned to use them strategically.

"Here's what you're going to do," she said. "Convince them that your business is about to go under. That you just walk around Lafayette pretending that it's a success, but that you're knee-deep in bills and obligations, and you'll do just about anything for money."

"Okay, but what if they ask about you? If they're stealing your gambling lines, they may know I work with you," he explained.

Glory tapped her nails against the dashboard, working it through. "Well, they clearly don't think you're rolling too deep with me, or else Grady wouldn't have invited you here. If it comes up, tell them that I haven't given you any work in months. That since my recent notoriety, my clients are mainly a bunch of lookie-loos that place small bets because they saw me on TV. And that a lot of my old clients have been scared away by the publicity."

He nodded, like he could execute this plan. "You just gotta promise me that you're going to stay in this car, Miss Glory."

"Of course I'm going to stay in the car. I wasn't invited, and contrary to popular opinion I am not actually looking for trouble." The car vibrated with skepticism. "I'm not!" she demanded.

"Don't worry," added Delphine. "I'll strap her down if I need to."

It seemed like Glory was the butt of everyone's jokes that night, which she would not forget.

"Okay, they asked me to meet them at the stables right about . . ." He looked at his watch. "Now. I better get going. Meet back up here for a regroup?"

"No," said Glory. "Best not to, in case they tail you, to make sure you're not coordinating with me. Just text me when you're in your car and we'll coordinate after."

"Gotcha. See you soon."

Franklin walked into the stable and was surprised to find a scene that felt more like a party than a backdoor deal about to go down. Music blared from a portable speaker that someone must have been controlling with their phone. Cigarettes and other herbaceous roll-ups were being smoked. Franklin winced. He had a new business meeting the following day with Benoit Industrial. He knew from past experience that the stink would soak into his skin and would take a good couple of showers before it washed away, if he was lucky. A man was kissing a woman's neck in the corner. Franklin rolled his eyes and looked the other way. It looked more like a drunken after-work party than anything else.

Bonnie, the card dealer, walked up to him. "Hi, I'm Bonnie. What's a handsome man like you doing here all alone?"

Franklin smiled on the outside and groaned on the inside. Was that a line that was actually supposed to work? He had standards. And a mission as well, which he was eager to complete.

He stayed focused, despite the smell of booze on her breath and cannabis in the air. "That's awful kind of you. Say, you don't happen to know where Grady is? I was supposed to meet him here tonight around this time."

She smirked, recognizing the deflection for what it really was—a rebuke. She pointed. "Over there, next to the straw and horseshit," and walked away.

When Franklin turned around, he was surprised to see the condition Grady was in. In the casino he seemed slightly agitated, but here in the stable, he looked downright panicked. He wiped his nose with the entire length of his forearm and made a beeline toward Franklin.

"Hey, good to see you, man. Afraid you weren't going to show," he said. "You're not here with anyone, are you?"

"Nah, man, I'm alone. I know how business is done. I'm not about to just roll in with anyone."

"Good, good," said Grady, wringing his hands for no apparent reason. "Let me ask you a question. I can't talk freely in that casino. You never know who's listening, but folks say you know Glory Broussard personally, and that you work for her. Is that true?"

"Man, I haven't worked for that broad in years. Let's just say she and I had a disagreement."

Grady backed away a tiny bit. "Disagreement? What kind?"

"You know how that old woman is. Just runs her mouth, ordering people around and ain't got nothing good to say about anyone. And the money wasn't what it used to be . . . got to be more trouble than it was worth." It wasn't exactly the script that Glory had laid out, but he didn't need all that detail.

"Good, good," Grady said again, seemingly satisfied. "That woman just can't keep her nose out of people's business, showing up in the casino, nosing around, stealing food from the buffet . . . acting all kinds of crazy.

"I heard about her acting up all over Lafayette. Even getting blackout drunk at some concert at the casino? I guess that's what happens your husband leaves you for another woman. Now he's gone and ain't ever coming back. And she'll be alone forever."

Grady snickered. "Yeah, I took care of both they asses."

Franklin laughed, if only to disguise his shock. "Yeah? How'd you do that?"

Grady opened his mouth but then caught himself. "So, let's talk business. And I know I don't have to tell you this, but this is real confidential. You can't tell anyone . . . not your priest, not your lady, not even your dog."

"I hear you, but I'm gonna need you to come out with it, because I ain't got all day."

Grady slung his arm around Franklin's neck, a half embrace and a subtle warning. "We got something going on at the casino. You see that gal right there?" He nodded toward Bonnie, the woman who had dealt blackjack to Glory, and also the same woman that had molested Franklin with her eyes just moments earlier. "You know that saying . . . the house always wins? Imagine if that wasn't the case. Imagine what might be possible."

"Come on, man. Come out with it."

"We enlist trusted . . . associates . . . to play blackjack at Cypress Downs. Bonnie provides very subtle signals that help our associates make more informed wagers, catch my drift? And then we all share in the proceeds. Some of our colleagues got scared off, what with Sterling getting murdered and the state gaming commission sniffing around like bloodhounds, but the groundwork has been laid. You know how it is . . . the heat gets turned down eventually. And there's money to be made. We just need someone we can trust to form a new partnership."

"And that person would be me," confirmed Franklin. In front of them, a bottle was being passed around a group, each person savoring a swig of the pale liquid inside. Franklin flinched. *Damn, they ain't got mixers or chasers or nothing*, he thought.

"That person would be you, if you're game."

"One question before I agree to this. Who exactly is 'we?'" asked Franklin. "You and this dealer going rogue, or do you have other folks involved."

"I can't tell you that."

"Then I'm afraid I'm out. I can't get involved in something where I don't know the scope," Franklin said. Trying to hide the arithmetic that was quickly adding up in his head. "This is how Sterling died, isn't it?"

Grady put a finger to his lips, urging him to be quiet. "Okay, I'll tell you. Ain't no one else involved except me, Bonnie, and T-Red. He makes sure we're covered off with security and the casino bosses. Ever since Sterling died, I got promoted, man. I'm T-Red's lieutenant. And I can tell you one thing—it's a tight circle. We get one whiff of a leak, that leak is taken care of. You in?"

Franklin nodded his head, indicating that he was game. Grady took him outside the stables to talk in private, and Franklin wondered the whole time what an old man with a limp like Grady did to deserve such a big promotion at the casino.

♣♦♥♠

Once he had gotten his instructions, he texted Glory, whom he had agreed to meet at a gas station parking lot about twenty miles away. From the backseat of her car, he filled everyone in.

"I really hate it when Black folks get wrapped up in this sort of thing," said Glory, shaking her head. "It gives us all a bad name!"

"Bonnie is apparently going to give a slight nod if I should hit and be as still as possible if I should stand. I'm not supposed to play more than six or seven hands. The idea is to get in and get out. Try not to attract too much attention to myself. Then I'll go back to my car, and T-Red gets a seventy-five percent cut."

"Seventy-five percent!" screamed Glory. "That's highway robbery. I knew this little scheme wouldn't be possible without his scammery, but you can't let your dime walk away feeling like he got cheated. You want them to feel like they're a partner in this, so you don't have problems later."

"You really did miss your calling as a mob boss, Mom."

"I know," she said, without a hint of irony. "When is this happening?"

"Ten o'clock tomorrow."

"Whew, child, that's my bedtime, but I guess I can make it to the casino for that."

Franklin shook his head. "No, ma'am. You seem to keep forgetting that you're banned from the casino. And you can't be anywhere near there when it goes down. The association would be bad for both of us."

"You right, you right," said Glory. She sipped a Diet Coke that had been in her cup holder. "I'm just sorry I got you deeper into this. I suspected something was going on. I didn't mean to get you wrapped up like this."

Franklin stretched his pecs. "I'm kind of interested now. And I've been wanting to invest in some online marketing for my business. Drum up some new leads. Do you know how expensive customer acquisition costs have gotten these days? A little extra money to target all those oil companies and their procurement officers would be right on time."

"If you say so," said Glory.

"So, I'll report to the casino at ten, and I'll call you after, if you can manage to stay up."

"Yes, I suppose I can, since you're doing all the heavy lifting." Glory felt uneasy, given all the people she had involved in this, like Justice and Franklin. She'd have to say a special prayer for Franklin tonight, and ask the Lord for forgiveness, should anything happen to him.

24

The next morning, Delphine and Justice stared into a computer monitor at the Edith Garland Dupre Library at the University of Louisiana, Lafayette. They were there to search whatever online records might bring them closer to Cleotus Farmington, knife maker to star chefs, and were coming up with precious little.

Delphine's purse was strewn across the wooden table, along with articles she had printed out and read about the man. She scrolled through yet another database. "How is he so unfindable? I've searched every national database, as well as the Louisiana Library Connection Databases, which includes dozens of references, and I can't find a trace of this man. Yes, there are stories in *Serious Eats* and *Bon Appetit* and just about every food website that exists, but nothing about the man himself—where he might live, where he's from—nothing at all. The only thing I've been able to find is his wedding announcement in the *Times-Picayune* from 1984 to a woman from Mississippi."

"That's part of his myth. Makes the knives more valuable," said Justice. Arranging a large stack of reference books in front of her as a shield, Justice pulled out a Styrofoam platter from a greasy bag and bit a piece of flaky meat off a turkey wing.

Delphine's mouth hung open. "You did not just bring a whole to-go container from Cajun Kitchen into the library."

"My favorite thing about Lafayette so far is the food scene. To have a thriving food ecosystem, you need a healthy number of small businesses," Justice said, taking a napkin from the bag and wiping her hands clean. "The flavor on these stuffed turkey wings is incredible. I don't know how people down here just eat like this every day."

"We don't," said Delphine.

A stern library worker crossed their path, catching Justice in the act of stuffing a biscuit into her mouth. "Excuse me, miss, there is no eating whatsoever in the library."

Justice closed the top of the Styrofoam dish and put it back in the bag. "Yes, of course. Sorry about that. Studying for midterms and needed a snack."

The woman lasered an angry scowl in her direction, not believing a word. She parked herself at a nearby reference desk, separated by a thin layer of plexiglass, and began to clack away at a computer of her own.

"You see, this is why I only lasted a semester in college. I'm not cut out for the library."

"It's not even midterm season," said Delphine.

"Can you please hurry up so we can leave? This place is making me itchy. Though I must say, I am really enjoying watching you work in the library. Those reading glasses are hella sexy." Justice inched her plastic computer chair closer to Delphine. "And that turtleneck is really accentuating your features, if you know what I mean . . ." Justice wrapped her arms around Delphine's waist and nibbled her ear. Briefly, Delphine enjoyed herself, felt pleasure. It felt odd being with Justice so much, given what had happened to her father.

The reference librarian slammed her hands against a leather-bound book with gold lettering.

Delphine sighed. "Let me hurry up and finish my research."

Justice hung her arm around Delphine's shoulder, and smiled defiantly at the librarian.

Delphine, unbothered by it all and hardly paying attention, looked through the scribbled notes in her notebook. "Wait a minute, I have an idea . . ." She began to type furiously at the computer, searching all databases and public records. She scrunched her face.

"Find anything?" Justice winked at the librarian, causing the woman to drop a stack of books she had been pretending to organize.

"Please leave that woman alone," said Delphine, writing in her notebook. "I had been looking for addresses in *his* name, but the wedding announcement gave me an idea. I should be looking for her instead. Anyway, I found a lead in Mississippi. There are a few commercial spaces near Jackson, but no phone numbers attached."

"So, what does that mean?"

Delphine stared down the librarian. These people, these attitudes, were why she lived in New York. She turned her attention to Justice. "It means we're going on a road trip, just as soon as I can confirm these addresses." She kissed Justice on the mouth to seal the deal.

25

Franklin stopped himself in front of the glass sliding doors of the casino. *Clothes make the man* was his motto, and for this he had wanted to look extra good. His barber had clipped a high taper on his fade that morning. He had chosen a pair of navy blue, virgin wool pants from Armani, but just the pants. A blazer would have been overkill. They were paired with a crisp white button-down with his initials embroidered in the cuff. And just for kicks, he wore his Christian Louboutin oxford loafers. The only accessory was his Omega watch, a new piece he bought with Glory's last paycheck. His proceedings had turned out to be more handsome than usual. He had a few fancy things, like his watch and tailored Armani suit, because he was still growing his new business. He knew how people saw him first and foremost: as a Black man. When they noticed his expensive watch, the tenor of the room changed. It communicated to everyone that he, too, deserved a seat at the table. He had won eighty percent of competitive bids since he got that watch and knew it wasn't an accident.

At any rate, he was more overdressed than anyone in that casino. The cool air hit him the second he opened the door. The second thing that hit him was the cigarette smoke. *Damn, not on my Armani*, he grumbled in his head. He passed the same terrain as Glory had on her last few visits. The sunken pit of slot machines whirring and clanking down coins, the buffet, the gift shop.

Then he saw Grady, who had been waiting for him. Franklin never thought Grady would be involved in something like this. He seemed too quiet, too meek, but circumstances do creep up on a person. A man gets older and can't get by and can't even get the hip replacement he so obviously needs. Franklin could understand how a man might feel like the world owed him something.

He found Bonnie working the blackjack table in the rear corner, just as he was told. She inspected him in a lascivious way, like he was a ham under the heating lights of the buffet carving station. This was a problem in Lafayette, he thought. You would think he'd be thankful for all the female attention he got, but the women in town could definitely use some expanded options. It might have given him the advantage, but it also made him sad. He could understand why Delphine, a woman with beauty and brains, would get out of this town as quickly as possible. He had heard through the grapevine that Delphine and Lieutenant Landry had feelings for each other, and he hoped she wouldn't fall for it, even if he seemed like a nice enough guy. She'd gotten out, and that mattered.

"Take a seat," she said, once Franklin neared the blackjack table. He obliged.

"You from around here?" she asked, as if they were total strangers.

"Yes and no. I'm from Shreveport. Just here visiting family." A cocktail waitress appeared to take a drink order. He graciously declined.

From here on out, they were all business. He peeked at his cards, face down against the smooth, green felt of the table. His two cards had totaled thirteen, a sum that he ordinarily would have hit with another card. But she gave a hard, stony look. The instructions had seemed clear when he received them, but now he wasn't so sure. But ultimately, he interpreted her cold demeanor as a "no," meaning he should not get another card. He was right. Bonnie was busted, and he had won $900 with the low-card count of thirteen.

This went on for precisely six hands, as discussed. He flicked his cards quickly against the table, tallying the total. She had given a single nod and smile to indicate when he should hit with another card, and then just as fast went cold again. The bets increased gradually but steeply. And within just six hands he had netted close to $18,000.

As Bonnie prepared to deal another hand, Franklin interrupted. "That'll be enough for me. Gotta have the discipline to stop when you're ahead, you know what I mean" he said, tipping her $200 before cashing out.

He was grateful for the fresh air once the doors opened. It felt like a tonic to the stuffiness of the casino. Maybe his pants could air out and save him a trip to the dry cleaners.

Within the vast parking lot, full of minivans and camper trailers, he searched for the hunter-green Cadillac Escalade, and as instructed, let himself inside where he found T-Red and Grady. He momentarily held his breath entering the car, which smelled like cheap car wash air freshener. There would be no avoiding the cleaners now. Playing on the stereo was The Isley Brothers' "Between the Sheets," and suddenly T-Red's entire persona made sense. He must have imagined himself as a lost member of The Isley Brothers, with his loud suits and hats. More like a pimp than a rogue employee of a casino, which was probably more or less the same thing.

"Well done, my brother, well done."

Franklin handed over the stack of money, allowing T-Red to peel off his sum, and then stuffed the remaining money T-Red handed back to him in his pocket. Grady reached for his share, only to be rebuffed by T-Red's shoulder. Grady sunk back into his seat, defeated.

"The well has gotten a little dry lately, if you know what I mean," added T-Red. "The gaming commission has been around here a lot, and then we had that Glory Broussard and her nonsense as well. And I don't think it's a coincidence, if you ask me."

Confusion scattered across Franklin's face. "You think she's working with the Feds?" he asked.

"All of a sudden, the woman starts showing up in my casino, asking questions about her ex-husband, who she didn't even like. And now I get the authorities on my tail. I have a mind to take care of her ass for good. I didn't get in this position by looking the other way."

Franklin cracked his knuckles as a byproduct of nerves. "What do you mean by that, exactly?"

T-Red reached into his back pocket and pulled out his wallet. He fanned out the tickets to the St. Agnes Red Hat gala, purchased directly from Glory. "All I'm saying is that I bought twenty tickets to that Red Hat gala, and I intend to make it a night to remember. You in?"

"Nah, man. I just signed up to play cards. Nothing else." Franklin pulsed his biceps and stuck his chest out, a reminder that he could still bench 400 pounds.

"Grady, you in, right?" Grady nodded and gave a miserable smile. He looked like his life had just sunken deeper in the mud.

"Man, forget you," T-Red said. He threw a hundred-dollar bill toward the back seat, Grady frantically trying to catch the bill with both hands. T-Red sucked his teeth in disgust. "Nah, this is too important. I'mma handle her on my own . . ."

26

Glory had somehow managed to stay up past 10 P.M., passing the time flipping through old issues of *Southern Living* magazine. When the phone rang, she excused herself from the living room where Justice and Delphine were also awaiting the call. "It's just Constance, harassing me again about some trivial Mardi Gras matters," she said, even though the caller ID said it was Franklin. Delphine's daddy was murdered after all. Maybe she didn't need to know *everything*. And though Justice appeared to be about as solid as they came, she didn't sign up for a murder investigation. She fell into her bedroom chair and took the call.

Franklin's voice was frantic. "Miss Glory, T-Red thinks you're the reason why the gaming commission is investigating the casino. They're blaming you."

"Well, that's just absurd. You know me, Franklin, I ain't no snitch. And he knows what I do for a living. I'm not exactly in a position to go placing calls to the gaming commission, if you know what I mean."

"And now he's vowing to show up to your Mardi Gras gala and cause trouble. Saying he's going to put an end to you," said Franklin. "Is it true you sold him twenty tickets?"

She groaned, remembering the tickets she forced him to buy at CC's Coffee House. "Damn. I had a bunch of extra tickets to sell, and the group was putting a lot of pressure on us to sell them. I'm the chair!"

"Miss Glory, I don't know what exactly he's planning on doing, but he seems real determined to teach you a lesson. Or worse. Promise me you'll stay away from the gala this year, please. And stay away from that Grady, too. I don't trust him either."

"Child, please, Grady couldn't hurt a fly."

"I know you think T-Red is the villain here, and he's a bad guy for sure. But I don't know, I don't see him killing anyone. He's too smart for that. But you know who is desperate enough to do just about anything? Grady."

She leaned back in the overstuffed bedroom chair and thought about this. Even Milton Knowles had believed that T-Red was the kind of man to issue orders, not carry them out. And there was no denying that every time she had seen Grady recently, his teeth were damn near chattering from nervousness.

"Okay, but why would Grady kill Sterling?" she asked, curious about his theory.

"Here's what I think. T-Red trusted Sterling, and Sterling profited from that association. And when he started to talk about leaving to open his fishing business, they got scared. Scared he was going to run his mouth to the police. And from there, it's possible two things happened. Either T-Red paid Grady to take him out, because he was putting their skimming operation at risk. Or Grady took it upon himself to do the job, hoping it would lead to a promotion in the eyes of T-Red. Either way, T-Red is sitting on a handful of tickets that you sold him, and he intends to wreak havoc. I heard it with my own ears."

She raised her feet on top of the ottoman, slowly, one at a time. "Look, what exactly does he plan to do? Kill me in front of five hundred guests at The Pelican Club? In front of the entire congregation? I can't stay home. The entire membership is depending on me!"

"It's a bad idea, Miss Glory. Just promise me you'll keep your eyes peeled. And do not go anywhere by yourself. To your car, to the kitchen. Nowhere."

"Child, don't worry about me. I'll be fine. That man ain't the first dog that come around barking, and he won't be the last."

She would never say this out loud, but Glory almost hoped he would come. She wasn't much closer to finding the rat who killed Sterling, though at least now she had a few suspects. You can't catch a rat when it's burrowed away in its hiding place. You have to lure it out.

"Louisiana is wild, y'all," said Justice, unpacking boxes of produce from a stint volunteering at the farm. She handed the produce over to Glory, who rinsed and prepped it for the food pantry visitors. "I've been here for a little over a week, and I've seen an old Black woman uncover corruption at a casino and a racetrack and learned to make boudin balls and turducken. Never in my wildest dreams."

She handed over a bundle of collard greens to Glory. "Who you calling old?" She plugged the giant kitchen sink and turned on the faucet. Behind her were rows of reach-in refrigerated storage for the patrons, and row after row of shelf-stable foods like pasta, beans, rice, and cookies. Glory made sure that there was always something sweet. She figured if you're going to a food pantry to make ends meet, you could use a little pick-me-up.

"You ever thought of becoming a private investigator, like for hire?" asked Justice.

"People keep asking," said Glory, hands on her hips as she watched the water fill the sink. "Sometimes I think about it because people do come to me with the smallest of problems. I feel like I could help straighten them out, you know? On the other hand, I don't especially like getting tangled up with people, especially folks I don't know."

Delphine, who was slicing off carrot tops, chimed in. "What you don't understand, Justice, is that what some people call friendship, my mama calls *getting tangled up with people.*"

Justice laughed.

"And what do you mean by that? I have plenty of friends."

"Name one."

Glory turned off the faucet. "Well, Noah Singleton at the coffee shop. And . . ." She stalled.

"Exactly," said Delphine. She threw a bunch of carrots into another sink. "It wouldn't hurt to try to make a friend or two."

"Well, Amity was my best friend, and she got murdered. I don't know how many more great friends are left out there for me to make, especially at this age. Sometimes you just have to be grateful for what you had."

Justice interrupted. "I read that one of the things that prevents dementia is having a strong social network. It could help you in your later years."

"My goodness. I invited you two down here to help me out, and now I'm getting lectures about becoming a private investigator, the importance of a social network, and dementia, as if I'm a problem to be managed instead of a person standing right in front of you." She pushed her sleeves up and drowned the collard greens underwater, giving them a good shake.

"We just want what's best for you, Glory," offered Justice, apologetically. "That's why I offered to make the king cake, because I wasn't about to let those ladies attack you for an ugly donut with purple icing, disguised as a king cake. I will not stand for those crusty old ladies disrespecting my girlfriend's mama like that."

Everyone froze. Delphine stopped cutting carrots, Glory stopped rinsing the greens.

Justice seemed to understand what she had unleashed. Scrambling and panicked, she added, "And you . . . you're my girl, too, Glory. And my friend, and I appreciate you letting me stay in your guest room. We've got to stick together, right?" Nobody was convinced. "Anyway, I got to run down to the kitchen to do some final tweaks on my recipe." She looked at Delphine, whose posture had surrendered. "See y'all later." She couldn't leave fast enough. Before they knew it, Justice was out the door and in her rental truck.

Delphine exhaled, seemingly preparing herself for the inevitable. "Mom, it's not what you think it is . . ."

Glory closed her eyes, like she was visualizing the words in her head before speaking. "I'm pretty sure it's exactly what I'm thinking. You and Justice have been running around behind my back, in my own home, pretending that you're friends when you're really together. Why didn't you tell me?"

Delphine readied to face her mother, literally and figuratively. "I didn't tell you because I'm still figuring this out myself, to be honest. And I didn't need your noise complicating things."

"My *noise*? And what does that mean, exactly?"

"You know how you can be. You create an entire backstory about a person based on the shoes they're wearing. You traffic in rumors, and gossip is currency to you. Everyone knows how judgemental you are. That's why I didn't tell you."

"Judgmental?" Glory tilted her head. "Okay, fine, I *can* be judgmental about some things. For instance, if you buy a jarred mirepoix from the grocery store, I have every right to look down on your cooking. And flip-flops. No one wants to see anyone's toes. But I am not going to let you paint me as some kind of homophobe. I'll have you know the kids at church listen to that Big Freedia, and I like it very much. It has a nice groove. I also walked in the Lafayette Pride Parade, along with the Red Hat Society. We might have our individual *grievances*, but we are not bigots."

"I . . . I didn't know you marched in the Pride Parade."

"Sure did. Even bought a little rainbow brooch and everything. But let me tell you, some of those men were acting a little too silly. Did you know they make pants without the ass in them? That's inappropriate, regardless of who they're sleeping with."

"Okay, okay, there's the mother I know," said Delphine, who cracked a faint smile. "Then what's with the tone earlier? You sounded angry."

"Oh, don't get me wrong, I'm livid. Not because of Justice. I quite like the woman, who has been nothing but helpful ever since she showed up here. And I can see how much you enjoy spending time with her. I'm just disappointed that you'd think I'm a prejudiced person."

"You have to admit it, you are a little prejudiced."

"Not against gay people. Just fools! And foolishness is an equal opportunity affliction. Since we're finally talking about secrets, there is something that I've been meaning to ask you."

"Okay . . ." Delphine said suspiciously, grabbing a broom to sweep away the produce scraps that had fallen to the floor.

"When I was at Valerie's house, I saw a picture of you, your daddy, and that man T-Red from the casino. When was that taken?"

Delphine began to sweep the floor, avoiding eye contact. "In December."

"December?! As in two months ago?" Glory asked, trying to keep her voice measured, even if she was raging inside.

"Yes." Delphine could see Glory conducting an investigation in her head, in real time, and spared her. "I know I told you that I was exhausted from working all those hours in the law firm, which was true. But then Dad invited me, and I don't know, I thought it might be nice to spend some real quality time with him. You see, we'd been writing letters for the past year. As you know, I wasn't really taking his calls. He had stopped calling because there's only so many times you can go to voicemail. So, he started writing letters instead.

"And something in him finally clicked. He had apologized for all kinds of things before. What was his go-to line? *Ain't nobody perfect.* But something shifted. He started to express a real understanding of what he had done, and how that impacted the family. I don't know if it was Valerie or therapy, or just the realization that there were only so many years left, but he was doing real emotional work. I didn't respond right away, but eventually I wrote him back, and that led to phone calls and FaceTime with him and Valerie. When they invited me for Christmas, I was willing to take that step."

Glory had never been in a physical fight before, but she suddenly knew what being punched in the solar plexus felt like. The air was forced out of her lungs. "Why didn't you tell me? And why did you come down to Lafayette and avoid me?"

"I wasn't avoiding you . . . I just made a decision to spend the holidays with Dad. I knew if I told you, you'd insist that I stay with you, go visiting at this person's house for dinner, go to Christmas Eve Mass, and head on over to another person's house on Christmas Day. I just wanted to have one Christmas with Dad."

"I am not some ogre, Delphine. Of course you could have spent Christmas with your dad." Glory could tell she did not deliver this with the conviction needed to really sell it. "I just don't see why you couldn't have stopped by my place as well." Sensing that her daughter was unmoved about her decision to visit Lafayette without informing her, she moved on. "And what about T-Red?"

"Honestly, I had no idea he was even in the picture. The only things I know about him are from you. Why don't you ask Valerie? It was her holiday party."

"I did. She said T-Red's her cousin and wouldn't get involved in anything unseemly." Glory also couldn't help but think about Landry, and how he might take the news of Delphine's new love interest. "And I bet Landry's gonna be real upset once he hears about this." She was wading in waters that she should probably leave untouched.

"Oh, he knows. Saw us together testing recipes at the commercial kitchen downtown and well, it was pretty obvious. He's not particularly thrilled, no."

"What did he say?"

"Oh, something about me not knowing who I am, taking on the personality of whoever I date, whether it's my ex-husband or Justice, and how I need to sit with myself for a while and figure things out before I go ruining anyone else's life."

"Damn. He really let you have it." *And it's about damn time*, which she kept to herself. Someone needed to set this girl straight. Maybe she'd actually hear it coming from someone else.

"He did." Delphine paused, and then added, "I have to admit that I'm surprised you took this so well, and I'm sorry I didn't tell you earlier."

A large delivery truck beeped its way into the delivery bay. Once in place, the driver popped out of the truck and then opened the rear, which was filled with more pantry items and paper goods. Glory nodded at the man, acknowledging his presence.

"There's still one thing that's not sitting right with me," said Glory.

"Valerie," said Delphine. "Because you're never going to forgive her for having an affair with Dad. You have such a bias against her, which is clouding your judgment and taking you off course. But I can also see that you're just not going to let this go."

"I'll concede that it's unlikely she committed murder. But there's something about the salon and all that financial business that I can't get over. I say that after we pack up here, we head over to that salon of hers for another round of questioning. I just want to see how she responds when the question is put directly to her face."

"Mom, you're really pushing it."

Glory waved the delivery man and his handcart into the pantry. "Yes, I know. That's my personal brand."

It was then that a muddy pickup truck also appeared in the delivery bay. An older woman in baggy sweatpants walked down the ramp, then up the stairs.

Glory turned to Delphine. "We have hours for grocery distribution, but folks are always turning up whenever they darn well please. I suppose I should be stricter, so folks respect the hours we set, but you know how it is. Work hours don't always line up with pantry hours. Help me get a box ready."

Delphine jumped into action, taking one of the boxes already loaded with pantry staples and adding some fresh produce from their recent haul, along with a dozen eggs and a quart of milk.

"Marguerite, is that you?" asked Glory.

Marguerite looked down at her shoes, then up at Glory. "Well, this is mighty embarrassing. I didn't know you worked here."

"I am the director of the pantry. I'm here several times a week. No regular schedule. Someone has to be here to receive deliveries, especially the fresh stuff. And there ain't nothing to be embarrassed about. This facility wouldn't exist if there weren't others in your exact same shoes. We serve over 6,000 members of the Lafayette community, and we're just one shelter."

Delphine walked over, cradling a box filled to the top with food. "We got some fresh produce today from a local farm, including some gorgeous collard greens. And turnips. They might look a little ugly but they're perfectly delicious. Just not the prettiest. And loads of shelf-stable food that should last a while."

Marguerite sheepishly took the box from Delphine.

"They don't pay a decent wage down at the stables?" asked Glory.

"Minimum wage to us stable hands."

"That's a damn shame, as much as those horses bring in."

"My wife passed away, but you know what lives forever? Hospital bills. They will harass you nonstop."

"I'm sorry to hear that. And don't be bashful. You come on up anytime you need something, you hear me?"

"Yes, ma'am. And thank you. I really appreciate this," she said, choked up. She moved the box to her hip and, with one arm, hugged Glory.

Glory screwed up her face. "All that isn't necessary, but you're welcome." She recognized the smell of horse manure, as well as the smell of something else, possibly alcohol?

♣♦♥♠

Glory and Delphine were parked across the street at the store that sold fabric and notions to local interior designers. Once only one car remained at The New Woman Salon, they drove over and went inside.

The single car in the parking lot, they knew, belonged to Valerie, who was cleaning, sweeping up hair, and arranging chairs so that they all pointed in the same direction. When the salon's door chime rang, she did a double take. "I wasn't expecting to see either of you today." She was pulled together as usual, in slender jeans, a hot baby blue button-down shirt, and matching heels of new heights, even for her.

"Oh hey, Valerie, how you doing?" Delphine took a seat under the bonnet of a hair dryer that was installed on the back of a big vinyl chair, the kind of hair dryer you might have found in a salon in the 1960s. Glory didn't sit. She leaned against a wall between the checkout and the mirrors, her arms crossed in a defiant stance.

"Well, judging by the glum looks on your faces I take it this isn't a social visit. Glory must be here to interrogate me again."

"That's right," said Glory, propping herself up against the wall with one bent leg.

"Enough is enough. I don't know how many times, and how many ways, you need to hear it, but I was not involved in my husband's death. I know it's hard for you to believe, but I loved the man. I only manage to carry on at work because I have to. I have bills to pay—a mortgage, renovation loans, and IVF bills for a child that never materialized. And because what else am I supposed to do? I tell you what, no one wants to have their hairdresser crying all over them. They want a hairdresser that's cheerful and gossipy. So that's what I do. I come to work and perform. Just because Sterling died doesn't mean I have the luxury of falling apart."

"My mother just has some questions that she feels she has to ask," said Delphine, almost apologetically. "Please."

"If asking these questions is going to make you feel better, by all means. I have nothing to hide. I'll go first, yes, Sterling has a life insurance policy and it's in my name. No, I haven't cashed it out yet, but yes, it is in process. This is no different than it would be with any married couple."

Glory unfolded her arms and pushed herself off the wall. She began to circle around Valerie. "That money is right on time, seeing that you're way behind on the mortgage on this place."

Valerie slammed the broom to the floor. "Yes, I do owe money on the salon. Got into a real bind last year with a roof that needed to be replaced, and doctor's bills, like I've already told you. But if you think I killed Sterling, the love of my life, you're wrong."

"*The love of your life*," mocked Glory. Delphine looked around in a panic, sensing that her mother was going off script. "I was married to that man, and for a lot long longer than you were. The only good thing he ever did was father Delphine, and even then, that took about ten minutes and I'm pretty sure that was mostly my doing. Tell me what this man ever did for you that's got you fighting for him the way you've been doing. I'm genuinely curious."

Valerie smoothed her shirt down with the palms of her hands. "My marriage is none of your business, but I can see that there's no personal boundary that you're not willing to stomp all over, so I'll tell you.

"When I first met Sterling, I was an assistant, sweeping up hair and making a few dollars a blowout. And you know what Sterling told me? He told me to quit sitting around and waiting for permission. To stop waiting for someone to walk through the doors of the salon, just hoping they'd be a client. He gave me the confidence to operate like an entrepreneur. So, I started handing out business cards, started networking, offering discount cuts and colors to just about everyone I ran into. And before you know it, I had the biggest clientele in the entire shop. But I'm sure you know what an entrepreneur he was already, since the business you now run was one that he started."

It took Glory every bit of self-control she could muster to not throttle Valerie. "Sterling may have started the business years ago, but it was me who kept it. Without my smarts, it would have gone belly-up like a rodent in the swamp. You know, I can see it now."

"See what?" asked Valerie.

"You and him have a lot in common. The both of you just take, take, take—consequences be damned. You wanted to take over the salon from old Caroline McGee, and you did it, right underneath her nose. You wanted my husband, you found a way to nab him, though in hindsight that was probably for the best. You didn't care that he had a wife, or a daughter. Never apologized to no one."

"That's not true," said Delphine. "She apologized to me, over Christmas."

That Christmas visit again. It was ironic that Valerie wanted Glory to solve his murder, but couldn't extend any contrition her way, with that awful thing she did. *Damn it,* Glory thought. *This woman does not deserve to see your tears.* They say being vulnerable is a gift, but that's assuming you've chosen the right recipient. Valerie wasn't worthy. She composed herself and hoped that neither of them had noticed. "The man is buried in the ground, and somehow you still believe in him."

"I do," Valerie said. "You know, maybe he didn't believe in you because *you* never believed in *him*."

Composure was also a gift for those that deserved it, and Valerie most definitely did not. Glory snatched a pair of hairdresser shears, and in a fit of blind rage, hurled them at a mirror. Chunks of mirrored glass flew, and the scissors fell to the ground. Valerie and Delphine's faces froze in horror. Glory's hands trembled by her side.

27

The final general meeting of the Red Hat Society of Acadiana before Mardi Gras was in session, and the membership came to destroy.

Glory stood at the podium before the firing squad. She steeled herself and got ready to run the ladies through the Mardi Gras plan. She had rehearsed it last night with Delphine and Constance, and Delphine had drilled her like a trial attorney. Glory was exhausted by the end, but also in awe of her daughter's skill. It was good preparation for the membership.

"Good morning, everyone," Glory started. "Thank you for gathering here today for the official Red Hat Society of Acadiana Mardi Gras run-through. I'm going to present the agenda for the entire slate of festivities, from our annual gala and the Mardi Gras float, so if you could save your questions until the end, that would be appreciated. First, let's start with the float."

"I heard Krewe de Yountville's float was twice as big this year," said Millie Broward. "And they have an inflatable fleur-de-lis that they can control like a puppet. I seen that on the Macy's Thanksgiving Day Parade." Millie was always veering off subject.

Glory conjured up as much patience as she could. It wasn't clear how much cognitive function Millie had these days. Sometimes she was as sharp as a tack, and other times the hinges came off like a broken door. It was important to err on the side of patience, especially in front of this crew. "I have heard these rumors, yes, but we don't know if they're true."

"Oh, they're definitely true, and we're going to look like absolute amateur hour now, thanks to your lack of foresight and keeping abreast of competitive floats," said Annalee Guidry. If Glory had thought that Constance was her enemy, it turns out she had been misguided. Annalee had been picking apart all of Glory's choices since the day she was installed as chair of the Mardi Gras committee. She had made one unreasonable demand after the other, including table linens that would have bust the budget, masks made of red Swarovski crystals, and a tower of shrimp for cocktail hour. She knew the Red Hat Society didn't have those kinds of funds, of course. She merely wanted to be adversarial, and she was doing a real good job of it.

"How other organizations celebrate is their business, not ours," said Glory. "If you would, please hold your questions to the end." At this point, Constance fired up the presentation that she and Delphine had worked on. Glory didn't know how to move the slides on the screen, so Constance did it for her. It turns out all the prep was working, because Glory didn't even have to look at the slides. She knew all the details cold.

The menu? Everything was catered from Poche's Market in Breaux Bridge, including the crawfish étouffée, boudin balls, alligator bites, and all the favorites. Music? The cocktail hour would be DJed by DJ Big Shaun, whom Glory had seen in action once at Miami Moon. Even though that modern style of music that they play on the radio was definitely not for her, it must be said that it got people moving, which was all that really mattered at the end of the day. Then Terrance Simien and the Zydeco Experience would headline, live. The beads? Secured from Bead City, which Glory was able to show in her presentation *and* hand out samples to the women, who inspected them as if they were gemologists scrutinizing diamonds instead of plastic beads.

It was time for the king cake, the most contentious part of the day. You don't mess with classics, and certainly with stakes as high as the Mardi Gras gala. It was akin to putting raisins in a potato salad or deciding at Thanksgiving that you were "trying something new" with the macaroni and cheese.

"I know that Gambino's has been a long-standing tradition, but sometimes there is an opportunity to evolve, and that is what we are doing this year. To further explain the changes we have made to the cake this year, I've asked Chef Justice Harris, James Beard Rising Star Chef of the Year, to discuss her inspiration for her interpretation of a classic."

"Interpretation my ass," Annalee heckled from her seat. Glory knew physical violence wasn't something she'd ever resort to, but she liked to imagine taking her pocketbook and smacking the woman across the head.

Justice walked to the front of the room, wearing her chef's jacket with rolled up sleeves, revealing her tattoos to everyone. She looked like a chef out of central casting, which judging by stares and oohs and ahhs in the room, tickled most of the women. But Annalee just made a face of disapproval, like her face had gotten stuck in the middle of a spasm.

Now at the podium, with the presentation advanced to the correct slide, Justice explained her updated version of the king cake. "Good morning. I know there has been some concern about this year's king cake. I get it. Holidays are a time when people want the foods that they know and love. But I think you'll appreciate what I've done to it. First, let's start with the pastry itself. It's made of a *pâte à choux,* which manages to have the sweetness you'd expect from a king cake, but with an airier texture. In the middle, you'll find a cream mixed with hazelnuts. I took the care to toast the hazelnuts, to coax out a more complex flavor profile. And because it's Mardi Gras, I've used an edible glitter on top, in the traditional green, gold, and purple. Without any further ado, I present samples."

At that prompt, Delphine rolled a cart into the room with the dessert samples. After Delphine passed out the plates the room grew silent as the women tasted. They didn't often have treats during regular meetings, and this was an unexpected one. Glory watched carefully and felt some measure of relief as the women greedily scooped up every last crumb.

"This sure is different," said Millie Broward. "But it's wonderful. I've never tasted anything like this before." Most of the women nodded along, shoving the rest into their mouths.

Annalee started in. "I suppose this does taste just fine, but I'd like to know what happened to our regular cake order with Gambino's . . ."

Glory suppressed a distinct sucking of the teeth, or maybe she didn't. She collected herself. Sort of. "I think everyone knows by now that there was an error with the cake, and I'll take responsibility for that," said Glory, loathe to admit any kind of shortcoming to these women, and especially to Annalee, who clearly wanted Glory to wallow in remorsefulness. "That said, everyone else is going to have a king cake from Gambino's. This is an opportunity to *distinguish* ourselves. One thing I know as a member of the Red Hat Society is that we never rest on our laurels. We stand out. We are well on our way to making this our best Mardi Gras ever."

Everyone nodded and every plate was cleaned. "And with that, this meeting is adjourned," added Glory, trying to end on a high note, adjourning the meeting even though she had no authority to. One thing she'd learned from Constance is that authority isn't real. It's an essence, something one claims.

Delphine and Justice collected the paper plates while Constance and Glory did a temperature check of the mood. "Well, I'd say that was an outstanding meeting, apart from that little outburst from Annalee," said Constance. "Don't pay her any mind. Everyone knows she comes from hateful people."

"I know, I know. I just can't stand that woman. If karma is indeed a real thing, I'd like to see it come around and bite her in the ass."

Justice and Delphine disappeared into the kitchen to finish cleaning, and Annalee circled back to Glory and Constance. "It looks like your highfalutin cake won the ladies over, but you don't have me fooled, Glory Broussard. There wasn't a so-called problem with our Gambino's order. This is all a cover-up for the fact that you forgot to place it. *You're* the problem with our Gambino's order."

"I believe I took responsibility for that," said Glory. "And please do not speak to me with that tone."

"And I've heard rumors that this chef is staying at your house as your daughter's friend, and they're swapping more than recipes, if you know what I mean. My daughter works as a reference librarian at U of L and even saw them kissing in the library. But that's Glory Broussard for you, willing to just let *anyone* in her house, without any kind of due diligence."

Glory leaned forward, readying to cut the bitch down with words alone, but Constance, in a surprise move, firmly grasped Glory's shoulder and inserted herself in front of her. "Is your life that empty, Annalee, that you'd cause a fuss over a *pastry*? It reveals so much about your character. And as for situations at home, don't get me started on that no-good son of yours. If you want to talk about rumors? Let's do it. Rumor has it that the cashier at Piccadilly had a baby by your son, and he doesn't do anything for her. No child support, no visits . . . can't even drop off a box of Pampers. And don't even get me started on why he's *rumored* to be banned from the Acadiana Mall on account of belligerence and threats, with his breath smelling like . . ."

"That is not true!" screamed Annalee. The volume and the frenzied pitch caused all other conversation to come to a screeching halt. Annalee smoothed down her hair. It was the Southern woman's equivalent to bringing the room to order. In a more measured tone, Annalee looked straight at Glory and said, "This organization will rue the day they ever put you in charge of Mardi Gras festivities, our most important fundraiser of the year."

"Go tell that to your son's baby mama," added Constance. Annalee stormed off.

For once, Glory stood in stunned silence. The women of the Red Hat Society fell back into their places, pretending to busy themselves over the coffee and folding up chairs.

Constance walked toward a table, swiping the leftover cakes with her forearm into the trash. Glory approached her. "I . . . I sure appreciate what you said back there."

"It's about time that someone set that Annalee straight. She takes things entirely too far!" She continued to pick up discarded paper plates and plastic utensils and put them into the trash. "How dare she talk to you like that?"

Glory joined in to help Constance with the cleaning. "I appreciate that," she said sheepishly. "Actually, I respect the hell out of you for that." Maybe she'd never be a bosom friend like Amity, but finally, she felt like at least one person in this group had her back, just a little.

28

After the debut of the updated king cake, Justice and Delphine headed back to Glory's house, unaware of the kerfuffle that ensued afterward. The house was always eerily quiet without Glory because she was its beating heart as well as its loud mouth.

"It looks like you won those mean old ladies over," said Delphine, reaching into the refrigerator for some cold brew she made the day before. She poured some into a glass and topped it off with oat milk then headed into the living room.

"Whew, why are those women out to get your mama like that? It's cold-blooded," said Justice.

"The level of disrespect is off the charts. And don't think I didn't hear the murmurs when you walked into the room. I can only guess what those awful women were saying under their breath."

"Yeah, I guess they aren't accustomed to seeing a masculine-presenting woman like me, but they seemed to get over it once they started eating. I guess what they say about the South is really true. They'll talk bad about you, then eat your food. Anyway, I guess all is forgiven."

"*Forgiven*, like you haven't slaved away for the last week in a rented kitchen making dessert for their little party that no one cares about." Delphine took a gulp of the coffee. "There is nothing they need to forgive!"

Justice sat beside her on the living room couch and grabbed her hand. "Don't get yourself worked up over a bunch of mean old women. It's not worth it. I tell you what though, I cannot wait to start my guest-cheffing next week at Pierre's. Your mama and her little crew got me hopping around here like fireworks on a national holiday."

"I'm sorry. You come down here to check in on me, and my mother enlists you into some shenanigans."

"I like your mama," said Justice. "And I told you she's not as judgmental as you think she is. She was fine about us, right?"

"Surprisingly so."

"Quit being so surprised by your mother. Yes, she's a lot, but she's a pretty dynamic woman."

"I guess she is."

Justice leaned her head back, finally able to relax after days slaving in the kitchen to get Glory's king cake right. "I'll just be glad when we're back in New York, so we can relax and get some sushi. And I keep meaning to tell you . . . a group of my friends are going to Tulum in March. You know how brutal it can feel at the end of winter, like there's no end in sight. We always try to get away just when it feels like you're going to snap. You should come."

"Friends, huh? I didn't think we were at the stage of meeting each other's friends?"

"Delphine, I've been living in your childhood home with you and your mama for over a week now. I think you're ready to meet my friends. Unless you don't want to?"

Delphine shifted down the couch, just a little. "It's not that I don't want to meet your friends, I do. I really do. It just feels a tad . . . early? Anyway, I like when it's just you and me, in the apartment cooking and dancing to Marvin Gaye."

Justice's relaxed posture disappeared. "First you didn't want to introduce me to your mother as your girlfriend because you were certain that she'd disapprove. And she was *fine*. Now you don't want to meet my friends because . . . you like it when it's just you and me?" Justice leaned forward, hands on her knees. "I have a feeling some of this has to do with the fact that you're uncomfortable being public in a same-sex relationship. And I also have a hunch that you're emotionally tangled up somehow with that man who stopped by the bakery."

"Why would you say that?" asked Delphine, putting on a somewhat convincing front, trying too hard to sell it. It was exactly what her mother would have done.

"Because of the injured look on his face when he saw us together. And your rush to talk to him privately, where I couldn't hear," she said. "You don't have to be Glory Broussard, private eye, to figure out something that's pretty obvious. I kept it to myself, on the off chance I was wrong, but I can see that I'm right."

Delphine grimaced. "I . . . I didn't mean for any of this to happen this way. Everything has collided in spectacular fashion. If I could go back in time, I would have told you that there was a man in Lafayette still in love with me, and that we had gotten together before Christmas. But I didn't know that he was getting a divorce, or that I'd meet you, or else I would have pumped the brakes."

"Yeah, it would have been helpful to know that," said Justice sarcastically. "So . . . I guess you have unfinished business, and that business doesn't involve me."

"You are a wonderful person, and per usual, I'm the one who's a mess," said Delphine. "I'm sorry I wasn't more clear. But I'm going to be clear now. I don't think we should see each other romantically anymore. You deserve someone who adores you and has the capacity to be in a reciprocal relationship. Right now, I meet only half of that criteria."

If Justice wanted to be angry, she didn't have it in her. "Honestly, I'm the one who should have known better. You straight girls are always a risky investment of the heart. There's only ever a thirty percent chance you'll come over to my team. I knew I was gambling."

"Thirty percent? Where'd you get that number?"

"It's a known fact. Probably from the Council on Straight Girls and their Bullshit."

Delphine glared at her quizzically. Justice's cheeks began to puff up and then she exploded with laughter, with Delphine shortly following suit, releasing all the tension that had been unknowingly building in her body since she arrived in Lafayette.

"But can I give you some advice?" asked Justice, her voice suddenly pivoting to a more serious tone.

"Sure, I suppose I deserve a lecture or whatever it is you're about to say."

"Not a lecture, but something I think you need to hear. Don't run away from the people who love you, starting with your mother. She's so proud of everything that you've accomplished, and yet sometimes you act as if you're burdened by all her pride."

"It is a tiny bit embarrassing that she's a bookie, don't you think? And the way she carries on?"

"If we were talking about someone else's mother, and that imaginary 'someone else's mother' was a bookie who had solved a crime and wears whatever delights her, no matter how loud, I'm pretty sure you'd feel differently about her. What I'm saying is, she's familiar to you, but she's actually pretty remarkable. I wish you could see that and brush off that stank attitude of yours."

"Stank attitude?"

Justice kept going. "And speaking of someone else that loves you, if you feel as strongly as I suspect you do about this Lieutenant Landry, you should sit in that for a while. We'd be lucky to have one great love in our lives, and I think you have one. He won't be single forever."

Delphine exhaled. "Here we are, breaking up, and yet somehow you manage to summon a tremendous spirit of generosity. How?"

Justice smirked and ran her fingers along the shaved side of her head. "I know I'll be okay, because what you never fully understood is how fine I am. Do you know the number of ladies that slide into my DMs since I was a guest on *Top Chef*? I've been ignoring them, but now that we're moving on, maybe I'll hit some of them up."

"You're going to go trolling in your DMs for a girlfriend?"

"It's not trolling if they come to me," she said with the swagger of a rap star.

"Well, I guess I'll tell my mom she'll have to order her king cake from Meche's. None of them deserved any special dessert anyway."

"Oh no, I'm seeing that through. We already presented the cake to the members and they're all excited. I can't have those Red Hat ladies talking trash about my girl. Your mama is about to have the best king cake in town, I will see to that personally."

"What did I ever do to deserve you?"

"You don't, really, but your mama does. I do not intend to let her down."

29

One thing Glory watched every morning was the weather report. It was essential for her trade to understand how the weather might impact upcoming games. She was also of the age in which weather was also entertainment. She monitored the precipitation and storms all around the country. *Did you see those wildfires they're having in Oklahoma? They're about to have some big snow up in Colorado. Big snow.* On this particular occasion she was watching because they were driving all the way to Mississippi, which was a little over three hours but might as well be Bermuda, by the way Glory was carrying on. By the time they set out, Glory knew the temperature, expected rainfall, relative humidity, and elevation of Jackson and every town in between.

Glory sat in the back seat, studying the clouds. "I told y'all the weather was going to be bad," said Glory, miffed that she had been forced to venture out in a well-publicized rainstorm. Rain pelted the roof of the car, pounding like nails. Glory's stomach tensed when the tires seemed to lose traction with the road.

Delphine nearly hydroplaned over a slick of water. Glory clutched the overhead grab handle near her window in dramatic fashion. "*Go easy*. I just got my brake pads changed."

Delphine spoke up. "I'm sorry for dragging us out in the rain, but it took me a few days to confirm these addresses. This may be our best chance to identify the owner of that knife. Feels like we needed to drive out immediately." She struggled to see through the windshield. "My God, this rain. Must be global warming," Delphine added.

"Severe storms are getting more common," said Justice. "It's going to affect our food supply, and what gets served in restaurants. We're living in the last golden age of food availability."

"Global warming has got this planet barking at us humans, and rightfully so," added Glory. "I sure am glad I lived my little life already, so I don't have to see how this all ends. That'll be your problem to sort out."

Justice looked up from her phone, horrified, which Delphine happened to catch. "I know, just when you think you've gotten used to my mother, she manages to say something even more shocking. I've known the woman my entire life and she still catches me by surprise."

Glory ignored them and changed the topic. "So, you mean to tell me that we're driving in this god-awful rain and this man doesn't even know we're coming?"

"Nope. He didn't answer the phone. I think the only way to confirm is to visit that location. None of the chefs I spoke to have met him," said Justice, who once again seemed thrilled to be on an adventure.

The ride had already been an hour, with two hours and change left. The rain had lulled Delphine into a kind of locked-in focus behind the wheel as she tried her best to avoid more hydroplaning that sent Glory into chest-clutching dramatics. Justice sat in the passenger seat content to tap away on her phone and occasionally cracking up to whatever was playing in the wireless earbuds, magically suspended in her ear.

It was really something to watch Delphine and Justice get along the way they did, especially now that they had broken up, Glory thought. Delphine had encouraged Glory to date, but they both knew that was never going to happen. Any goodness Sterling had in him, any ability to be the halfway decent person that Valerie seemed to enjoy? Glory did that. She'd rather pour that energy into herself now, for how many days remained. And men her age? No, thank you. Glory was not about to let some aging man who needed a caregiver more than a wife latch himself onto her. Even in exchange for a few good years, she was not going to sign up to be a hospice wife. Glory's introspection was interrupted by the blinking of the car's turn signal and a hard veer to the right.

"This gas station has the best crackling in the whole state. Justice researched it," said Delphine. A few moments later the car was parked, the women entered, and Justice was chatting up the gas station manager/cook about his recipe and methods for coaxing the best flavor and texture out of fried pork skin.

Glory leaned against the counter and chomped into the crispy fat. "Y'all got me eating at a gas station like I'm some kind of long-haul truck driver. They should at least have a counter with some little stools if they're going to sell food, don't you think?"

"Nah. That would ruin the vibes."

"*Vibes.*" Glory tsked.

The dramatic lights of a diesel truck shone through the store window. Delphine sipped on her fountain root beer and worked up enough gumption to address the situation between her mom and Valerie. "So . . . you're just never going to talk to Valerie again?"

Delphine had had to forcibly block Valerie from physically harming her mother after the scissor incident, and it had rattled Glory more than she could have anticipated. She trembled on the ride home, hoping her daughter hadn't seen her shaky hands on the steering wheel, but knowing that she probably did. Glory had tried to put the argument out of her mind. "You make it sound like we were friends to begin with. You can't love someone less when you don't like them in the first place."

"I know she regrets what she said," offered Delphine. "I think if you would just apologize everything could be forgiven . . ."

Glory's face looked like it might if she had hydroplaned on a slick of water and drove off a bridge. "I didn't do anything wrong! She is the one who tried to attack *me*!" The fluorescent lights of the gas station flickered above, and Justice was happy behind a deep fryer, taking notes.

"Mom, you—"

"Yes, I know I threw a pair of scissors at her mirror, but she had that coming the way she was running off at the mouth. How dare she talk to me like that?" She remembered her blood pressure and took a few beats. "And if anything, I'm the one who's courting disaster, breaking a mirror and bringing all that bad luck down on my head."

"Yes, Mom, you're the victim here." Delphine went to the fountain station to refill her root beer. Glory was grateful for a few seconds to compose herself. What had angered her most was this ongoing conversation between That Woman and her daughter. The fact that her daughter appeared to be brokering some kind of peace between the two of them meant, of course, that they were still talking.

It made her blood boil hotter than that vat of grease Justice was standing over.

The quiet that filled the space between them was punctured with the question that had been in Glory's head the entire car ride up. "How is it that you and Justice aren't at each other's throats since you guys broke up?" As far as Glory could tell, Justice had admirably rushed down to Delphine's hometown to comfort her, only to be broken up with by her daughter who appeared to be in love with a local boy.

"Not everything needs to be a battle. We dated, and it didn't work out. It doesn't mean our lives are over. And it doesn't mean we hate each other." She took a bite of her dessert—a popcorn ball held together with Steen's cane syrup.

Glory mulled this over. When Sterling left her for Valerie, her life really did feel over. Panic seized her chest every night when she wondered how she would pay the real estate taxes and the car note. She made it work, but it had felt impossible at the time.

Delphine continued. "If you could somehow reprogram your brain to realize not everything is a war, I think you'd feel a lot lighter. Not everyone is out to get you, you know."

Little does she know, Glory thought.

With the rain slowing the journey to a crawl, they drove another four hours before arriving at an anonymous warehouse clad in galvanized steel. Delphine drove through a narrow opening in the chain-link fence that surrounded the property. Naturally, the rain had stopped the moment Delphine turned the engine off and they parked in a gravel lot.

"So, I've been thinking about a plan of attack," said Glory, back in a wartime mindset. "Justice, we are going to need you to do the talking." Delphine nodded in agreement.

"Me?" Justice responded. "Oh no, I don't even know what to ask. You two are the private investigators. And no one gets people talking quicker than you, Glory."

"I've made up my mind and you, Miss Justice, will be taking the lead. I don't know anything about this man, or knives, or chefs, or that world. But you do. You speak his language."

Justice sighed. "First you got me making pastries and I'm not even a pastry chef. Now you got me out here looking for clues of a murder weapon."

"Yes. It's my singular charm."

"Fine . . . what information am I trying to extract, exactly?"

"I've been thinking about this. I highly doubt Sterling knew some fancy chef, let alone was murdered by one. But we need to know who the knife belonged to, and then I guess we go about figuring out who might have worked in that kitchen."

Justice seemed to be getting over her hesitation of being conscripted into this caper. "Got it."

The women did their best to dodge puddles of water as they made their way to the front door. *Cleotus Farmington, Fine Blades* was forged into a large plate of steel, which hung from chains above the door. Glory looked around to make sure everyone was ready, then rang the buzzer. The doorbell made a roaring sound, like a lion. Or a dragon. Glory rolled her eyes. "Men are so dramatic."

The man who opened the door had a bald head, a long gray beard, and a face that looked like a calloused hand. He had the look of one of the men she grew up with in her neighborhood, the kind that used the weekly Knights of Columbus meeting to discuss Klan business. Fortunately, she was experienced in handling these kinds of men.

She thrust a ramrod-straight hand in his direction. "Glory Broussard. Nice to meet you." You couldn't show any weakness with these old rednecks, thought Glory. At the very least, they sometimes had a begrudging kind of respect for an older Black woman, who probably raised them and cleaned their homes.

He paused, looked at them suspiciously, and then wiped his hands against dirty overalls, which seemed pointless. He shook Glory's hand.

"I know you're not expecting us, but we need to speak with you about a murder, and a knife of yours that may have been involved."

He gathered his beard in his right hand. "Ahh . . . so that's why the police have been calling around."

"You talked to the police?" asked Glory, surprised. It was true she had told the officer to look into the knife, but she was amazed that they had narrowed it down. But it was also true that she would like to be the one to solve this case. After all, she had invested a lot of personal time in this matter.

"They been leaving messages," he said.

Delphine tilted her head to the side. "We would have liked to call first, but I couldn't find a number. I did find this address. The man who was murdered was my father, so I hope you'll forgive us."

"Don't worry, I didn't talk to the cops. Not a big fan, if you know what I mean."

Glory prodded Justice to the front.

Justice took this as her sign. "Nice to meet you, Mr. Farmington. I'm Justice Harris. First, let me say I'm a chef and a huge fan of yours. Daniel Boulud once allowed me to use one of your blades for the day, and it was remarkable. It's almost like your knives have two personalities . . . strength and flexibility. Leather and lace. It's strong but bends when you need it to."

He had heard enough. He opened the oversized door and let them enter.

A pit of fire was the first thing that Glory noticed. Orange flames leapt like trained gymnasts inside a shoulder-height cauldron. Hand tools were strewn across a large wooden table that took up at least half of the studio. Justice gasped when she saw the wall at the other end of the table.

Dozens of knives clung to a magnetic wall. As if in a trance, Justice walked over to inspect them. Some had handles of ebony or rosewood. Others, mahogany. Each had carvings of his signature celestial designs, though no design was exactly the same. From the knives dangled white tags with names of the chefs who had ordered them. The three-starred Michelin chef who had recently lost a star and would now have to face the world with this shame. The chef in Sweden whose restaurant had a years-long waiting list. The restaurateur who was seldom seen after his #MeToo scandal and had retired, permanently, to his vacation home in Michigan.

Classical music filled the air and wood shavings crowded the floor. "What are you listening to?" asked Delphine. Their organized front seemed to be falling apart inside the wonder of his studio.

He inhaled deeply, the way a person does when they are consuming something they love. "Ah, that's Florence Price. The first Black woman recognized as a composer of symphonies, and the first to have her compositions played by a major orchestra. She's just now getting the credit she deserves in the canon of American classical music."

As much as Glory liked to think she could play it cool at all times, her face occasionally betrayed her. Cleotus laughed. "I know you must think I'm some kind of redneck, with my knife making and dirty overalls. I don't blame you."

Then, it was Justice's turn to lose her cool. Her hand trembled, and she pointed at a red box of chocolates at the table. "Is that what I think it is?" she asked.

"One of the perks of working with the best chefs in the world is that they routinely send me treats. For those I decline as customers, they sometimes send me bribes. Help yourself."

"You said no to Jean-Pierre Beaumont?" She took a piece of chocolate into her mouth and groaned in ecstasy.

He sat down on a stool at his worktable. "So, one day, this guy calls me up with a French accent, sounding just like that skunk from the cartoon. You know, all Pepé Le Pew. And says he wants to outfit his entire kitchen with my knives and wants to fly me to Paris, all expenses paid, for a tour. Now, I don't normally do things like that, but it was my wedding anniversary, so I thought . . . why not? Free trip for me and the wife. I toured that man's kitchen, and he's all professional and shit. Everything is on point. Then an assistant knocks over some melted chocolate onto the floor, and this guy goes apeshit. Loses his goddamn mind at this young woman. And I decided right then and there—he would never get one of my knives. He still sends me a box of chocolates every month, hoping I'll change my mind."

Glory let her guard down. "Now I gotta get me some of that chocolate." She marched over and popped a piece into her mouth, tasting carefully to see if it was worth the hype.

"But I gotta say, this is the first time one of my knives has ever been used in a murder. That's a new one. You got the knife with you?"

Glory reached into her handbag. "That's evidence now. Property of the Lafayette Police Department. What I do have is a picture, though." Landry, convinced she'd have more success than his own department, complied. She unfolded a color printout and smoothed it on the table. Cleotus reached into the front pocket of his overalls for a pair of reading glasses.

He stared at the picture and caressed his beard, like it had powers of divination. "It's usually pretty difficult for me to tell my knives from a photograph. But I remember this knife precisely. I made it for Chef Donna Gibson, owner of that restaurant down in Galveston. Specialized in Gulf Coast seafood. It's one of my early knives. You can tell by the design on the handle. I was only doing just a few stars at that time, not entire constellations."

"Are you still in touch with her? Can you let us know how we might reach her?" asked Delphine.

"Afraid not. Passed away about five years ago. Tremendous chef, terrible drunk. Cirrhosis of the liver."

Defeat sunk into the women's faces.

"Any idea what might have happened to her knife? Or who might have been the last owner?" Delphine asked.

"Once I sell a knife, it's out of my hands. Afraid I can't help you out."

Silently the women racked their brains to ask whatever last questions they might have about the knife, or how it ended up in Sterling's chest, but there were none. Cleotus walked over to his wall of knives and loosened one. He worked it into a canvas roll and handed it to Justice. "For you."

She was nothing short of astonished. "For me? Whoa . . . I can't."

Glory rolled her eyes. "Girl, you better take that knife and say thank you."

He smiled. "This, my dear, is for the James Beard Rising Star Chef of the Year honor bestowed to you a few months ago. Won't be long before your first Michelin star."

"How did you know that?" asked Justice, astonished.

"It's my job to know the comings and goings on the scene."

"You just be a foodie, too," added Glory.

He flinched. "I guess you could say that, but I don't prefer that word. It's a little common. Minimizes the craft behind the food." He looked at Justice and winked.

The women were gathering to leave, and right before Cleotus closed the door, he walked over to a chest and pulled out a glossy red bag, sagging at the bottom from its weight. "I'm not really into sweets," he said, and handed Glory a bag of chocolates from Jean-Pierre Beaumont. Justice later estimated the chocolates to retail at over $1,000.

30

"Stop tugging on my hair like that," said Glory, seated at the kitchen table, her daughter towering over her. "I'm about to be bald by your hand because you're being too rough."

Delphine ignored her, stretching her wet hair taught with a bristle brush and wrapping it tightly in a large roller. "Well, you could have gotten your hair done by Valerie and her stylists with the other Red Hat women. Heard they rented the entire salon for glam before tonight's gala. But no, you went ahead and torched that bridge to the ground."

A bridge is only useful to get where you want to go, and Glory wasn't interested in traveling any further with That Woman. But she kept this to herself. *Personal growth*, she applauded herself and rewarded herself by biting into another chocolate from Cleotus Farmington's workshop.

Delphine looked a little closer at her mother's scalp. "You know, I think your hair would look a lot thicker if you cut it. Maybe even a short cut! You'd look like Judi Dench. Here, let me show you." Delphine whipped out her phone to show her mother a picture.

Glory didn't mention that Valerie had told her the same thing. She scrutinized a picture of an older, but sturdy, woman with chic gray hair. "I'm not opposed to doing something like that, but this isn't New York City. We don't have those kinds of hairdressers in Lafayette. If I ever find someone good down here, though, I'll inquire about this Judy Blume haircut."

"Judi *Dench*."

"You know me, I can't remember these names like you do."

Justice entered the room wearing her starched chef jacket and clutching a notebook. This notebook had been a constant companion ever since she arrived in Lafayette. Inside were the culinary secrets of southwest Louisiana. The seasonings used for Billy's Boudin off I-10. A step-by-step tutorial for making the turducken at Herbert's Specialty Meats. And as of last night, the crackling recipe from the gas station.

Justice poured herself a lukewarm cup of coffee from the coffeepot.

"Girl, I can practically see the nerves jumping off of you," said Glory. "Relax. Everyone loved your dessert. It's already a hit. Believe me, those women would have torn you limb from limb if they didn't."

Justice nearly spit out her coffee.

"It's just a figure of speech," Glory assured her.

Justice wasn't as sure. "I can't wait to get back to New York, where I'm safe from the over-sixty crowd." She took a final sip of coffee and smoothed her jacket. "Anyway, gotta run. See you both tonight."

Glory stopped her. "Don't forget your new knife."

Justice, relieved for the reminder, took the rolled-up knife from the kitchen counter and waved goodbye.

Delphine continued to section Glory's hair, yanking her head again in the process. Glory bit her tongue, not wanting to hear yet again about how Valerie would have done it. Once you throw a pair of scissors at a mirror, you really can't go back.

"So, I've been doing some research about who worked with Donna Gibson in Galveston, and this isn't going to be easy," said Delphine. "Restaurant workers are nomadic, ready to jump ship for an extra dollar an hour. And a lot of people work off the books. I stayed up last night reaching out to about a dozen people I found who were connected to the restaurant, and so far I don't see any connection to Dad."

She pinned a final curl into place and wrapped Glory's roller-set up in a black hairnet, tying it with a bow in the front.

"Keep working whatever connections you can find online, and I guess I'll keep working the casino and the horse track. One thing I do know for sure is that both places are cesspools of illegal activity. They are shooting up those poor animals at that track. And you know me, I do not prefer animals. The only reason I have this damn cat is because that five-dollar psychic convinced me it was some kind of talisman. But what they are doing to those animals is wrong. And then we've got the casino, where I know that dealer is in cahoots with players to steal money, which bothers me less in the grand scheme of things. If you can find a way to beat the house, good on you. Also, it's not my problem. But it seemed your daddy hated working there toward the end. Maybe there's not a connection to his death, but I'd sure like to find out."

Delphine wheeled the portable hood dryer from the laundry room into the kitchen. "Maybe Daddy knew about it and was going to expose them as part of his role as security?"

"Possible. But he wasn't exactly the type to go snitching to a boss. If anything, he'd have tried to figure out how to get a cut."

"I guess." Delphine positioned the hood over Glory's head and turned on the heat.

"Girl, my hair is fragile. I can't be having all this heat on my strands."

Delphine lowered the heat on the dryer and yawned. "I'm going to take a nap while your hair dries. Do not take these rollers out until your hair is completely dry, or else you'll show up to tonight's Mardi Gras gala looking like a cotton ball." She yawned again, and her face was thin with worry. Glory could tell that she was wearing the stress of Sterling's death and all the tumult from her personal life heavy.

Glory's hair had thinned so much over the years that it didn't take but twenty minutes for it to dry. It was another indignity of aging, along with painful feet and a sore back.

Once her hair was dry, the real preparations for the gala began. First, she loosened the rollers from her hair and then smoothed the curls with a large brush. What remained were loose bouncing curls, which she arranged just so. She then hit up her hairline with a bit of mascara to camouflage the grays that she couldn't manage to get colored.

She pondered the full-body shapewear that Delphine had encouraged her to buy. Maybe it would smooth out a few of the lumps, but you don't get to be Glory's age without a few imperfections. She decided against it. She knew she wasn't fooling anybody.

Glory's clock radio, an ancient Sony Dream Machine, had a CD player. The top of her dresser was dotted with jewelry as well as a row of CDs. She thumbed through them, skipping *The Commodores Greatest Hits*, which would only resurface bad memories. She settled on Aretha Franklin and one of her favorite songs, "I Say a Little Prayer." Now it was time to get ready.

Unofficially, every member wore red for big events, and the Mardi Gras gala was the biggest of them all. But as she was chair of the committee, she decided to set herself apart. A white sequined jumpsuit dangled from a padded hanger against Glory's bathroom door. She had seen it first online, and then asked Delphine to buy it for her because she hated buying things on the internet. She tried to pay her daughter back, but Delphine refused. Glory intended to hide four, one hundred dollar bills in her carry-on before she went back home.

Glory knew the white sequined jumpsuit would get those old women talking, and if she was honest, she was excited at the prospect of being talked about. Something in her had changed since she had solved Amity's murder. Everyone in town had started talking about her. And not under their breath like they usually did, but openly. Maybe it wasn't a bad thing? She'd decided that, given a choice, she'd rather be the talk of the town than be boring.

The jumpsuit looked good on her, especially with the belt Delphine bought for her to complete the look. It was thin and had two red tassels at the end, a nod to the membership. Delphine had lectured her on the importance of accessories and also bought her a pair of white platform sandals with red soles. Truth be told, her feet were still aching from the flat ballet shoes she had worn to see Milton in prison, but the sandals did look phenomenal with the outfit. And she knew the red sole was supposed to signify some kind of designer that she didn't know or care about. But her fellow members would, and she didn't mind that the shoes would get those tongues wagging yet again.

Soon enough, she could hear the sink running in the hall bathroom, which meant that Delphine didn't take much of a nap. Her daughter walked into her bedroom like her old self. The braids were gone, and so was the nose ring.

"What happened to your braids?" asked Glory. The stiff, straight braids had vanished. In their place were soft curls that reached just below her shoulders.

"I couldn't fall asleep, so I decided to take them out," she said. "I guess it was time." Glory said nothing as her daughter fussed over her belt and arranged Glory's makeup on the bed before starting to apply to to her face. A crisp, thin line of black opened Glory's wide, almond eyes. With tear-shaped sponges Delphine buffed away the darker areas on Glory's skin, providing a smooth canvas for the rest of her makeup. Brows were filled in and made symmetrical. Cheekbones were contoured to their best advantage.

Glory knew she shouldn't be meddling, but she couldn't resist. "Have you heard from Landry recently?"

"Mom—"

"I know, I know, as your mother I am on a need-to-know basis. But as Glory Broussard, I simply cannot help myself."

"You're always acting as if you have no control over your emotions and actions, Mom. That isn't true. I've seen you exhibit a tremendous amount of restraint, with your clients, with the police . . . just about everywhere, in fact. Except when it comes to me."

Glory held a mirror up inspecting her face and listening to Aretha sing about feeling like a natural woman. "I'm just saying. When a man has harbored a love for a woman over years, and in your case decades, that flame does not get snuffed out so easily. You walk around like it's common."

One of the outcomes of Glory's difficult marriage was that it made her something of an expert on identifying good men versus bad men. Landry? He'd always been good. From a kid to now. Sometimes the nice ones get overlooked.

"So, you're suggesting I go begging to Landry?"

Glory dabbed her lips with a tissue. "No, I am merely telling you to think twice before you throw that away. You hear me?"

Begrudgingly, Delphine agreed. "I hear you." She went to Glory's dresser and found a pair of bejeweled Mardi Gras mask earrings. One earring was of a downturned face, the other in a state of crazy surprise. "You look good, Mom."

She'd take it. The gala was bound to be full of surprises. Even though she had maintained an air of unflappable calm on the phone with Franklin, she knew it was time to walk into the hornet's nest.

31

Preparations were in full effect by the time Glory arrived at the St. Agnes gala. The Grand Oak Ballroom of The Pelican Club was designed to impress. The walls had a French Regency–style wallpaper, and crystal chandeliers dangled from the ceilings throughout the venue. Tables were draped in gold tablecloths and topped with purple and gold masks, not to mention Mardi Gras beads of every hue and size. To the side of the room, at least two dozen chafing dishes were being set up by frazzled workers, which would warm every Louisiana specialty possible—from étouffée and gumbos to maque choux and fried oysters. For dessert, Justice's unique version of king cake would be served, and either their five hundred or so guests would love it or whisper about how Glory had ruined Mardi Gras.

She heard a clicking of heels that she would recognize anywhere. Wherever that clicking sound could be heard, Constance Wheeler could also be found with a clipboard in her hands. In fact, she carried *two* clipboards.

"Oh Lord, must be a lot of things to check off if you brought two clipboards," said Glory.

"I brought one for you. So we could review all the open items together."

The two women shared complicated circumstances, but it was clear to Glory that her stubborn insistence on not thanking Constance for her efforts was petty, even for her. "Constance, I just want to thank you for your help with planning all of this. I suppose I didn't realize how in-depth this would all be, what with the logistics and all. I just want to say I appreciate your help."

Constance couldn't disguise her surprise, but she was a lot like Glory—neither could stand to linger in an emotional scene. She quickly reverted back to her default high-handed nature. "You are quite welcome. When the annual gala is a success, the entire organization wins." A few other Red Hat members wandered in early, turning over the tableware and inspecting the quality of the beads. "You know, I'm beginning to see how you've been treated a little unfairly by the other women. Look at them, inspecting the tabletops as if this is a state dinner," Constance added.

"Turns out your life depends on this trivial shit when you've got nothing else to do."

"I suppose you're right." She gave Glory a good look up and down. "I must say, you're not helping matters with this shimmering getup. They are all going to fall out when they see you. You know we wear red on these occasions." Her tone was cautionary.

"I have a red belt. And the soles of my sandals are red."

"Don't think I didn't notice those shoes." Constance pointed at Glory's feet with a pen. "You look about a size nine? If so, I do intend to borrow those." She gave the shoes another glance and raised an eyebrow. "Here. Take this clipboard so we can do our final walk-through. We might even be able to pregame with some champagne before any more members arrive. We're going to need it."

Past the swinging doors of the kitchen they found Justice behind a burner, stirring the raspberry sauce for the cake and reducing it until it was the correct consistency. The beautifully etched handle of her Cleotus Farmington knife was visible from a holster tied around her waist.

"That looks real good," said Constance. "How we got to this dessert no longer matters. This will be a grand finale for the ages."

Glory was humbled and in the mood for more acknowledgments. She had been saved from total humiliation by these two women. "I want to thank you again—"

Justice interrupted before she could launch into her full statement of gratitude. "No thank you needed. I was glad to do it."

Now it was Constance's turn to weigh in. "Young woman, I would advise you to let Glory praise thanks upon you. It's not often she recognizes others."

"You see, that is why we can't have anything nice," Glory retorted. "Someone always has to ruin the moment."

The hired caterers prepared the étouffée and the boudin balls behind them at a kitchen worktable. Glory was surprised to see Marguerite dicing tomatoes for the salad and marched her way.

"Marguerite, what are you doing here? I'm surprised you're not tending to the horses on a busy night like this."

Marguerite grabbed a towel and dried her hands. "Busy night for the casino, not the horses. I do catering jobs here and there for some extra cash when I can."

"Now that is a hard worker," piped Constance, who clicked her pen and continued to check things off her list.

"It's a shame that they don't pay their people more at that stable. That is some real backbreaking work."

"Hard for anyone to make a living wage these days," said Marguerite.

"Ain't that the truth." Glory grabbed a mini boudin ball as a snack.

"Stay focused, Glory," snapped Constance. "We have thirty-seven items on this list left to review."

"Good to see you, Marguerite. My task master demands that I follow her . . ."

Marguerite saluted her, like Glory was a general inspecting the troops before a battle. It wasn't that far from the truth.

Not long after, ticket holders to the evening's festivities began to trickle in. Within an hour, a sea of red washed over the dance floor. The zydeco band's lead singer was a well-known celebrity in town. His honeyed falsetto could have loosened the panties on any woman in the ballroom. Even religious women are not immune from temptations—not from a man that fine and with a voice so sweet. Along with the dessert that Justice was preparing, the band would be a triumph of the evening.

Her head was on a swivel for T-Red, or anyone who might have the look of mischief in their eyes. But so far, everyone was just enjoying the evening. Her feet were beginning to swell in her designer sandals. She thought of sitting down, just for a minute, when her moment of peace was interrupted. Glory's teeth clenched when she saw that none other than Valerie was headed her way. It was just like her to show up at an event that had been planned by Glory. She truly couldn't have anything of her own. Valerie LeBlanc would be sure of it.

Valerie wiggled about, wearing a red bustier and cigarette pants. But you want to know what really incensed Glory? The train. Or was it a bustle? Whatever it was, it was entirely too much glamor for Lafayette. Who did she think she was? The Black Marilyn Monroe?

Valerie headed toward Glory, who did not budge. Whatever happened, it was going to be gossiped about for a long while. Glory was determined to hold her own. "Thank you so much for the invitation. I figured after everything that happened I wouldn't be hearing from you again. But you, Glory Broussard, are full of surprises. A ticket to the annual Red Hat Society Mardi Gras gala usually sells out by Thanksgiving, so I appreciate the invite."

"It was Delphine," Glory said. "But I am glad you could make it." She clenched her toes to avoid visibly clenching her fists and popping the woman in the face.

"I figured as much, but I do appreciate it. I've always wanted to come to this gala but could never buy a ticket because of . . ." She struggled for words.

"Me."

"Yes, I suppose. That would have been awkward after all that transpired. At any rate, I've been meaning to say this for some time—"

Glory interrupted. "It's good to see you. Enjoy the party." She had no patience for whatever little speech That Woman had planned. And besides, she had members to mingle with and other things to do, like keep this gala on track.

From the corner of her eye, she could see a number of contemptible Red Hat members lifting up the glassware and holding it up to the light, hoping to see spots. When none could be found, they rifled through the floral arrangements on the table, praying to find a wilted blossom to complain about. Glory laughed to herself. The only thing withered in attendance was Annalee, who probably brought her own king cake to spite Glory. She tracked Annalee's large chest that seemed to drag down to where a belt should reside. Even though Glory despised Annalee, especially after the snide remarks she had made about Delphine, she lamented the sad state of brassieres. Someone along the way convinced women that comfort was a priority, when what they needed most was underwire. Annalee could keep dissecting every element of the gala. She would find no flaws.

Glory startled at a push from behind. She turned around to see an apologetic server, who had just nudged her with a tray. She scanned the room again for trouble. Franklin had warned her that T-Red threatened to cause problems, and she had not forgotten. The good news was that if she didn't see him, his loud suit would announce itself. So far, there was no sign of either.

Glory saw Lieutenant Beau Landry walking her way. He looked better in a suit than he ever looked in his uniform, and something about the boutonniere in his coat jacket indicated that maybe there was still hope between him and Delphine. He was clearly trying to look good for someone, and Glory doubted she was the intended target.

He leaned in for a hug. "Miss Glory, the early reviews of St. Agnes's 31st Annual Red Hat gala are in. Everyone is raving. They're surprised you pulled this off."

"You know you're winning when the haters start chirping," she replied. "And look at you! Sometimes I forget that you are now a handsome eligible bachelor. I'm sure there are many women who would love to help you ease back into dating, if you know what I mean."

He looked down briefly. "I don't think I'll be doing any of that any time soon."

Glory hesitated, but then made her move. "Well, when you're ready, just file away in that head of yours that Delphine is single. She broke up with that Justice. Between you and me, I think that was just an experiment anyway."

He tugged at his bow tie. His face reddened and then he spoke quickly. "Maybe that's true. But I was thinking about things. I've spent too long chasing after women that don't want me half as much as I want them, whether it's my wife . . . or ex-wife. Or Delphine. I think next time around, I'm going to find someone whose heart skips a beat when I enter the room."

Glory stood there, in a rare moment, unsure of what to say next.

He already looked like he had said too much, betrayed too much of the heartbreak inside of him, and was eager to change the subject. He looked over to the Red Hat table where Millie Broward and some of the older members of the Red Hat Society were sitting and waving him over. "I went over to say hello to Miss Pearl and somehow committed to dancing with all the women at that table."

Glory sucked her lip. "We call that group The Black Widows, on account of all their husbands being dead. You watch out now, you hear?"

He nodded and headed over to the table where The Black Widows devoured him with their eyes.

She'd have to revisit this Landry and Delphine situation another time, because the party was now in full swing. The band had launched into their zydeco-tinged covers of popular songs. The keyboardist raked his fingers across his electric keys, and it took just a few notes of "I Want You Back" by The Jackson 5 before the crowd erupted, ready for the second half of the evening. Diners were finishing up their bowls of crawfish étouffée, made from a homemade stock of shrimp shells and rich butter and cream. They were so full that they didn't seem to notice that the wine had been purchased in bulk from Costco, which Justice had recommended. She claimed that, because they were bought in volume, they had better quality than most. Glory knew any kind of cheap rinse would be met with approval, especially after a few warming sips.

Speaking of cheap rinse, Glory decided she wouldn't mind a little herself. She had declined a pregame party drink with Constance, but now that the party was deemed a success, she could relax. A server with a silver tray floated by with a prepoured glass, which Glory lifted from the tray and thanked the woman. She was about to finally allow her shoulders to settle down into a natural position when she saw T-Red behind the server. He was smiling directly at Glory.

T-Red was as ostentatious as usual, in a purple pin-striped suit and a matching hat with a green feather. Where does one even buy such loud clothes? She would have commended him for adhering to a theme if he wasn't such a vile human being.

"Glory Broussard, imagine finding you here," he said, taking her hand and bending at the waist.

She snatched her hand back toward her chest. "Everyone in Lafayette knows I'm here tonight, so you can take your little performance elsewhere. Not to mention the fact that I'm the one who sold you tickets."

"My, my, my. As the organizer of tonight's festivities, I'd expect a little more hospitality."

"Oh, you mean like the hospitality I got when I was booted out of your casino?"

"Look, I know it's real embarrassing for a woman of your age to be exposed with a drinking problem. You must have had too much wine, like that swill you're serving tonight."

Glory had been cut down by men like this her entire life. It never seemed to stop, but at least she wasn't surprised. "I suppose you get used to talking to people of all sorts way down there at the casino. But here, at my event, I expect you to comport yourself with some semblance of manners. I see that you tried to dress the part tonight, which I appreciate. Where do you even find attire this tacky? At any rate, I hope you will address the other women of the Red Hat Society with more kindness than you've spoken with me tonight. If not, you're welcome to take yourself back to that house of ill repute." She turned around, but then faced him again. "And please remove your hat indoors." Glory walked away, happy to see Franklin and Noah nearby, watching closely. She could count those two, along with Landry, as the good ones.

The partygoers were oblivious to the confrontation. The music played on. Folks danced drunkenly, all pretenses gone, and Glory headed toward the kitchen. It was clear that no one was going to be handing Glory easy wins tonight. Even though everyone agreed that this was the best Mardi Gras gala that they'd had in recent memory, somehow the devil managed to send enough emissaries to ruin her night. It started with Valerie, trotting in like some kind of show pony in her little costume. And in front of the Red Hat membership? She should have predicted this. A harlot only cares about the spotlight. And then T-Red strutting in, looking like Grimace in his tacky suit? It was almost enough to dampen the evening. Almost.

What she needed, in addition to more of the house wine, was a taste of that dessert Justice had prepared for the party. She was hungry and had barely eaten anything from the buffet, which was being carted away. Surely a little sugar in her blood would calm her nerves. When she swung the kitchen doors open, she was surprised to find Justice with her face in her palms. Panic sprinted across her face.

"What is going on back here?" asked Glory. "I've never seen anyone look so depressed at a party."

Delphine rubbed Justice's back, the way a mother does with a child who is ill. "Worse. All the desserts are burned."

"How the hell did that happen?" snapped Glory. Missing the king cake cutoff from Gambino's had been disastrous enough, and she had worked hard to sell Justice's vision. The night was turning into a disaster of epic proportions.

"I told you both I'm not a pastry chef. I told you!" screamed Justice, who seemed to be unraveling with the pressure. "Put me on a grill, I'm fine. A sous chef, I can handle anything. But I just can't with these pastries. It's just too much detail. Too precise. I set a timer but still managed to ruin everything."

"Now, now," said Glory, seeing now that her harsh tone had not helped one bit. "I'm sure we can figure out something. These are not astute diners. Just douse it with powdered sugar or something, these women are not going to know."

Delphine nodded her head in agreement. "The *New York Times* food critic is not here for a review. This is a bunch of tasteless elderly women as soused as a fruitcake right about now. No one knows left from right at this moment. They won't know that your dessert is overcooked by a few minutes."

Glory first did a double take, on account of her daughter's snap judgment, and then agreed. "She's right. Just take that fancy knife of yours, scrape off the burned bits, and dust a mountain of powdered sugar on top."

"It's the same thing just . . . *deconstructed*." Delphine could see Justice starting to come around.

"I suppose we have no choice," Justice agreed.

"I can help," said Glory, reaching for one of the kitchen jackets and putting it over her sequined jumpsuit.

"Me, too," piped Marguerite, who had been washing dishes. "You wouldn't know it, but I'm real good with a pastry bag. Once worked as an assistant pastry chef down in Galveston. With a real famous chef named Donna Gibson, or at least she was famous down in Texas. Justice, you ever heard of her?"

Justice was right. Louisiana was truly wild. "Oh yeah . . . I think I've heard of her."

"Real shame she passed away the way she did," said Marguerite, closing the door to the dishwasher. "I'm happy to help if I can."

Had the entire kitchen witnessed the revelation sink into the faces of Glory, Delphine, and Justice, all at the same time?

32

"Come on now, tell me how you want this plated, and I'll get started." Marguerite was eager to help a trio of women who wanted none of her assistance, and who were horrified by what they now believed to be true. Marguerite snapped them out of it. "Those women are going to get violent if you don't get some sugar in their bloodstreams in about fifteen minutes. You know how they are. They will absolutely slaughter you. Won't they, Glory?"

Glory's throat had dried out. If she spoke, her esophagus might rip. "She's right," said Glory, forcing the words out. "Justice, please provide Marguerite with plating directions so we can get these desserts out to our members, who have paid good money for fine dining *and* dessert and will deliver suffering into our lives if they don't get something sweet on a fancy plate in a few moments."

With wide eyes and slow movements, Justice created a sample plate for her unwanted assistant. She took the slightly burned pastry foundation and crumbled it onto the plate. It was ladled with a pillow of cream infused with whole vanilla beans, and then topped with powdered sugar sifted from a sieve. She took a plastic squeeze bottle, then dotted the plate with raspberry sauce, and then spread it around the plate with the back of a spoon. Marguerite watched intently, taking mental notes, and jumping into the task. She got to work, prepping one plate after the other.

"I need to get back to the festivities," said Glory. "Thank you both for jumping in and making it work. I know everyone is going to love it."

Justice looked over her shoulder and watched as Glory and then Delphine walked out, disappearing behind the swinging doors that separated the kitchen from the dining room. If Justice's strained face could talk, it would have begged them not to leave her alone with a killer. All Delphine could do was shrug and follow her mother out of the door.

Once Delphine and Glory were in the ballroom, they talked almost at once. "*Ohmygod,* do you think it's her?" asked Delphine, looking around the room to make sure they weren't being watched. They couldn't be too careful.

"Of course it's her. I simply cannot believe that I didn't figure this out until now."

"But why would she do it?"

"Why does anyone kill another person? What I do know is that she is the only person with a tie to the knife—Donna Gibson was her *girlfriend*! And she lived upstairs from Sterling. Who else could it be?" said Glory. "But I tell you one thing, I am not about to confront her. The last time I confronted a killer I ended up unconscious at Lafayette General Hospital. We need to tell Landry."

"It'll take him at least twenty minutes to get here, Mom. I don't know if we've got that kind of time."

"He's here. Talked to him not fifteen minutes ago." She pointed at him on the dance floor, coupled up with old Millie Broward who was grinding against him in an inappropriate way.

Glory and Delphine raced over to the dance floor and tapped on his shoulder. "I'm sorry to interrupt, but this is important. Landry . . ." She gestured with her head to the outdoor patio, signaling that she needed to talk with him outside.

"Glory Broussard, can't you see I'm dancing with a handsome gentleman? Don't be jealous now, let an old woman have her fun."

"Your fun's over," barked Glory. "Landry, we need to talk with you. *Now.*" Not a person in that ballroom would have disobeyed Glory with that tone. Landry followed her outside. Millie sulked and carried on dancing the zydeco two-step on her own.

They stood on the small, red-brick patio and closed the door behind them. "I can't believe you'd interrupt my dance with Miss Millie." He avoided eye contact with Delphine.

"Landry, Marguerite Dunlop is Sterling's killer."

"What? How?"

Glory explained everything as quickly as her lungs would allow. The knife. The visit to the blade master. The restaurant in Galveston. They had linked the murder weapon to her, and she had ample opportunity to commit the gruesome crime.

Landry struggled to make sense of it. He paced the brick patio. Multiple times he looked at both of the women with a mix of anger, admiration, and fury. "Why didn't you take this information to the police?"

"We just put it together a few moments ago. And we *are* taking it to the police. We're taking it to you so you can make an arrest," said Glory.

"It doesn't work like that," he said. "First of all, I'm not allowed to be on this case. I was forced to recuse myself."

"Why wouldn't you be allowed to have anything to do with a case involving murder in Lafayette, when you've worked these kinds of cases in the past?"

Delphine averted her eyes from Landry. The love between those two always seemed to come out sideways.

Landry sidestepped the backstory. "I can't get into it, but I have specific instructions not to be a part of this investigation! And I just can't go around arresting people in a kitchen for murder. I have to have a warrant, which requires evidence, though in this case I'd suspect there'd be enough circumstantial evidence to at least bring her in for questioning, but again, I'm not working this case."

"What if I reach out to someone else in the department? Get them started?" offered Delphine. "How long might it take?"

Landry scratched his head. "We have to do our own police work, confirm your suspicions. If we can reach this guy who made the knife and confirm he made the knife that killed your father, we can probably bring Marguerite in in a few hours for questioning. Have a warrant a few hours after that."

"And I can keep her busy in the meantime," confirmed Glory. "Someone has to keep an eye on her while you guys get it figured out."

"No, I'm not leaving you here alone," Delphine insisted. "It's too dangerous. I'll stay here and you go with him, Mom."

"Ordinarily I would agree with you," said Landry. "But in this case, I think it makes more sense for you to come. I've got to explain not only how I've learned of the evidence in the case, but why I need an emergency warrant. It would be helpful to have a lawyer, especially if I end up in front of a judge."

"*Go*, both of you," Glory demanded. There's no time to debate this. I'll be fine. Just hurry."

Everyone ran through the ballroom. Landry and Delphine headed to the police station, Glory peeled off to the kitchen. Once inside, she found dozens of desserts, plated and nestled onto serving trays, ready for the guests.

"My goodness, will you look at all these desserts? Wait until they get a taste of this. It's going to be the talk of the town, or at least at Mass come Sunday. Marguerite, I just want to say thank you for helping out. We would not have been able to do this without you."

"I'm just real happy to help out. And I got to taste some, too. Best thing I've eaten in a long time, I can tell you that."

"Service," demanded Justice. Servers descended in white jackets and bow ties. They stacked dessert trays in the crook of their arms, and ushered them into the ballroom. Glory peeped through the scratchy plastic windows of the kitchen doors to watch everyone's response to the dessert. There had been such a fuss about not securing the right king cake. If this didn't go over well it might be as bad for her reputation as the ill-fated crawfish that nearly got her booted out of the Red Hat Society. But eventually, she saw one of The Black Widows loosen her belt and knew that all was good.

The bandleader then made an announcement. "If everyone could please step outside, I've been told that the fireworks are about to begin." That was an understatement, thought Glory.

"Come on now, y'all worked so hard in the kitchen, might as well grab a glass of champagne and head out to watch the fireworks," insisted Glory, figuring that everyone would be safer in a crowd. The kitchen workers, including Marguerite and Justice, wiped down a few more surfaces before heading out for the display. All the members of the Red Hat Society were gathered, as well as other members of the community. T-Red drank from a champagne flute and continued to snarl at Glory each time he managed to make eye contact.

Glory wrapped herself in a sequined shawl that she had bought to match her jumpsuit and was glad that she had. The air was nippy. She just hoped that Landry and Delphine would get back fast, and it would be nice if they could arrest Marguerite without causing a scene. Her gala had gone so well, it would be a shame to mar it with an arrest. She watched the explosions above, taking a few small sips of champagne to calm her nerves.

Fireworks of red, green, and purple erupted, and Glory wished they had been able to afford drone fireworks. She and Constance had taken a meeting with a company that sent hundreds of drones into the sky, and could form any kind of shape you wanted, including a fleur-de-lis. As it turns out, they didn't have enough money, and these fireworks alone were making every dog in the adjacent neighborhood bark. Truth be told, Glory had always hated the fireworks, because she felt that they were right on top of the guests, and it was uncomfortably loud. But it was a tradition, and she had already ruined the king cake tradition and could not tamper with another. In short order, her ears began to ring from the noise, aggravating her tinnitus.

But it wasn't just ordinary tinnitus. She felt as if the planet Earth had tilted sideways, forward, and back. At first her ears were roaring like the sea, but then the volume lowered, and she could barely hear a thing. She became so dizzy, so completely out of her body, that she barely noticed that Marguerite was gently ushering her away from the fireworks. Glory clutched her forearm and tried to push Marguerite away, but the strength in her body evaporated.

Once inside the kitchen, Marguerite guided her down a set of stairs that Glory had not noticed before, closing the door behind them. Glory, no longer possessing the balance to stand on her own, stumbled against the wall, unable to stop the momentum. Inside the basement, boxes were stacked upon each other on metal racks. A mop and bucket were stashed in the corner. Bunches of paper towels and toilet paper stared directly at her.

"We know what you did to Sterling," Glory slurred.

Marguerite turned over a bucket and sat on it. "Yes, I know. I figured it all out about an hour ago."

With heavy eyelids, Glory wheezed. "How? How did you know?"

"When I saw that knife handle sticking out of the chef's knife holster, I knew you all had figured it out," replied Marguerite, pushing up her sleeves, preparing for what was next. "I'd recognize a Cleotus Farmington blade anywhere. Murder is a funny thing. It moves so quickly that it's impossible to track all the details. By the time I realized I left it at Sterling's place, it was too late. And then once I saw Justice with another Cleotus Farmington knife—a real beauty, I may add—I assumed you had visited him and put it all together. At any rate, I better get to work. They'll know it's me, but I have a history of dropping off the grid. I guess you could say that I'm accustomed to living in the shadows."

Glory's eyes flickered. "This. You drugged me at the casino. It was you."

"No. That wasn't me, but an old casino trick to get meddlesome people out of their hair. Ply unsuspecting people with alcohol, slip them one of those special concoctions, and watch as they get blind drunk and belligerent. Then kick them out of the casino or racetrack, probably for life. We call it the Cypress Downer, for people making too much noise. But that's what you've always done, isn't it? It's why half these women hate your ass."

Glory struggled to make sense of the words. Everything sounded distorted, warbled. She was losing her grip on consciousness, and needed to ask just a couple of questions before the medicine took full effect and she passed out, or worse. "But why, why did you do it?" She swallowed hard, trying to lubricate her throat. "Sterling took care of you. He gave you a home."

Fireworks exploded in the background.

"Oh, you know how Sterling was. So full of promises, most of them empty. I suppose I can tell you, since you won't be here for much longer. It would feel good to unburden my soul. He was in on every corrupt thing that happened at the casino, from the doping the horses to the cheating at the blackjack tables."

Glory's breath left her. Whether it was from the drugs or the revelations, she was too out of it to know. Marguerite continued. "I learned about all of it. So, he promised to cut me in on the blackjack scheme. Had his friends from all over town coming to play blackjack with Bonnie, all while he's peeling off all this money for himself. So, he cut me in. And you know how he was . . . *oh sure, that won't be a problem. More than enough to go around.* And I was starting to finally get a handle on my life. On Donna's hospital bills, which I've been paying off for years. I was even on track to pay off my truck. But then it started drying up. Said he needed to save for his fishing business, and he needed to save for his new family. It was like I didn't even exist anymore.

"So, one day when I heard him at the duplex, I went down to confront him. I brought a knife. Now mind you, I had no intention of doing any harm. But sometimes you need a little prop to be taken seriously, kind of like you and your friend Constance walking around with those clipboards. And when he tried to stall again, I just lost it." She quieted for a moment. "You ever do something that isn't logical at all, but in the moment, you just can't help yourself?"

Glory slumped further down the wall. She looked around the room for something that could be used as a weapon, but her eyes wouldn't focus. The single lightbulb in the center of the room was a smear. She thought, *that's it . . . the white light people talk about before they die.* She said a final prayer.

Lord, if this is the end . . . please give my daughter the peace I was never able to find for myself. Please, give her peace.

And her eyelids shut. Marguerite loomed over her.

She had no idea how much time had passed, but she must have still been hallucinating, she told herself, because otherwise why would Justice, Constance, and Valerie be standing on the staircase? This must be hell, with the three of them laughing from above. Then, a flurry of action. The whoosh of Valerie's train smacked Glory in the face, and if she was seeing things correctly, Valerie had pounced on Marguerite and pinned her to the ground. Marguerite continued to flail, her shoulder smacking Valerie in the chin. Justice, just inches behind her, joined in and forced Marguerite's shoulder into a position that looked unnatural. Judging by the agony on her face, she may have required orthopedic surgery by the time all was said and done.

Constance didn't join the melee. Instead, she propped Glory up and tried to force some water down her throat. "Thank God for this cheap jumpsuit. You left a trail of sequins from the patio to the basement."

A few IV bags later, the stupor was lifting and Glory began to feel more alert. Constance was flapping around, first calling Delphine to fill her in on the happenings in the basement, and then calling the police, telling them to arrive without sirens. Constance had then stood out in front, directing all first responders to the entrance closest to the kitchen, like a crossing guard. Turns out she didn't need a clipboard at her side to have an air of importance.

By the time Landry and Delphine had returned to the scene, T-Red was in handcuffs. His purple hat was lying in the parking lot, and his suit jacket was torn down the back. "All I did was burn the king cake! Y'all are arresting me for intentionally burning a cake?!" As it turns out, it wasn't the Lafayette Police Department that had arrived so quickly, but the FBI, who had been surveilling T-Red, Grady, and Bonnie, and their various crimes for months. Glory would later learn from news reports that once the feds got wind that there was another crime underway, they figured they might as well get their man. They had enough evidence and didn't want a jurisdiction dispute with the local cops.

"Oh hush." Constance gave a wink. "Let me get back out there before those women start to suspect something is amiss. They can just smell a commotion." Constance went into the ballroom and circulated rumors that one of the kitchen staff had become locked inside the walk-in freezer. It was not just Glory's reputation on the line, but hers as well.

Glory was in the same position as she was when she passed out, slumped on a concrete floor, propped up against a wall. A crew of EMT workers surrounded her. Delphine held one hand; Landry grabbed the other. Her eyes fought to open. After rounding her mouth a few times to find words, her speech returned. "Just what I needed. Another embarrassment in front of the Red Hats."

Constance stepped in. "Not on my watch." She explained all she had done to contain the situation, including enlisting and diverting the police crews, ordering the DJ to play another set, and giving another complimentary round of bourbon to everyone in attendance. She'd have to explain this extra cost to the members, but that was a problem for another day. "As far as anyone knows, a member of the kitchen staff accidentally locked themselves in the freezer and needed medical assistance. The Lafayette Police Department and emergency services answered with a show of force, due to our standing in the community and stature as women of God."

"Thank you, Constance. For everything."

Delphine, Landry, and a gaggle of police officers crowded the basement. "Where's Marguerite? Did you shoot her?" asked Glory, still groggy.

Landry gave a hint of a smile but kept it together. "She's been apprehended and taken downtown. At the minimum we've got her for administering drugs to an unsuspecting person, a Class E felony, which in the state of Louisiana is punishable by hard labor. At most we've got her for murder. Either way, she'll be locked up for a very long time." Glory struggled to her feet.

"You sure you don't want to go to the hospital?" asked Landry.

"I am absolutely certain that I do not want to go to the hospital. Millie Broward's daughter is the night shift nurse, and I already got half the town thinking I can't handle my liquor."

"Who cares what anyone says," said Justice, offering a forearm so Glory could steady herself. "You should get looked at."

"The only thing I want to look at is my own bed. Just let the record show that I was not intentionally blitzed at the Commodores' concert, while screaming disparaging things about the band and Lionel Richie. That was just whatever Mickey they slipped into my drink. I am far more composed than that, which Marguerite confessed to, you know."

Delphine rushed to Glory's other side, offering another forearm. "I will make sure that the record has been updated and that your reputation remains untarnished, at least with regard to the Commodores," said Delphine. "Landry, can you get your car so we can take her home?" He nodded and disappeared.

"You can ride with us," said Delphine to Justice.

"I'm not done here. This kitchen is a mess. As a professional chef, it would ruin my reputation to leave a kitchen in this state, even a rented kitchen. I can't have anyone here saying that the James Beard Rising Star Chef of the Year left a kitchen in tatters, and then post a video on social media. Your mama has a reputation to worry about, and so do I."

Delphine rolled her eyes. "Everyone is so worried about their reputation and 'letting the record show' when we've had a killer in our midst all night. I for one would like to get the hell out of here."

Glory complained only slightly at having to climb the steep stairs that led back to the kitchen. There, a few workers from the catering company lingered, scraping dishes and staring sideways at Glory at the same time.

The cab of the truck was silent on the drive back home, except for some vintage country music droning from the speakers. Delphine wanted to laugh. It was just like Landry to listen to some old George Jones song about a love gone wrong, and all the memories that were collecting dust in someone's soul. He must have had a lot of wear and tear on his heart.

After what seemed like an eternity but was actually closer to thirty minutes, they arrived back on Viator Drive. Landry and Delphine helped Glory into her bedroom. She was gaining her strength back by the minute. "Okay you two, my bedroom is my sanctuary. I don't need you meddling in my drawers and nightgowns. I'm fine now . . . leave me be while I change and put myself to sleep. Go on, now. Go." Patti LaBelle jumped on the bed and tucked her front paws into herself, as if she had been waiting for her all along. Glory shut the door.

Delphine, hands shaking, put on some coffee in the kitchen. Not that she needed any more stimulation for the night. She'd had enough. But she felt like she needed to *do* something. What they needed, she decided, wasn't coffee but a stiff drink. She reached into her mother's hutch and pulled out two juice glasses and a bottle of whisky. Landry cocked his head in surprise.

"Don't look at me like that. It's my mother's stash." She poured and sipped, the aroma of oak and brown sugar singeing the hairs inside her nostrils.

"You don't have to explain," But the truth is, she had a lot to say to this man who had confessed his love to her months ago and had showed it through his actions for at least twenty years.

She inhaled the drink, not to screw up some kind of false courage, but so the words would come out the way she wanted them to. "You were right. I've spent the last decade or so of my life trying to make myself acceptable to other people, trying to look and act like they want me to, so that I could be loved. I've twisted myself every which way. The thing is, I've never had to contort myself for you. I've always had your love. But I kept thinking there was something bigger out there. That if I dated someone rich or important, that I'd be important, too. Instead, just the opposite happened. I only ended up feeling small."

She reached for his hand. "I guess this is my way of saying that I'm sorry. That you were always good enough for me, too good for me, actually. I was the one who had to wake up and realize it. And well, if you'd have me, I . . ."

He took her face in his hands and kissed her. It felt like the kind of kiss that swept away the past and ushered in a new beginning, if only she'd let it.

A couple days later, Glory walked through the doors of The New Woman Salon. Delphine had made the appointment, and Glory knew she'd have to confront Valerie eventually. At the very least, she had to thank her for teaming up with Justice and Constance to take Marguerite down. Why was she being forced to apologize to so many people? She'd like a word with the universe about this.

The string of bells rang as she opened the door, heralding Glory's arrival in a way she wished they had not. The two women stared at each other like a bull and a conquistador. She walked into the salon, past a station with a broken mirror that had been patched top to bottom with duct tape.

"You're fifteen minutes late. Put a robe over your clothes and take a seat," said Valerie. Glory did as she was told. Once she was seated, Valerie ran her fingers through Glory's hair, inspecting the thin and patchy areas. "I've told you this before, but I think you really need to cut this shorter. Shorter hair looks thicker. Right now, it looks stringier than it has to."

Glory spoke before she could regret it. "Fine. Cut it."

"Really?" asked Valerie, shocked.

"But if this looks terrible, I swear to God, I'm telling everyone in town that your hand was responsible."

"I have no doubt that you will." She sprayed Glory's hair until it was damp, combed it out and, using two fingers as a guide, began to snip away. "I can't believe it was Marguerite. After Sterling gave her a job and a home and everything!"

"Are you going to be okay, the salon and all?" asked Glory.

"Just settled up with insurance the other day. Should be enough to catch up on my mortgage . . . maybe even replace that mirror you broke."

Glory was tempted to remind her that she had pushed her to do that, but seeing that Valerie had helped save her life, and was also wielding a pair of sharp scissors close to her head, she kept it to herself. "I suppose I'm sorry about that."

Valerie tilted Glory's head to the side and gathered more hair between her fingers to trim. "I guess I deserved it. Look down." Glory stared at the floor while Valerie trimmed the hair closest to the back of her neck. Hair cluttered the floor. "If anyone owes an apology, I guess it's me. I never should have violated your marriage the way I did, no matter what was going on between you and Sterling. If he never apologized, and I suspect he didn't, then I'm apologizing. For both of us. I really am sorry, Glory."

The salon grew quiet as the apology washed over her. Glory's eyes grew cloudy, and a few tears fell from her eyes onto the robe along with a smattering of hair. She had no idea how much she needed those words. Glory had carried a mountain of anger with her for too long. In that chair, she allowed herself to feel the weight of it.

Valerie massaged her shoulders, and more tears fell from Glory's eyes. "Come on," Valerie whispered. "Let's shampoo you."

Glory wiped her eyes and leaned back into the sink while Valerie pumped pink shampoo into her palms and rubbed them into Glory's scalp. She massaged Glory's temples and the back of her neck, then rinsed her hair with warm water. Then she worked conditioner into Glory's hair, taking even more time with a gentle massage over her scalp. When she had rinsed it all out, she straightened Glory's chair and kneaded her neck, just a little. Glory could not recall the last time anyone had touched her with kindness, beyond the pats on the shoulder that Landry gave her.

"Okay, blow-dry," said Valerie, pointing her back to the hairdresser chair. "Now, you must tell me what is going on with that fine-ass boy that's been following Delphine around." Valerie sectioned her hair and began to smooth it with a big round brush.

Glory was all too happy to oblige. "Oh, he's been in love with her since he was eight years old. And Delphine seems to have finally come around. They're going to try to work it out, I guess. She's even thinking of moving down here. Can you believe it? She's spent her whole life trying to get away from Lafayette—and *me*—and here she is talking about moving back to give it a go with a hometown boy."

"I tell you; you don't know what you've got till it's gone." She worked product into Glory's hair, molding each area with her fingers. "It might not be the only reason she has to come back."

In the mirror, Glory stared at her quizzically as she continued. "You'll probably be outraged, and I'm half afraid to tell you, but . . . she's going to have a half-sister." She told Glory that both she and her IVF doctor thought the last round had failed, and it had. Rather, one of the embryos had. The other was still thriving. The size of a cherry pit, the pregnancy website had informed her. "Look, I know you have no reason to be happy for me, and you and those hens at the Red Hat Society will probably talk bad about how old I am, but I loved Sterling. And now I have something to remember him by, just like you have Delphine. At least, the good days with him."

Now that Sterling was dead and buried, maybe it was time to stop maligning the man. Was there anything new to say? If the past couple weeks had taught her anything, it was to mind whose house you were in. And at the moment, it was Valerie's. "I'm happy for you," said Glory. "But can I at least gossip about how you're too goddamn old to have a kid? When that kid is in high school, you'll be . . . how old?"

"I'm going to need knee brace just to play with her."

Her. It sunk in. Sterling was gone, but there was going to be another Broussard woman. A Broussard woman that would need to be nurtured and loved. Was Glory going to babysit? Or change diapers? Not a chance in hell. Maybe Delphine would want to participate in that, but not Glory. That said, there was no telling what kind of child-rearing ideas Valerie had that needed to be corrected. At the minimum, Glory would see to it that the child had proper manners and house training.

Valerie handed Glory a mirror and swiveled her around in the chair. "Well, I'll be damned," she said, smoothing her hand over the back. "You got me looking just like that Judy Blume."

Valerie put a hand on her hip. "Who?"

Glory paid up. She left a $300 tip for the haircut and the mirror. As far as she was concerned, they were even.

34

Glory sat at CC's Coffee House, checking in the reflection of the window to see how her new hairstyle was holding up and patting it on the sides. A notification on her phone interrupted her primping.

Justice: *When am I going to see you at Pierre's? I'll make sure you get the tasting menu, kitchen tour, the whole shebang.*

Glory: *Girl, you know how much I hate driving long distances. And don't even get me started about parking in the French Quarter!*

Justice: *I went ahead and made a reservation for next Saturday.*

Glory: *You know Delphine is back in NYC, right?*

Justice: *Yes, I can only manage one crazy Broussard woman at a time. Bring someone! It's a great way to make a friend . . .*

Glory: *I already told you. I don't need any friends . . . see you next Saturday.*

Justice closed the conversation by inserting some image of a girl jumping up and down in excitement. Glory put her phone down on the table. People were always doing too much in these text messages.

Noah walked out of the kitchen and did a double take when he saw Glory. As if the dramatically different hairstyle wasn't enough, she was dressed in a leopard print blouse and some wide-legged jeans, along with the same heels she wore the ill-fated night of the St. Agnes Mardi Gras gala.

"I'm surprised to see you sitting down here on a Thursday. To what do I owe this midweek honor?"

"I am your favorite customer and the source of at least ten percent of your business. Not to mention Lafayette's most notorious amateur crime fighter. I suggest you show me respect." She noticed a longer than usual line, and just as many baristas and cashiers as a busy Sunday morning, even though it was Thursday afternoon. "What is going on here? Why is it so busy in here?"

He sat down at her table, as if he'd been hoping for her to ask that very question. "Glory, my drink is taking off. First, I put it on the spring menu and sales went through the roof. The folks at CC's headquarters got wind of it, so their CEO came to personally visit and taste my *Praline Perfection*. And now they're trying to figure out if they can launch the recipe in all locations—'operationalize' it—I guess that's what they call it."

"Well, damn. Looks like you were truly onto something after all. Just remember I was one of your first taste-testers."

"And best part of all, if it works out, they're going to source all local products. That means Gus's House of Bees could be on the cusp of getting some very large orders." The line was nearly backed up to the door. "Let me go and help my employees. Had to hire a couple new ones and they're still learning how to make it."

"Go on, tend to your customers," she said, shooing him away. "Just bring me a cappuccino when you get a break in the action. No, make that two."

"By the way . . . I like that haircut. It suits you."

Unaccustomed to compliments, she touched the sides of her hair before waving him back to the kitchen.

Glory was tickled to watch Noah at work, possibly on the verge of a big business breakthrough. He deserved it. If she were open to dating, it would probably be to a man like him—strong, industrious, and able to hold his own with her. She caught herself. That's exactly the kind of man Sterling had been. Success, of course, was always evaluated through the lens of the times. Sterling was a Black man who came of age when it was hard for a Black man to thrive. In another time, maybe he could have owned a legitimate business like Noah did. Was that an excuse for his philandering? No, but maybe it was finally time to give Sterling a little bit of grace.

Franklin, her hired muscle, walked through the door and leaned down to kiss her on the cheek. He took a seat, and then looked around nervously. "I heard Cypress Downs has been shut down. This better not come back on me, Glory?"

"Don't worry. From what I hear they're only focused on T-Red, Grady, and Bonnie as the masterminds. And besides, it's not shut down, just changing ownership. It will now be owned and operated by Benoit Industrial. Given how greedy they are, I suspect it will be up and running in a matter of weeks, if not days."

"Oh yeah, I think I saw something about the son taking over. Went to jail last year?"

"Yes, he went to one of those federal prisons, with Verizon Fios and pickleball. And because he's got the best lawyers on retainer, he's out in a couple of days."

He shook his head. "You'd think there'd be some rule that prevented a convicted felon from running a casino."

"I'm sure there is. But who is going to enforce that in Louisiana, especially when you've paid off all the law enforcement agencies? They'll find a work-around." The people waiting for their *Praline Perfection* were growing restless. "Anyway, that's not why I called you here."

She reached under the table and pulled out a rust-colored box, trimmed in turquoise, with fancy lettering on the top. "I have no idea what transpired between you and my daughter, but she did say that you gave her a lot to think about, and she wanted to give you a little gift."

He pointed at the box, astonished. "This, this . . . it's not a little gift."

"I suspect not. My daughter knows all kinds of fancy things I do not, and I know you've got a taste for fine things, too. All she told me was that she bought the lightweight version so you could wear it in Louisiana. Go on . . . open it."

He opened the box and found a light-blue sweater inside. "I called her out on all her fancy brands. So, she sent me a Loro Piana sweater, Italian cashmere."

Glory pursued her lips. "Goodness gracious. Here in Louisiana, you'll be able to wear this about ten days a year." Weaving her way through the throngs of customers was Constance. "If you don't mind, I . . ."

He stood up. "Tell Delphine thank you." He grinned like a straight-up country boy on the way out.

Constance walked through the people, also doing a double take at the crowds and the lines. Glory waved her over to her table.

"My goodness, what is going on in here? Are they doing a give-away or something?" asked Constance, dressed in burgundy slacks and a matching top.

"Get this. Remember that drink Noah Singleton had us try? *Praline Perfection*? Apparently, it's doing gangbusters. Might even become a permanent menu item across the entire chain."

"And you never once thought of—"

"No, not once," said Glory. It was a partial truth. She had thought about it, but not seriously. When it comes to men, she had played one hand. And as she had been reminded several times over the past couple of weeks, the house always wins. Sometimes not playing at all is the winning move.

"Well, I must say I was quite surprised that you invited me out for coffee. I was so intrigued that I took my lunch break now so I could see what else you were cooking up. No one's really watching me at the DMV anyway. Do you have another murder to solve? Whose husband is stepping out? Don't leave me in suspense any longer."

Noah arrived with their cappuccinos and a couple of scones. He was always throwing in a little something extra. Constance gave him a lingering glance, from head to toe, as he walked back to the kitchen.

"No, Constance, there is no news. I was thinking . . . maybe you and I could be friends."

Constance raised an eyebrow and gave a nervous laugh.

Glory interrupted before she could answer. "You know what? Never mind. And just promise me that you won't turn this into some kind of story hour at the next Red Hat meeting. I can hear you already, over beignets and coffee saying, 'And then you know what she asked . . .'"

"Oh Glory . . . I was joking. I think we can bury the hatchet." She tore off the corner of her scone.

"And while we're at it, now that we're friends, maybe you could waive off that last court-ordered visit."

Constance's hands fell hard on the table. "Absolutely not, Glory. I take my civic responsibilities seriously! And if I were you, I'd get to tackling that bedroom. Don't think I can't see what's going on in there. Where do you even sleep?"

Glory could see a lot of herself in Constance, once she left the pettiness behind. The two talked for nearly two hours about whose license was suspended, Millie Broward attempting to dirty dance with Landry, and Delphine's pending return. She had even invited Constance to Pierre's in New Orleans the following weekend. Maybe Delphine had been right: maybe everyone wasn't out to get her. She would try to keep this in mind moving forward. It was true that Glory had already lived most of her little life, but she was damn sure of one thing—she wasn't done yet.

ACKNOWLEDGMENTS

I would like to extend my deepest gratitude for those who have worked behind-the-scenes to bring this book to life. Writing a book is a solitary experience. Publishing one involves an entire group of people who come together and try to make another person's dreams come true. It's magical.

Facetime Studios continues to deliver gorgeous covers and puts up with my detailed PowerPoint "inspiration" decks, so thank you. Maria Fernandez, interior book design, makes my book readable with delightful surprises throughout.

I marvel at the attention, skill and knowledge of Lis Pearson, copy editor, and Susan McGrath, proofreader. You think you know about words and grammar, and they get their hands on your manuscript and you are humbled.

And then there is the team at Pegasus, which includes editor Jessica Case and marketing and publicity ace Meghan Jusczak. Thank you both for your care and attention to my girl, Glory.